W9-BEZ-678

Acclaim for Annie Solomon's Previous Novels

BLACKOUT

"FOUR STARS! Fantastic story! . . . Tough, suspenseful, and we have a heroine who is even tougher than the special-agent hero. Whew! Never a dull moment. Solomon has outdone herself this time, and that's not easy to do."

—RomanceReviewsMag.com

"Twisty and diverting, with well-written action sequences."

—*Publishers Weekly on Blackout*

"Talk about edge-of-the seat! I have never read a book with such relentless suspense. . . . A superb example of showing over mere telling of a story. I highly recommend Blackout."

—*Romantic Reviews Today*

BLIND CURVE

"FOUR STARS! Riveting and emotionally intense."

—*Romantic Times BOOKclub Magazine*

"A perfect ten . . . nail-biting, intense drama that will leave you breathless with anticipation."

—MyShelf.com

more . . .

"Annie Solomon does such an outstanding job creating taut suspense. From the very first page . . . to the riveting climax, you can't help but be glued to the story."

—RoundTableReviews.com

"An action-packed novel . . . a feast for suspense fans, and the added mixture of romance . . . . another winner for an author who clearly has a gift and is on the rise."

—TheRomanceReadersConnection.com

TELL ME NO LIES

"Infused with raw emotion and a thirst for vengeance. Excitement and tension galore!"

—*Romantic Times BOOKclub Magazine*

"Full of simmering emotions that lovers of romantic suspense will devour."

—*Rendezvous*

"Another success! Miss Solomon's latest novel is a testament to her gift for crafting intelligent, sexy novels."

—RomanceReadersConnection.com

DEAD RINGER

"Just the ticket for those looking for excitement and romance."

—*Romantic Times BOOKclub Magazine*

"An entertaining . . . exceptional . . . emotionally taut tale . . . offers twists and turns that kept me enthralled to the last page."

—*Old Book Barn Gazette*

"Thrilling and edgy . . . Dead Ringer delivers excitement, suspense, and sexual tension . . . Highly recommended."

—RomRevToday.com

LIKE A KNIFE

"A nail-biter through and through. Absolutely riveting."

—Iris Johansen

"Fast-paced . . . exciting romantic suspense that . . . the audience will relish."

—*Midwest Book Review*

"A powerful character study . . . [Ms. Solomon] blends the elements of romance and suspense . . . with the skill of a veteran."

—The WordonRomance.com

Also by Annie Solomon

Like a Knife

Dead Ringer

Tell Me No Lies

Blind Curve

Blackout

DEAD SHOT

ANNIE SOLOMON

NEW YORK BOSTON

The characters and events in this book are fictitious. Any similarity to real persons, living or dead, is coincidental and not intended by the author.

Warner Forever is a trademark of Time Warner Inc. or an affiliated company. Used under license by Hachette Book Group, which is not affiliated with Time Warner Inc.

Warner Forever is an imprint of Warner Books Inc.

Cover design by Diane Luger
Book design by Stratford Publishing Services, Inc.

Warner Forever
Hachette Book Group USA
1271 Avenue of the Americas
New York, NY 10020

ISBN-13: 978-0-7394-7985-8

Printed in the United States of America

To Larry, who helped me pull another one out of the hat.

Acknowledgments

I'd like to thank Katie Wellborn of the Frist Center and Nathalie Lavine who both gave me their time and their insight into the world of art museums.

Thanks also to photographer John Guider, who explained the mysteries of the 8 × 10 camera, and shared his beautiful photographs of his river trip to the Mississippi.

And once again, I'm indebted to Detective Patricia Hamblin of the Wilson County Sheriff's Department.

DEAD SHOT

1

From the edge of the angry crowd, he watched the fat black limousine crawl to the entrance of the Gray Visual Arts Center. The place blazed, lights piercing the night like knife points. Flags celebrating the art museum's first anniversary flapped against poles in the night breeze, snapping like skins.

Someone bellowed a chant. "De-cen-cy! De-cen-cy!" The crowd joined in, fisted arms raised in time to the beat. "De-cen-cy!"

A protester broke from the police lines and rushed the car, attacking the windshield with a homemade placard on a stick. The man couldn't read what it said, but he could guess from the others around him: GO HOME, SICKO, NO TO DEATH ART, JESUS IS THE TRUE SACRIFICE. A phalanx of uniformed cops pried the scraggly man off the car and dragged him away.

Amid the swirl—the multitude of TV trucks with their satellite antennas, the angry crowd, the police trying to maintain a barricade—the man stood still, hands buried deep in his jacket pockets. The eye of the hurricane.

He inhaled deeply, absorbed the chaos through his skin. It leached into his veins and up his bloodstream, pumped hard and fast through his heart. The noise, the excitement, the energy of the night juiced him with a seething envy he could hardly contain.

For her. All for her.

The crowd pushed against the police line as the limousine stopped at the foot of the museum steps. He stood in the back, and from that distance, the four passengers appeared like tiny dolls climbing the stairs. But he imagined them. Wrapped in silk and glitter, six-thousand-dollar tuxedos, three-thousand-dollar shoes.

And her pale, white body, such fragile beauty, soft and perfumed.

A swarm of reporters descended from all sides of the steps and overwhelmed the four passengers. The shape of the swarm bulged and contracted as people shoved each other for position.

Jealousy churned into white-hot resentment. It should be him up there. Him in the newspapers, him on television. It should be his name the crowd chanted.

She was a liar, and a cheat.

He was the real thing.

She only imitated death.

He created it.

2

Be careful what you wish for. As the limousine crept through the enraged protesters, that little piece of irony reverberated in Gillian Gray's head.

Outside the car, the protesters formed pockets, dispersed, and re-formed again, like a giant snake undulating in fury. Gillian narrowed her eyes so the group's edges blurred. She imagined a dragon. A monster. As if she'd summoned Godzilla from the depths.

Maddie leaned over and murmured, "Regrets?"

Gillian could smell the perfume on her. Something strong and spicy. Venom or Vengeance. She smiled. "Are you kidding?"

Maddie smiled back. "You are not a nice person."

"Look who's talking."

It was Maddie who had convinced Gillian to come in the first place. Maddie, with her long, scary face and Morticia Addams hair, who, as Gillian's assistant, had taken the message and passed it on to her. "It's the museum's first anniversary," she'd said. "They want to bring in a local."

Oh, Gillian was a local all right. Not born, and because of boarding school, not even bred. But branded just the same. The way the building they were creeping to was branded. Gray. Gillian Gray. Daughter of a murdered daughter. Photographer. Aristocrat. Demon. Artiste.

But not Maddie, lucky girl. She was from some other godforsaken place. Some other nightmare. One where food itself was scarce. Not rich, not famous. Just glad to go to school with them, be friends with them. How long had she known Maddie? Longer than she wanted to count.

Gillian watched her friend out of the corner of her eye. She was pouring a small snooker of liquid courage for *les grandperes*.

Helpful Maddie. Lean and spare and strong as a tree limb weathered by winds.

Of course, Gillian had initially refused the invitation. She'd shrugged and climbed the ten-foot ladder to the platform in her Brooklyn studio where a bulky eight-by-ten camera sat on a tripod overlooking a set of a kitchen. An ordinary, commonplace suburban kitchen. But nothing in this life was ordinary, a kitchen least of all.

"The museum has your name on it," Maddie had said.

"My grandfather's name," Gillian had corrected.

"It would be a great tie-in. Good publicity."

"I don't need publicity."

Too true. Her name and face had been famous since she was a child and, as an adult, her work had always been controversial. So, she couldn't avoid publicity even if she wanted to. And she didn't want to. Not really. How could he find her if he didn't know where she was?

Maddie had held the pink message slip between two fingers. Waved it like the devil offering temptation to a sinner. "Yeah, but think how much you could rock their world."

Gillian stared at her friend. Maddie's lips had twitched, not a smile exactly, but the smug suggestion of one.

Gillian had snatched the message out of Maddie's hand.

Rock their world.

It sure to hell was rocking now.

And this was only the VIP party; the show hadn't even opened yet. What would happen on Friday?

A thud. Someone with a sign flung himself at the slow-moving vehicle. On the seat opposite, her grandmother, Genevra, gasped and clutched at her fur-encased throat. It was early April, but she still wore the silver mink, more out of status than a need for warmth, although she did always complain about the cold. Not enough fat on those patrician bones. Above the stole's rim, Genevra's throat rose tall and tapered, the cords stretched tight in her too-thin neck. She stared in horror at the half word "obsceni," which hung on the window, then slipped out of sight as a cop dragged whoever it was away.

"It's all right," Gillian's grandfather said grimly. He squeezed his wife's other hand, curled tightly in her lap. His own was beefy, his fingers squat and well manicured.

"Of course it is," Genevra said through tight lips, pretending, as she always did.

Of course it was.

They made a handsome couple. The college quarterback and his homecoming queen. Growing up it seemed no surprise to Gillian that their only child had become an icon of beauty. At least to everyone with a subscription to *Vogue*. Not much of an icon to her own parents, however, but that was an old story.

Gillian turned, pressed her forehead against the glass like she was seven again.

"Get away from the window," Genevra snapped.

Gillian ignored her. She peered into the face of the furies. Was he out there? Watching her? Would he come for her, too?

"Gillian!" Genevra's voice grated into the hum of silence inside the car.

"Is your glass empty, Genevra? Let me take that from you." Maddie's voice behind her. Smooth interference. "Wouldn't want to ruin that beautiful mink with spilled gin."

"Thank you," Genevra said, the words a sniff of stoicism, a warble of concealment, a disguise.

"Vintage?" Maddie asked, and like that she distracted Genevra into a discussion of fur and color and shape.

And Gillian could stare out the window at the faces. Would she see his face? The face of the man who'd killed her beautiful and famous mother? Was he out there, watching?

Be careful what you wish for.

3

Ray Pearce stared hard at the enormous photograph mounted on the museum wall. At the strange light coming in from a window, making the ordinary kitchen with its pink-and-green floral curtains and Winnie the Pooh cookie jar look ominous, even without the body on the floor.

But there was a body. A dead girl lay on her back. School uniform mussed, book bag lying beside her as though she'd been surprised and dropped it. An algebra text and a notebook with a mottled black-and-white cover spilled out of it. The girl, eyes wide and glazed in a bloodless face, stared unseeing at something beyond him. Her attacker? The viewer? He'd seen plenty of crime-scene photographs, but this one made him shift his feet and step back.

Not that moving away lessened the impact. Wider than Ray was tall, the huge picture pulled you in, making it impossible to ignore the girl's plaid skirt, which lay crumpled above her knees. Or her thighs, which were parted and blood-streaked. A shirt embroidered with a school crest was untucked and unbuttoned. Three red splotches marred the once-crisp white cotton. The blood had soaked through as she bled out, fuzzing the edges of the wound marks. A suspicion of lace beneath hinted at her virginal white bra.

Close to her outstretched arm lay a bloodied knife. The fingers of her hand curled outward toward it as though beckoning: Come closer, they seemed to be saying. See me. That hand, that tender, fragile hand made him feel like the voyeur he was.

"What do you think?"

The voice of Carlson, his boss, and head of Carleco Security, broke the photograph's eerie hold. "One sick puppy," Ray said, and reminded himself to keep as far away as possible from her.

Carlson shrugged. "Well, let's make sure she stays that way."

Carlson nodded toward the exhibit entrance and beyond, where men in black tie and women in little black dresses sipped champagne. "They're here."

Ray followed Carlson out of the exhibit and into the reception area. Amid the black-coated waiters who mingled with trays of wineglasses and hors d'oeuvres, stood a tall, gangly man with black-rimmed glasses that matched his shock of black hair: Wilson Davenport, director of the museum.

Ray nodded, shook hands, filed his face away under "friendly." At least, for now.

They left the reception and moved out into the hallway that led to the entrance. Once away from the crowd, the museum's marble floors echoed with their footsteps. It was cold in the empty hallway. Cold the way a room is when all the people have gone.

Ray hunched inward, the collar of the tuxedo shirt tight around his neck. He never liked wearing the things, but babysitting the rich and famous meant blending in. And after three years of it, he had the money to buy all the trappings.

They turned a corner, passed the glass wall that skirted the closed and lifeless gift shop, past the unmanned information desk, and bore down on the metal detector at the other end of the long passageway. The museum had balked at installing it, but Carlson had insisted. Given the tumult outside, Ray guessed Davenport and his crew were glad they'd acquiesced.

Beyond the metal detector, the museum's front door beckoned. For half a second, Ray imagined what it would be like to keep going. Walk into the night, get in his truck, and drive, baby, drive.

The lines from the Dylan song reverbed in his head: *with no direction home. Like a complete unknown. Like a rolling stone.*

Soon he'd make his plans. Pack his bags. Clip the guide wires and float free.

Tomorrow. Or the next day. Or the day after that. Soon.

He nodded at the uniformed officer manning the security station, and they all passed through. The little group planted itself just inside the museum's front door and waited.

Exterior lights illuminated the center's imposing front entrance. A columned portico. A slope of long, graceful steps. At the bottom, a black limousine was disgorging four people.

Beyond the four, the distant crowd still seethed. Fisted arms shook in the air and ugly, twisted mouths shouted slogans Ray couldn't hear. He could hardly blame them for being incensed. Gillian Gray and her friends could call it art, but the photographs he'd seen were rightly labeled obscene, and if it had been up to him, they'd meet the woodpile. All of them. With a nice hot flame. No one but his former colleagues in homicide should have to look at those nightmares.

But it wasn't up to him. He was no art expert; he was simply the guy who would escort Ms. Gray and her entourage to her party, then stand around while they ate stuffed mushrooms and drank champagne until they all got back in that limo and drove away to her granddaddy's mansion.

Away. Far away.

The words played in his head as he watched the four ascend, the patriarch in front.

Although he was past seventy, Charles "Chip" Gray still had a broad, ex-footballer's frame, though golf carts and country-club meals had turned it into paunch. Red-faced and huffing, he blocked Ray's view of Gillian and her companion. Chip's wife, Genevra, held his arm with one hand while the other clutched closed her silver fur as though it were armor. Ray knew who they were because most people in Nashville knew who they were. The Grays were local royalty, founders of an insurance conglomerate worth billions. Their name graced the front of the museum they were climbing toward.

The Gray Visual Arts Center was a cultural landmark for Nashville. For years the arts community had lobbied for an art museum of national standing. The Gray millions had finally made it possible, and a year ago the museum had opened to great fanfare. What better way to celebrate than to bring one of their own back for the first anniversary festivities?

He shot a sideways glance at the museum rep—what was his name? William? No, Wilson. Had it been his idea to bring Gillian Gray back to town? He'd bet Willy boy was regretting it now.

The group below hadn't gone five steps when the swarm attacked. Swelled with national press and tabloids, a herd of reporters and paparazzi descended from both sides, surrounding the Grays. Now he couldn't see any of them.

One glance at Carlson, and they both burst through the doors and raced down the steps. Elbowed to get through. Voices screamed questions as they got closer.

"Given community anger, will you withdraw from the exhibit?"

"How do you feel about public reaction to your work?"

A sea of faces, voices, and microphones buffeted the group. Cameras flashed, and the lights of news cameras shone in their eyes.

"Gentlemen! Ladies! Let us through!" Chip Gray pushed relentlessly through the thick sea of bodies and dismembered voices.

"Does your work contribute to violence?"

"Are you violent yourself?"

"Don't respond," Genevra Gray said. "Don't say a word. Just one foot in front of the other. Forward."

"Do you expect the museum to cancel the show?"

"What will you do if the museum cancels?"

Ray reached them first. He pulled the elder Grays through and handed them to Carlson, who threaded a path for them. Chip and Genevra plowed through, and Ray caught his first glimpse of their granddaughter alongside a tall, black-haired woman.

If he had to pick which of the two was the photographer, he would have guessed the dark one. There was an amused, cynical cast to her long, witchy face. It was a hard face, with a tough, brittle beauty that seemed more capable of handling a corpse than her companion's.

But the brunette wasn't the main attraction in the photographs. All the victims were incarnations of the angelic blonde beside her. And it was the angel, the small, slight angel, whose work was mounted on the museum's walls and whose name was reviled by the protesters below.

The night was cool, but Gillian Gray wore no coat or shawl. No mink stole of any kind.

Only a pale violet dress that skimmed her shoulders and floated down her arms, as delicate as the dead child she pretended to be in the photo. She was older than the photograph; then again, she would be—she wasn't pretending to be a schoolgirl now.

And yet her adult face and body had the same fragility as the dead girl's. Wispy fair hair piled on her head. Big eyes that stared out from an elfin face with childlike innocence.

If Ray had let them, they would have pulled him in like her photographs. But he didn't. He zeroed in on her. Linked an arm around her shoulder and another around the black-haired one. Pushed through. The pack continued shouting questions.

"You found your mother in the kitchen. Is that why you like kitchens?"

"Are you obsessed with death?"

"Ever killed anyone?"

"Let's go," Ray said, shoving the two women through.

"If they found him, what would you say to the man who killed your mother?"

He felt Gillian stiffen.

"Not now." He tightened his grip on her. "Keep moving."

But like a barge hitting ice, she ground to a halt. Turned back. "What would I say?"

The pack of reporters leaped closer, mad dogs salivating over the sound bite. They jostled Ray, and he swayed but didn't let go of the women.

"What would you tell your mother's murderer?" another reporter shouted.

Ray tensed, braced to keep his stance. Kept a roving gaze on the encroaching crowd. The last thing he needed was an incident before she even got inside the museum.

But the blonde didn't seem to care. "What would I tell my mother's killer?" She smiled sweetly as the pack closed in. "I'd tell him to come and get me."

4

Ray couldn't believe it. If she wanted to set them off, Gillian Gray couldn't have given a better response. Follow-up questions came so fast they blended together in a screeching, shouted racket.

Gillian swiveled to face the museum entrance again, a poised, confident move. No helpless little girl here. "I'm ready now," she said, and without his help, shoved her way through, leaving the mob screaming behind her.

Ray was sweating beneath his bow tie by the time they reached the door, but the woman beside him seemed revved up, excited. As if she'd faced down a challenge and won. There was a sharpness in her eyes as she greeted Davenport, who met them inside.

"Are you all right?" He took her arm. "Wilson Davenport, the museum's director."

"Ah." Gillian's smile could have cut glass. "The money man."

Will escorted her into the museum's foyer. "I am so sorry about all that outside."

"Oh, don't bother, Will." Chip eyed his granddaughter balefully. "She likes being in the thick of things." He shrugged out of his topcoat and dumped it on Will. "My God, a bunch of rabble."

"Never mind." Genevra Gray turned her back with a steely-eyed look and waited for Chip to take her fur. Underneath, a cream-colored floor-length gown clung to her frame. She looked all bone and sinew, as though she'd spent a lifetime on half rations and hard labor.

Ray waited for the business with the coats to finish so he could escort the group to the reception. The adrenaline had receded, and he felt the chill of the night and the pull of that red neon exit sign. Meanwhile, Chip was piling his wife's fur on Will, along with Maddie's coat, and Will was turning to Gillian, quirking a questioning eyebrow at her.

"No coat." Gillian raised her arms as if he couldn't see what was obvious.

"Ah, must be all that New York air." Will released one arm from around the coats to make a muscle. "Thickened your blood."

"It's not my blood, Wilson; it's my cold, cold heart."

Ray's glance swiveled to her. A sudden awareness, keen and interested. She'd surprised him again.

Davenport just chuckled. But it was an embarrassed, did-I-hear-that-right kind of laugh. He cleared his throat. "Call me Will, please."

"All right... Will."

"Well..." He lifted the outerwear as if that were the signal to move, then left, presumably to stash them in the coatroom.

"What a night," Chip said to no one in particular.

"Mr. Gray." Carlson stuck out his hand. "Ron Carlson. Carleco Security. The museum hired us to beef up security tonight."

Chip Gray shook Carlson's hand. "Thank you for the rescue out there."

"No problem. We've got everything under control inside. Museum security guards at all the entrances—they're the ones in uniform. My own people are plainclothes and will be floating, mixing with the crowd. And, of course, the metal detector. I'm afraid you'll have to go through it like the rest."

"Of course," Chip said. "My wife, Genevra." He turned to the other two women. "My granddaughter, Gillian, and her assistant, Madeleine Crane."

Carlson acknowledged the two women with a nod, and Gillian extended a long-fingered, delicate hand, the one that had beckoned in the photograph. The sight of the fingers, now moving and alive, sent an unnatural shiver through Ray.

"You've met Ray," Carlson said.

She glanced at him, swift but intense. A reading more than a glance. "Yes," she said.

Will returned from stashing the coats, and Genevra Gray turned her hard, pointed gaze on him. "Will, can't you do something about that mob outside?"

Will looked embarrassed. "The police are out there. Can't do much more than that. Freedom of speech and all."

Genevra sniffed.

Gillian leaned over to Will. "My grandmother isn't a big fan of the Constitution."

"I heard that," Genevra snapped.

"Never mind." Will clapped his hands and smiled, though Ray thought he still looked uneasy. Well, why wouldn't he? He had a lot riding on the night. "You're here; you're safe." He winked. "And the champagne is suitably chilled." He gestured for them to precede him. "Shall we?"

The group moved away, and Ray followed, watching intently but from a discreet distance. He wasn't part of the show, just the watchdog.

The Grays ignored him, but their companion hung back.

"Hey, good-looking. You gonna follow us around?"

He spared a fast look at the assistant, then returned his gaze to Gillian and her entourage. "That's what they pay me for."

She slid an arm through his. "Good. I like those decorative touches."

He disengaged himself, but if she recognized the hint, she didn't take it.

"I'm Crane. Madeleine Crane. Maddie."

"Nice to meet you, Maddie." He was professionally polite. No point in alienating anyone until he had to.

He followed Gillian to the party area. Davenport snagged glasses, handed them around. Word quickly spread, and soon the Grays were surrounded by a small crowd again. But it was made up of overfed men with golf course tans and their brittle wives, so he wasn't nearly as anxious as he'd been outside. He took up a post where he could keep an eye on Gillian's admirers.

"Drink?" Maddie grabbed two glasses of champagne from a passing waiter and held one out to him. He saw it out of the corner of his eye, his gaze solid on the crowd.

"No, thanks."

She shrugged, sipped one, held on to the other.

"Name?"

"Ray."

"Not much for the small talk, are you, Ray?"

He didn't answer.

"But you're cute. You know that, don't you? All dressed up in your little monkey suit with your earpiece and gun."

He slid a sideways glance over to her. She was laughing at him. Well, at least this one didn't look like she'd fall apart if he breathed on her. She looked like she'd survive a gale-force wind.

"Down, girl. I'm working."

"You know what they say about work... and dullness."

He didn't respond, hoping silence would send her away.

She threw him a sly, knowing look. "Well, I guess there's plenty of time to swap stories." She ran a finger down his arm by way of good-bye, then drifted toward Gillian.

Maddie slunk into the circle beside her friend. She was a head taller than Gray and had to lean over to whisper in her ear. Gillian looked up, her eyes landing square on him. She laughed.

He didn't move. Just met her gaze head-on.

Come and get me, she'd said.

Not on his watch.

5

The Gray Visual Arts Center was built around a glassed-in central lobby that was marble-floored and softly lit. A high ceiling gave it a cool, lofty feel, and a wide marble staircase leading up to the second floor gave it sweep and depth. Exhibit rooms branched off the lobby's outer rim, each with discreet gold labels: the WINSTON PARKER SCULPTURE GARDEN; the DAVID AND ANNETTE MILLMAN CONTEMPORARY WING. Above the contemporary wing a banner touted VIOLENCE AND MEDIA: WE ARE WHAT WE WATCH. Works by five artists were listed, along with *Dead Shots* by Gillian Gray.

A half circle of people had formed in the exhibit room, with Gillian in the center. Around them, nine of Gillian's huge photographs showed grisly death in a variety of guises, all located in what critics were fond of calling "jarring banality." Over her shoulder, *Kitchen in Suburbia* hung potent and threatening, though the women surrounding her didn't seem to notice.

"Your work is so... interesting," a woman in red satin said.

"Fascinating," said someone in gold.

The various shades of the evening gowns blurred like

a rainbow on an oil slick, and a picture framed itself in Gillian's head: the group scattered, movement distorting the shapes into streaks of color.

Gillian smiled, egging them on. "Unpleasant . . . but in a nice way."

"Exactly," the woman in gray said eagerly.

The embarrassed silence that followed was interrupted by a server with a tray of champagne. The group helped themselves, and the waitress, a young woman, sidled close to Gillian.

"We're not supposed to talk to the guests," she said softly. "I hope you don't mind." Her brown hair was pulled into a tight ponytail, stretching the skin on her forehead like a botched Botox job. She looked like she was in her late twenties, maybe a little younger. Gillian's age.

"Of course not," Gillian said, relieved to talk to someone real.

"I'm a huge admirer of your work."

"Thank you. Fellow photographer?"

She blushed. Shook her head. "An artist in my own small way."

"Good for you," Gillian said. "And good luck."

"Thanks." She hefted the tray. "Better get rid of these." She moved off, and Gillian looked for a way to retreat.

But she was trapped by the evening gowns. The hairspray and the perfume. Lips mouthing the same questions she'd heard a thousand times. "How does such a small, feminine woman come up with such awful things?" "How do you manage all the details?" "Where do you get your ideas?"

She pulled out her stock answers.

"I don't know how I think of these things."

"I hire people to manage the details."

"I don't know where my ideas come from."

But of course, that was the public lie. She knew exactly how she could think of awful things. They'd been in her head since she was seven and found the bloodied, battered body of her mother. She glanced at the faces around her, but *his* face wasn't there. In the crowd, she didn't hear his voice. But in her head, it was always there.

Tell, and I'll do the same to you.

He was a gorilla in her imagination. Big, dark, hovering. He growled low in his throat. "*Don't tell.*" The words came out of his mouth like snakes and frogs in the fairy tale. They boomed in her memory, deep and ominous and distorted. "Don't tell," they snarled, "or I'll come back and do the same to you."

His face was always obscured, a black shadow surrounded by mountains of shoulders. But his hands, those she could see. She was small, and his hands were close to her face. They were smeared with red. With blood.

He'd cast a spell on her, a wicked, evil spell. Her throat had dried up tight. She couldn't speak. Couldn't move. Then, in all that silence and stillness, his massive arm had shifted like a turnstile and pushed her out of the way. She fell. Tumbled like Alice, down, down, down. And he lumbered away, a thick, giant beast.

The memory took hold of her now, making the museum and the reception disappear into a mist. She let it come. Took the rest of the journey.

Watched in her mind as the intruder left. Suddenly, she was free. Free to run toward her house. To scream for the one person who meant safety and shelter.

Mommy!!! Mommy!!!

The screen door slammed as she pounded inside.

Mommy!

The sound of her heart was huge in her ears, the hammering frightening.

How funny for Mommy to be lying on the kitchen floor. Not funny ha-ha, but scary funny. She was on her back. The floor was wet all around her. Red and dark and wet. A knife lay in the muck. Her mother's eyes were wide-open, but she didn't see her little girl. She didn't turn her head when Gillian shook her. Her pretty dress with the pink flowers and the green ribbon was pushed to her waist. She had no panties on. Gillian felt shaky and strange to see what her mommy looked like down there. She lowered the dress. Her hands were now red, too.

Gillian never remembered screaming, although stories said she did. They found her wandering down Highway 100 in west Nashville, bloodstained and crying. She didn't remember that, but at some point someone gave her a sedative, and time blurred. Memory blurred.

And twenty years later she still believed that she, too, would die on a floor somewhere. Pointless, random. Too soon.

Stay in the limelight. How else to catch the bastard?

Her best hope. Her worst nightmare.

Come and get me.

Around her people were fawning, their voices less real than the ones in her head. She was breathing too hard and too fast. She clutched the metal strap of the evening bag Genevra had thrust on her as they were leaving home, felt it bite into her skin until she was no longer gasping for air. Until she was back, back in the present, the museum, the party.

Eyes hounded her. She glanced over the heads of the group to the tall man who'd been staring at her ever since she arrived. Museum security, someone had called him.

Maddie had tested him, then whispered in her ear, calling him "fine," "steady," "undistractable." Gillian called him what he was. Watchdog.

She should be grateful.

But if a watchdog was around, how would *he* get to her?

She excused herself from the group but had only taken a few steps when she heard a shout, then a bloodcurdling scream.

She whirled. A blur of movement raced across the room toward her.

"You want to bleed?" a crazed voice screamed. "I'll make you bleed!"

Gillian froze, and the server from earlier tossed something at her.

Before it could hit, someone pushed Gillian out of the way. Tackled her. She went down with a thud. A body landed on top. Her head cracked against the marble floor. Something cold and liquid splattered over her. Blood. Oh, God, there was blood everywhere.

6

A moment of stunned silence, then shouts and screams ricocheted around her.

When she could focus again, she saw the security man—what was his name? Ray something or other—pinning her down. Her arms were flung out; Genevra's purse lay a few feet away.

"What happened?" She pushed against him. Tried to get up.

"Stay down."

"There's blood!" The image of another body, another pool of blood invaded her thoughts. "There's blood all over!" She fought to get away, but he was so strong.

"It's not blood. It's someone's idea of a joke. Stay still."

But her lungs felt like they were going to collapse. He was a big man, over six feet if she judged correctly, which meant nearly a foot taller than she. With all the extra pounds to go with it. He was squeezing the breath out of her. She pushed against his shoulder again. "I can't breathe."

He didn't seem to care. "Don't move." He looked around wildly. People scurried toward them. "Get back!" He reached beneath him, pulled out a gun, and waved it at them. More screams. People ran away. Someone dropped a glass, and it shattered against the marble floor. Feet gathered in a rush around her. Shiny shoes topped by pants with tuxedo stripes. More security circling close.

A shout. People pointed. Between black-clad legs, she saw the waitress dash across the room, chased by two uniformed guards. The crowd slowed the pursuers, and the waitress darted away. Almost made it out of the exhibit room. The security men shoved, pushed people aside, cleared a path. One leaped and brought the fleeing woman down.

She sprawled on the floor. Two seconds later, her hands were imprisoned behind her back in plastic cuffs. One of the men hauled her to her feet.

"Poison!" she screamed in Gillian's direction. "You're poison!"

"Shut up!" Her captor shook her.

A few minutes ago, her face had been shy and polite. Now it was screwed into a vicious snarl. "Pig! Rich fucking pig!" Her screaming accusations faded as they dragged her away, but everyone could hear her distant rant: "De-cen-cy! De-cen-cy!"

Only when the sounds had disappeared did Ray roll off Gillian. He stood, held out a hand to pull her up. "You all right?"

She nodded grimly within the circle of men that enclosed her. The open plastic bag of whatever it was lay crushed at their feet. Ray had taken the brunt of the goop—paint, blood, thick, colored water. Oh, God. She swallowed. His neck and chest were soaked with it.

"She...she spoke to me earlier," Gillian said, still stunned. Despite weathering virulent protests, she'd never been physically attacked before. "She admired my work."

"Yeah?" Sweat streaked down the side of his face. He hardly seemed to hear her. He was watching the crowd intently, drawing her back, the other men—three of them—coming with them out of the room. But he had heard. "A few hours before he killed him, Mark Chapman asked John Lennon to autograph an album for him."

She repressed a shudder. Hushed murmurs now replaced the shouting and the screams. Through the wall of bodies shielding her, she glimpsed people staring and whispering. They gaped fearfully at the men beside her and their drawn weapons. Looked over their shoulders toward the lobby, trying to decide whether to flee themselves.

Ray backed her up against a wall, around a corner, out of sight. His body shielded her, his hand gripped the gun conspicuously. The other three men formed a screen around them. "Landowe," Ray said. "What do you see?"

From over his shoulder, one of the men said, "Nothing."

Ray spoke into what looked like the air, but what quickly became apparent was a wireless radio mike. "Carlson, what's going on? Everyone okay? Yes, she's fine."

One of the other three circled a finger in the air, signaling okay. Only then did the men around her holster their weapons and relax their stance.

The man Ray had called Landowe spoke. "You got her?"

"Yeah," Ray said.

The men eased away, and she headed back to the exhibit room, Ray shadowing her. A crowd had gathered around the wall that held her photos, blocking her view of them. When they saw her, they stepped back, parting like the Red Sea. Davenport was there. Even paler than usual.

"I'm…I'm so sorry," he murmured as Gillian stepped closer.

The view to *Kitchen in Suburbia* was unobstructed. Dripping streaks of red blotched the photograph and spattered the wall beside it.

"We'll take it down," Will said. "Get it cleaned up."

Gillian contemplated the damage. The fake blood marring the fake death scene struck her as perfect commentary.

"No. Leave it. Let it become part of the piece."

Will opened his mouth to object, but before he could, Maddie elbowed her way in. "Gillian!" She gasped. "Oh, my God." Flinging an arm around Gillian's shoulders, she pulled her close. "I'm sorry. I'm so sorry."

Ray stepped back, gave the two women room.

"Don't be." Gillian straightened. "This is what we live for. I'm fine." She stood square-shouldered and stiff. But he'd felt the tremors as he held her. And she was breathing hard. She was breathing very hard. And she didn't shrug off Maddie's comforting arm.

Carlson ran up to him. "She okay?"

Ray assured him she was. "That piece of crap though…" He indicated the marred photograph and the fake blood, which dripped down, a bright, ugly mess.

"Yeah. The woman was one of Dobie's." Matthew Dobie was leading the pack outside. Head of the self-proclaimed Citizens for American Values, he'd brought his show to Nashville and, abetted by area churches, had been drawing crowds all day. "We got her stashed in an office upstairs until your friends from Metro get here."

A pulse of fury was throttling Ray. "How the hell did she get in?"

Carlson looked rightly upset. “Came with the wait-staff.”

“You’re kidding.” Ray shook his head, looked away. “That’s what comes of letting the client do the vetting.”

Carlson’s eyes flashed with the implied criticism. “You like that new pickup you bought?”

“What the hell does that—”

“We don’t work for free, Ray, and we’re expensive. The museum cherry-picked the services.”

Ray didn’t answer. In security, as in everything else, money talked.

“Gotta go,” Carlson said. “Police won’t release the crowd until a detective gets here.” He nodded to Gillian. “Keep your eye on her.”

Carlson left, and Ray maintained a clear view of Gillian. Maddie’s arm was still around her, and she still stood stoically in front of her bloodied photographs. Ironic, that.

A woman in a shiny dress approached. “Excuse me. I think this is Miss Gray’s.” She held out a tiny glitter of a purse, and Ray took it. “Thanks. I’ll see she gets it.”

He stared down at the feminine thing, barely bigger than his hand. Reaction set in all of a sudden, and the shakes started. It was only adrenaline again, and he knew it wouldn’t last, but Jesus, the line between safe and unsafe was slim.

7

"I think we should go," Maddie said. She'd seen Gillian like this before—terrified and damned if she'd admit it—but it had been twelve years ago, when they were both fifteen and roommates at Hadley. Back then, Gillian was shut down so far the only place she'd open up was on her own skin. Maddie didn't think anything could bring Gillian back to that place, but seeing her blood-spattered dress and the haunted gleam in her eye, she was suddenly not so sure. She touched Gillian's elbow, guiding her from the people staring at her.

Gillian skittered away. "I need a minute."

But Maddie knew better. How many times in school had she seen Gillian spiral down the dark rabbit hole inside her own head? How many times had Maddie lugged her out of the quicksand? Besides, Maddie had her own part to answer for. A flicker of guilt touched her, and she made a more concerted grab for Gillian's arm. "No, you don't."

Too late. Gillian slipped away, leaving Maddie to distract the crowd.

* * *

"All right?"

Gillian's shadow, the security man—Ray—watched her with sharp brown eyes as she crossed into the lobby and found a vacant corner.

She smoothed down her dress, ignoring the dots of fake blood, which were already drying. "Of course. Nothing like a little assault to liven things up."

"I can have one of the men bring you a glass of water if you—"

"I'm fine." But her voice was a little too loud, a little too definite, and those keen brown eyes didn't miss it.

"Sure you are." Meaning the opposite. "Able to leap off a tall building, too, I bet."

She gave him a swift, assessing look. How dare he see through her? Before she could respond, she saw Genevra approach, and groaned inwardly.

"It's time we left," her grandmother said. She had that determined look in her eyes. The one that brooked no arguments. The one that made Gillian want to try.

But Ray, her new savior, did it for her. "Sorry," he said, his voice equally firm, "but no one's leaving. Police will want to talk to everyone first."

"Everyone?" Genevra managed to get both concern and disdain into the one word. "What is there to talk about? Isn't it clear? We all saw…"

But she didn't have time to finish. Chip Gray and Will Davenport closed in on them.

"Are you all right, Gillian?" Chip breached the gap between himself and his granddaughter in three hefty steps.

"Can I get you anything?" Will asked.

"I'm fine." The phrase fell off Gillian's lips with practiced ease. Because what else was she going to say? That the woman who was happy to pour fake blood over herself and take pictures was now a jellied, shaking blob just because someone else had done it? She'd deny it. She'd defy anyone to say it.

Never mind that in the pictures she was in control. She said when and how much. It was her choice, always her choice. That was half the point, wasn't it?

"Would you like to sit down?" Davenport said. "We could go to my office."

"What the hell happened?" Chip was hectoring Ray. "How could you let that lunatic in here?"

"You will not make a scene," Genevra said. "The police can handle this. We are going." She turned, but no one followed.

"Uh... my office is just upstairs," Will offered again.

"I want an answer," Chip said, badgering Ray with a pointed finger.

"Try saying thank you, first," Gillian said.

"Talk to Carlson," Ray said calmly, and Gillian was impressed. Wasn't easy to keep your cool when Chip Gray was bullying you into losing it. "He's the boss. He'll explain it." Ray gave Will a severe look that Will didn't see.

"I will," Chip was saying. "You can bet on it."

"Miss Gray?" A compact man in a blue velvet tuxedo elbowed his way over to her. His perfectly round shaved head popped out of his jacket like a melon in the moonlight, and with his silver mustache, he looked like the reincarnation of Hercule Poirot, only less Poirot and more Pierrot. "Benton James, *Tennessean.* So sorry about the... incident." He smiled and didn't appear sorry at all. "I wonder, could I ask you a few questions?"

"For God's sake, Benton," Will Davenport said, "leave her alone."

"Might be best to wait somewhere else," Ray said to her in a cool, low voice.

Out of the corner of her eye, she saw Maddie hurrying over. Gillian extended a hand to the reporter. "So nice to meet you." She smiled and walked past him. Ray was right behind her.

Maddie stepped in front of Benton, preventing him from following. "Miss Gray will issue a statement later," she said, and whatever the reporter replied was lost in the growing distance between them.

Gillian glanced at Ray. For all that had happened, she hadn't really studied him, and now she wanted to. What kind of man risks himself to save a stranger?

The ones she knew never put themselves on the line for anything, least of all her. Then again, that was why the last of the rat bastards was six months gone.

But this man... Ray. More fair than dark, with a broad face that looked corn-fed and farm-raised. The kind of face that should have freckles and didn't. With the wrong kind of food and a desk job, it could go to fat and sink into his neck, but that didn't look imminent. At the moment his jaw was hard-edged, the hair close-cropped, the brown eyes alert.

"I haven't thanked you," she said.

He nodded. "Glad it wasn't more serious."

She waved a hand toward the mess that was his jacket and shirt. "You can send me the dry-cleaning bill."

"No big deal. Carlson will take care of it."

She'd never felt comfortable with large men. They were like trees, tall and straight and impossible to see what lurked behind.

But Ray put her at ease. Even with blood all over him, he was direct. Quiet. Purposeful. His calm detachment grounded her. Hard enough to handle her own reactions, let alone someone else's.

They left the reception area and turned into the hallway that led to the front entrance. Footsteps echoed behind them. Ray turned, stepped behind to shield her. But it was her grandparents.

"Will the car be waiting?" Genevra said without preamble as if Ray had stopped to speak to her.

"When Metro releases you, I'll have the driver paged," Ray answered.

"I want to go now," Genevra insisted. "We can talk to the police in the morning."

"You can make a run for it." There was muffled amusement in Ray's voice. "But I don't think you'd get past the sentry." He thumbed over his shoulder. Beyond the metal detector an officer in the dark blue uniform of Nashville Metro Police stood guard.

Genevra wobbled, clutched Chip's arm.

"Genevra!" Chip buoyed her up.

"Whoa." Ray took the older woman's weight. "Here, sit down." He led her to a bench against the wall.

She fanned herself. "I'm fine," she said, though her face was pale and drawn. "Don't fuss." She slapped at Chip, who hovered over her.

The elevator was a few feet away. Gillian punched the UP button and looked at her grandfather. "Do you know where Will's office is?"

"Like I know my own. The man persuaded me out of ten million dollors there."

"Take Grandmother up. If the police want to talk to either of you, I'll tell them where you are."

When Chip hesitated, Ray said, "It's a good idea, sir."

The elevator opened, and Gillian ushered her grandparents through. With Ray in tow, she escorted them to the fourth floor and saw them ensconced in Will's office. "You can rest here," Gillian said, and turned to leave.

"Aren't you staying with us?" Genevra asked.

Gillian heard the worry behind the icy tone and gestured vaguely to the door. "No. I'm going back down." But she couldn't quite meet her grandmother's eyes, and Genevra knew it.

"No, you're not. Where are you going?"

"I told you—"

"Don't lie to me, Gillian."

Heat crawled up Gillian's face, but she didn't acknowledge it. Instead, she gave her grandmother what she wanted. The truth. Straight and fast. "I'm going to see the woman."

"Excuse me?" Ray shot her a baffled look.

"The woman. The waitress. I want to talk to her."

"Don't be ridiculous," Genevra snapped.

"For God's sake, Gillian," Chip said. "What is the point? You can't talk to fanatics."

There was a watercooler in the corner. Gillian dispensed a cupful and handed it to Genevra. "I'll be fine."

"Gillian—"

"I'll be fine."

She slipped out of the office before her grandparents could object further. They would never understand, and she was beyond explaining it.

8

Her shadow followed her out. Caught her leaning against the wall trying to gather herself together.

"What's wrong with your grandmother?"

"Besides being seventy-five?" Gillian ticked off the answers in her head: her daughter murdered, her granddaughter attacked. The sight of uniforms brought back memories. Bad memories. Enough to make anyone feel faint. "Family reunions." Gillian pushed off the wall. "Always hell."

She continued down the corridor to the elevator. "Where to?" she asked Ray.

Ray said, "Look, you're not really going to—"

She didn't answer.

"I mean, I don't think it's a good idea," Ray said.

"This floor?" Gillian punched the elevator call button. "Or downstairs?"

Ray looked annoyed. Shook his head. "Carlson said they stashed her in one of the offices until Metro shows up."

"If I remember, the second floor contains more exhibits and classrooms. That means this floor or the one below. Or the basement. Which is it?"

He leaned against a wall, crossed his arms. "Why are you doing this?"

She felt his eyes on her, another being wanting another explanation from her. Someone else who wouldn't understand the overpowering need to stare down the face of violence.

"Because I have to."

"Glutton for punishment?"

"Since birth."

"And if I don't tell you where, you'll just open every door on every floor?"

"Probably."

He sighed and touched his earpiece. "I'm bringing Miss Gray." He listened, his eyes on her. "Not my idea, no." Nodded toward the elevator. "One floor down," he said, and checked the elevator before he led her into it.

They made their way to a workshop with a double-paneled door that swung inward. Wide drafting tables and workbenches dotted the space. Shelves lined the walls. They were stacked with wood, foam core, supplies, and tools. The design room. Where the exhibits were built.

Someone had cleared a space in the middle. The server was in a chair, her hands cuffed to the legs. It was a horrendously distorted position. As she was unable to sit up, her back was bowed like a hunchback's and her head hung down.

"Couldn't get her to stop screaming," the man guarding her said by way of explanation. "All that decency crap."

"For God's sake, let her sit up," Gillian said.

Ray nodded, and the man guarding the waitress complied. But he relocked her hands to the chair arms.

Slowly, the woman sat up. Her eyes were red, her face

tear-streaked. She drilled Gillian with a hot, angry look. "What did you do that for?"

A weird kind of peace rippled through Gillian. *Not him.* Not this time. Not tonight.

The relief made her giddy. Of course it wasn't him. Couldn't have been. Not if it was a her. So, no monster with big hands. Just a fragile woman, bound in anger like she was bound in cuffs.

Been there, done that.

Gently, Gillian asked, "What's your name?"

The woman looked at her sullenly. "Ruth."

"I didn't like to see you like that, Ruth. The position they had you in looked painful."

"So? What do you care?"

Gillian shrugged. "Couldn't talk to you that way."

"Talk about what? Don't expect me to say I'm sorry. What you do is disgusting. The blood, the cruelty. It's sick. You're sick." Another surly stare from the waitress. "You have no right."

Nothing Gillian hadn't been accused of before, but there was something else in the other woman's face. Something more. "No right to do what?"

"No right..." Huge tears gathered in Ruth's eyes. She looked away. "To make money off it. Sell art. Get famous."

Gillian didn't bother saying she inherited her money from her mother after she was murdered. Or that whatever fame she had was swollen out of proportion because of that murder. Or that she needed the fame to draw out the monster who'd given her both.

She only observed the bound woman. The chair, the tied wrists, the aura of submission. Automatically, she framed the shot, lit it, titled it: *Victim.* She'd spoken about her work to hundreds of people. Received dozens of e-mails daily on her Web site. Those who were the most vehement were often wounded themselves.

She took a guess. "Did something happen to you?"

Ruth didn't answer.

"What happened to you, Ruth?"

She shook her head fiercely. "Not me," Ruth said at last, her voice tight and broken.

"Someone you love?"

"My sister. That picture..." She swung around, and Gillian swallowed at the raw loss in Ruth's face.

"I'm so sorry." She pressed her hand over Ruth's cuffed one. "I hope they caught whoever hurt her."

"He'll die in jail."

"That's good. You're safe." Ruth's hair had come undone from its ponytail. Sweaty strands clung to her forehead. Gillian brushed them back. Ruth shuddered under her touch. "Remember that, Ruth. How lucky you are. You're safe."

"No one is safe," Ruth said bitterly.

Couldn't argue with that.

She held Ruth's gaze a moment, then turned and left.

Ray exchanged a look with the guy on guard duty. A look that said they were each a little unsure about the sanity of both women.

Silently, Ray followed Gillian to the elevator. Hers was a weird kind of craziness, though. Took guts for a victim to confront the person who hurt her and do it with little or no rancor.

He punched the call button. "Why'd you do that?"

"Do what?"

"Why were you kind to her?"

Truth was, he wouldn't have expected the person who created such intensely violent photographs to be kind.

"Kindness?" She shrugged and gave him an amused smile. "It was just common decency."

The word hung in the air, a sardonic twist on the voices that still shouted outside.

They stepped in the elevator, and Ray punched the button for the main floor.

On the way down she said, "Ever see a dead body?"

His awareness of her sharpened. The things she said. Like he never knew what would come out of her mouth next. "I was a cop. I've seen my share."

"It's not like on TV, is it?"

He shook his head.

"We're so used to sanitized violence; we don't even know it's not real."

He made the obvious connection. "Not like your photographs."

"My work is as real as I can get short of dying myself." She laughed shortly. "And don't think I haven't tried that, too." He gave her a swift, startled look, but she rode right over it. "But it's important to see the truth, don't you think?"

For some crazy reason, a picture of his mother flashed in his head. Christ, the last time he'd thought of Sherry Pearce . . . he couldn't remember the last time. But a clear image arose: her thin, wasted form sitting by the phone, waiting, hoping, hour after hour, day after day, week after week, year after year. Sucking on Virginia Slims and swishing the ice in her glass. She'd spent a lifetime waiting for that phone to ring, for that crook of a husband to come back, and nothing Ray did, no amount of truth telling could dissuade her from that hope.

"Not everyone is strong enough for the truth," Ray said.

That's what the gin was for, Sherry always told him.

The elevator door opened on a squat, broad-shouldered man about to enter. Gillian started, and the man paused. Saw the passengers inside. His face split into a grin.

"Well, well, well. Lookie here. Hey, Ray."

Ray stopped. Stared into the eyes of the man who'd been his professional mentor and his friend. Could the night get any worse? "Burke." He nodded stiffly and escorted Gillian out of the elevator.

Burke glanced at the blood on Ray's shirt, over to Gillian, and back again. "Didn't know babysitting could be such rough work."

"Package is upstairs. Tied in a nice neat bow so you can handle her."

Burke acknowledged this with another grin and stepped inside the elevator. "Seen Nancy lately?"

"You know I haven't."

He held his arms out front, framing a giant invisible stomach. "Big as a house." The door began to slide shut. "Twins." Just before it sealed him up, Burke laughed.

"Asshole," Ray muttered, but he stared at the doors.

"Who's Burke?" Gillian said.

Ray flicked a glance at her, then back at the hard, closed elevator doors. "Detective Jimmy Burke. My brother-in-law." He paused. Frowned. "Ex-brother-in-law."

9

The police herded everyone into the hallway while one of their own snapped pictures of the ruined exhibit; the remnants of the blood-filled plastic bag; and its contents, which were still smeared all over Ray's shirt and tuxedo and spattered over Gillian's arms.

An hour after she'd seen him in the elevator, Gillian spoke with Detective Burke.

"And she just came flying up to you?" Burke asked after Gillian described what had happened.

"Yes."

"And that's when Pearce—"

"Tackled me. Like I told you. He... got in the way. Prevented her from hurting me."

Ray was a few feet away, leaning against a wall and watching the crowd. Burke waved him over.

"So you're the hero tonight," Burke said.

Ray's face was a mask. "I just did my job."

"You were always good at that, weren't you, Ray?"

"Look, Miss Gray isn't interested—"

"I heard you were related," Gillian said to Burke, as if Ray was no longer there.

"Damn good cop," Burke told her.

"Really?" Curious, Gillian examined Ray, watched his face darken, then turned back to Burke. "Why'd he leave, then?"

"I'm right here." Ray scowled. "You want to know, just ask."

But it was Burke, not Gillian, who did. "Why'd you leave, Ray?"

"You know damn well why."

Burke sniggered. "And look where it got you."

"Are we done? Because I'm thinking we're done."

"Yeah, we're done. You come down to the station tomorrow and sign a statement."

Ray grabbed Gillian's arm and dragged her away.

"Hey, farm boy. Slow down."

He dropped her arm. "Farm boy?"

She shrugged. "It's what you look like. Iowa, Nebraska. Pigs, cows, sheep."

He threw her a puzzled scowl.

"What's wrong with that? Hey—you're not one of those roots-rejecting country boys?"

"My 'roots' are on Long Island. You live in New York now, so you should know all about it. Malls, traffic, subdivisions. No pigs and definitely no sheep. Unless we're talking the human kind."

Well, well, well. A transplant. No wonder she felt a bond.

"So what are you doing here?" She couldn't keep the scornful disbelief out of her voice.

"Miss Gray," he said with mock deference, "aren't you originally from Nashville? You're not one of those roots-rejecting country girls are you?"

She smiled. Saw the gleam of humor in his eyes. "Okay, busted. Let me rephrase. What brought you down here, Ray?"

"Circumstances."

She knew an evasion when she heard one. "Ever think about going back?"

"Going back? Oh, yeah, going somewhere."

"So what's keeping you?"

Just then, Carlson waved him over. "Excuse me," Ray muttered, and left. A little too eagerly in her opinion.

It was nearly midnight before the police released the crowd. Gillian and Maddie huddled together on one side of the exhibition room waiting to be dismissed. Across the way, an empty patch of wall marked the spot where her photograph had hung. The blood on the wall around it had dried into a flaked and faded brown. Despite her suggestion, Will had taken it down. By Friday, when the exhibit opened to the public, it would all be sanitized. As if nothing had happened.

Chip stood in front of the bald spot, immersed in a heated discussion with Carlson and Ray. Ray had stashed his bloodied jacket over the back of a nearby chair and stood in his blotched shirt, black tie hanging loose against the white shirt neck, sleeves rolled up on strong arms. She liked the way he looked, rumpled and tired, the black and white an intense contrast, the blood streaked and splattered. Another title popped into her head. *Aftermath.* If she had her little Nikon, a couple of strobes…

"Ole Chip ripping them a new one?" Maddie murmured, cocking her head curiously.

"Ray said the museum handled the catering staff, so if anyone's getting ripped, it isn't him or his boss."

"Well, they're certainly going at it."

Gillian didn't respond, knowing all too well what the

group was probably talking about. Keeper number thirty-three in a never-ending list.

She reframed the shot in her head. If she could catch Ray just like that, leg bent, hand straddling his low-slung hip. Maybe shoot two-and-a-quarters with the Hasselblad, get more detail.

Maddie nudged her. "What are you thinking, woman?"

Gillian shrugged, tore her gaze away. "Nothing." Then couldn't help looking again.

"Yeah, right." Maddie snickered. "You can take the girl away from the lens, but you can't take the lens away from the girl."

Ray shot a swift glance over his shoulder. At her. Gillian Gray. Bloodstained, exhausted. The sight set something off inside him. A warning bell. An alarm about to go off. Nothing loud and clanging. Just a deep, low tolling. He could feel her eyes pulling at him. Soft, needy, defiant eyes. Troubled eyes.

"Look, it's a few days, right? Just until the hospital fund-raiser—the whaddyacallit—gala, art auction—next Saturday night." He was talking to Chip Gray's frown, knowing he wasn't getting through.

"Ten days," Chip corrected.

Jeez. Ten days was plenty long to get into all kinds of trouble Ray didn't want to think about. He waved the implied objection away. "Okay, whatever. Not a lifetime. If she stays low, is careful, I don't think there'll be a repeat. I really don't think protective service is necessary."

"You don't know her," Chip said. "She's incapable of keeping a low profile."

He thought of the scene with the reporters. The way

she barged in to talk to her attacker. "Landowe, then." He grabbed a name out of the air, turned to Carlson. "He's good with creative types."

"You've already established a relationship with her," Carlson said, pointing out the obvious.

Ray opened his mouth to deny that, but Chip forestalled him. "I'll double the fee."

"Look, Ray," Carlson said. "Like you said, not a lifetime."

Ray didn't like his own words used against him. "I don't th—"

"And throw in a personal bonus for you," Chip added.

Christ. He felt himself weakening. It wasn't the money. He had plenty of that. There was only him to buy for, and he didn't have expensive tastes. So it wasn't money. It was those eyes. Why couldn't he turn his back on them?

Because he didn't cut and run, that's why. Sticking was his specialty. Not to mention his private little torture chamber.

"I'd consider it a personal favor," Chip said.

Oh, well, then. A personal favor to Chip Gray. He wanted to tell him, *personally,* that he didn't give a shit. Not about Chip. "All right." Ray sighed. "You got your ten."

Chip's frown broke into a victorious smile. He extended a hand to seal the deal. "I won't forget this," he said. "The Grays have long memories. You won't regret it."

Ray already doubted that, but he didn't say so. He'd made the deal, he wasn't going to carp about it. Carlson left. Ray grabbed his jacket, and he and Chip headed toward Gillian.

"They're bringing the car around," Chip told her. "Let's go."

She didn't jump when the old man said jump. She only flicked a sardonic glance at Ray. "They rope you in?"

Chip frowned. "Mr. Pearce will look after you until you can return to New York. A few days. It's all arranged."

Gillian nodded. Things were always arranged, and somehow the arrangements never stuck. Her mother had arranged to move them here, away from her fast-track life, away from the pressure and the drugs and the all-night parties. She had wanted a safe place to raise her child. A nice place. A quiet place. The irony was staggering.

Chip gestured for Gillian to precede him. "Your grandmother is tired. Let's not keep her waiting."

The Gray house was miles away, but Gillian felt its suffocating walls close in on her. And outside, the night beckoned, thick with danger, but also possibility. She'd been attacked, but not by him.

He was still out there.

She looked over at Maddie. "Can you see them home?"

A silent message passed between them.

You up to trouble, girl?

Help me out. I can't go home yet.

"You come soon, okay?" Maddie said at last.

Gillian nodded, but Maddie knew her too well.

Chip peered at her, his square, mottled face irritated but resigned to it. "How will you get back?" he demanded.

She squinted up at Ray. "Mr. Pearce has a car, don't you, Ray?"

Exasperation flashed across Ray's face, then was quickly gone. "I'll see she gets home," he told Chip.

"Come on." Maddie tugged at Chip's arm. "Let me find Mrs. Gray and get you two out of here."

Her grandfather allowed himself to be led away, and Gillian was alone with Ray.

10

"You have plans?" Ray asked. "Because it's twelve-fifteen on a Wednesday night in Nashville."

"You miss your church meeting, Ray?"

"Just wondering where you think you're off to."

She watched her grandfather head through the arch and into the lobby, where the dregs of the reception were still sputtering out. He shuffled a bit, stooped and worn down by the night. Something turned over in her heart. He was getting so old. "Oh, I don't know. Downtown. Second Avenue is still jumping."

"Yeah, but you don't look like the tourist bar type."

She debated. Briefly. Decided to tell him the truth. Or at least part of it. "I don't want to go home until after lights out," she said. "Too much worrying."

"After tonight, maybe justified."

"Doesn't make it easier to live with, though."

"You'd be safer at home."

She thought of the night, heard the pump action of her blood pounding through her heart. "I'm not too good with safe," she said. "That's why you're here."

He didn't look happy about that.

"Oh, come on, Ray. Lighten up. You're getting paid,

aren't you? Ole Chip is great with that stuff. What'd he bribe you with?"

Ray took her arm and led her away.

She laughed and stumbled along. "Must have been good. Come on, spill."

He turned a corner and lugged her toward a back door delivery entrance she hadn't known was there.

"What's the big secret?"

"It's none of your business."

"Are you kidding? I *am* the business."

They arrived at the wide metal door, and he turned to her. "Double my fee to the agency plus a personal bonus. Happy?"

She smiled, but it felt all too wintry. "For you? Sure. I'm just helping you earn your keep. Besides, I'm starved. Can't eat at these things. Bet you are, too." She poked him in the belly. Hard as a rock. "Big guy like you."

He unlocked the door with a key card, told her to stay put while he peeked outside.

"Okay," he said after a few minutes skulking around. "Let's go." He beckoned at her impatiently.

His car turned out to be a full-size pickup. Black as onyx, all shiny and new. She couldn't help laughing when she saw it.

"What did I tell you?" She high-fived the air. "Farm boy all the way."

He opened the door for her and helped her up. "I gotta haul stuff; I can haul stuff."

"Yeah? What kind of stuff do you haul?"

"People like you." He slammed her door shut.

He yanked off his loose tie, threw his ruined jacket in the back, and slid behind the wheel. Then he backed out and headed to Broadway. But when he should have taken a right toward Second Avenue, he went left.

"River's that way," she said, pointing toward the eastern tip of Broadway, which ended at the Cumberland.

"My time as an extra on *Night of the Living Dead* is over."

He headed west, past what was left of the railroad shed at Union Station and farther on toward the brick gates that marked the beginning of Vanderbilt. Carefully placed spotlights gave the university's name a ghostly glow.

Traffic was almost nonexistent, so he sped through the lights, and she tried not to note the changes since the last time she'd been there three years ago. She wanted Nashville to remain a blur, an imprecise dot on the map of memory. A place she didn't even have to visit in her mind.

But some things linger no matter what. At Murphy Road he made a right. The Shoney's and Mr. Gatti's that used to occupy the corner were gone. In an effort to make her feel normal, her grandparents had once taken her to Mr. Gatti's, an all-you-can-eat pizza joint. She didn't eat much in those days and didn't remember whether they got their money's worth. She did remember lots of screaming kids, balloons, the whistle and ring of video games. Someone was having a birthday party, and the faces of the children had looked so strange to her. Smiling. Laughing.

Suddenly she wished she were out of the cab and standing in the truck bed, black wind flying through her hair, arms out to possess the dark.

She rolled down the window and stuck her head out. Screamed into the night like a teenager after a keg party.

Ray swerved. "What the f—" He yanked her back in. "What the hell you think you're doing?"

She bounced back in her seat, laughed. “God, that felt good.”

“Are you crazy?”

“You’ve seen my work,” she said lightly, the butt of her own joke.

He cut a hard glance her way. “Put your seat belt on.”

She didn’t move.

“Put your damn seat belt on!”

“Yes, Dad.” She leaned back, let the air wash her face with shadow, and fastened the belt.

They were heading into Sylvan Park, a vintage neighborhood of tiny bungalows on small lots. The streets were laid out alphabetically by state. He turned onto Nebraska and pulled in front of a small gray clapboard house.

Nebraska. She looked down to hide a smile.

He yanked the parking brake so hard it screeched. “You do anything like that again, and I’ll tie you down and cuff you to the floor.”

“That might be interesting.” She threw him a sly smile.

“Not the way I do it. Now don’t move until I come around.” He swiveled to collect his clothes from the back. “Take me five minutes to change.”

He threw the jacket over his shoulder and came around the front end to her side. Opened her door, took her elbow, and escorted her to the house. As he’d done at the museum, his big body shielded her again. Odd to have another person look out for her. To face the night on her account. Especially since he was so pissed at her.

At the front door, he handed her the key. “Keep my hands free,” he told her.

She looked out at the darkness with cold assessment. Would it be here, now? With Ray beside her? Would he keep the beast away or dare him to attack?

Her back prickled as she inserted the key. But the door opened, and Ray turned on the light. It snapped the world into brightness, cold, clear, and normal.

She looked around. The entrance bled right into a sparsely furnished front room with an air of impermanence about it. Temporary digs.

"Live here long?"

"Three years."

Not so temporary.

A random set of white plastic shelves stood against a wall. A hockey stick leaned against it. In a corner across from a wide-screen TV, an easy chair, the kind you buy at one of those giant furniture outlets. A long-sleeved jersey with a faded number lay over one arm.

Ray whisked the shirt away. "Have a seat. I'll be right back."

He went toward the back of the house, but she didn't sit. She wandered over to the shelf. Wedged between a pile of *Sports Illustrated*s and a bunch of CDs was a framed picture. Ray Pearce in a game uniform, holding a trophy, one arm clutching a hockey stick, the other around a woman. Well, hardly a woman. A girl. Young woman at best. Dark-haired, dark-eyed. Too much makeup. But excited, sparkling. A younger version of Ray wore a goofy, happy grin himself. High school?

She put the photo down and trailed down the hallway he'd disappeared into. The kitchen was off to the right, and she detoured there. It was a tiny square rimmed by counter space. She opened the fridge. Milk, eggs, apples, cheese. Sheesh, the guy was a health nut. The cabinets proved equally unpromising.

"Where's the beer and chips?" she yelled.

The water swooshed on. "What?"

"The beer and—" She trundled down the hallway, found him in the bathroom, shirtless, washing off the stains from his face and neck.

He didn't notice her at first, so she looked her fill. Great back, tight ass. Broad chest, rippled arms. God, she wished she had that camera.

He grabbed a towel and scrubbed his face. Saw her standing in the doorway gaping at him. Slowly he straightened. Stood there in plain view for a second, like he knew exactly what she was doing, and it was fine with him. Then he pushed past her.

"You ever hear of knocking?"

She followed him into the bedroom. The bloodied jacket was puddled in a corner, the tie and shirt on top. "You ever do any modeling?"

He whirled to face her, burst out laughing. "You're kidding, right?"

"It's good money for standing around."

He opened a drawer, took out a T-shirt. "Do you ever think about the things you say? I mean, before you say them."

"You have a great look."

"Put me in a pair of overalls and stick a pitchfork in my hand kind of look?" He pulled the shirt over his head.

She smiled. Over his shoulder she saw the open closet. A full dress uniform hung inside a plastic dry cleaning wrapper. She wandered over, saw the NPD pin on the blue uniform chest, all shiny and gold.

She wondered what had happened. Had he grown tired of the bad guys? Since he was still in the protect and serve business, that didn't seem likely. Maybe it was the lousy civil service pay. Looking around his house, she doubted that, too. So . . . what? Had he taken a bribe? Shot the wrong guy and started a riot? He didn't look like the screwup type. He looked upright and decent.

She turned to ask him about it, but he reached over and shut the closet door. Shoved a towel at her. Not particularly politely either.

"Want to get cleaned up, the bathroom's free," he said.

11

No one would ever call Margaret Pulley a pretty thing. She was a little too plump around the middle and a little too sad around the eyes. But he liked to watch her while he worked. Her suit just this side of tight, her hair just a hog's breath short of neat. Not perfect, but was anyone? Perfection was reserved for what people did, not who they were.

And so it was with Miss Margaret. A hard worker, she often stayed long into the dark night, ticking away at her computer, signing forms and laying them in piles that never stayed straight. Hidden, he'd watch her from the alley across the office on Nolensville Road. The turn of her face, the sigh in her shoulders. Through the front window, he could see her fluffy blond head, green with the glow from her computer screen.

His heart pounded with the possibilities. Sometimes he would touch himself.

Once, during the day, he had to go in to have his order signed, and she'd smiled at him. She was older than he would have liked. A bit too hard-used. But still, tonight, she was the perfect model. The perfect stand-in.

She'd gone down easier than his last. That one had

kicked and fought 'til the end. Miss Margaret just kind of gave in.

Maybe it was because he whispered at her how famous she'd be. How, for the first time in her life, she'd be important and respected.

He couldn't figure it exactly. Only knew that beneath the plastic bag, the fear in her wide and terrified eyes turned to resignation, and her shoulders slumped against him like a lover's.

He had a bit of a time dragging her body into a space wide enough to get his shot. And getting her into the plaid, that was a job. Miss Margaret had been eating too much banana pudding, and he couldn't get the skirt to fasten around her middle. But that was okay; no one would see her from the angle he was shooting. He had the book bag and the algebra book. He'd had a time hunting that one down. He placed the knife with care by her side, scooted back to check the frame in the lens.

A blast of excitement, like a heat wave, rolled over him. He wanted to touch himself, but he resisted.

This was pleasure enough.

12

Gillian didn't take Ray up on his suggestion to clean up. Didn't want to take off her dress and risk exposing her arms. Too many questions there. Besides, the blood, or whatever it was, had hardened into dried specks across her sleeves and shoulders. It looked bad but wasn't uncomfortable. And in the dark light of a bar, no one would notice.

"I'd rather eat." She threw the towel back at him. "Don't you have any beer? Chips?"

Ray attached a leather holster to his hip, shoved a gun inside it. The sight sent a ripple of awareness through her. A real gun meant real danger. Her throat tightened suddenly. The voice in her head boomed.

"*I'll do the same to you.*"

But she drowned it out by concentrating on the fine man in front of her. The man who was saying, "Don't keep beer in the house." She blinked. "And I don't eat chips," he added.

What was wrong with this guy? "You got the hockey stick, the whole jock thing going. I thought—"

"What is it? Jock or farm boy?" He crossed his arms, peered down at her from his superior height.

She glared right back up. "Can't you be a farm boy and a jock? I thought most of them were."

"I'd bet good money you never saw a farm in your life."

She answered in a mock huff. "I've been to the movies."

"Uh-huh. Let's go." He nodded for her to precede him.

But when he opened the door, an elderly man was stumbling up the walk.

"Shit," Ray murmured. A beat, then, "Stay here."

The approaching man was broad and squat as a bulldog, but an old, flaccid one. A once-white undershirt showcased a chest that sloped into his belly and hung over a pair of drooping pants. The top of his white head was squared off in a marine-style haircut, but the rest of him was round and wide, a roly-poly derelict. One foot was bare, one foot dragged a worn-out slipper. He weaved backward, then headfirst, plowed forward again.

Ray met him at the bottom of the two steps in front of the door. "Aw, hey, Sarge, what're you doing out so late?"

The man splayed a hand on Ray's chest, as if Ray were a lamppost he was steadying himself by. Gillian opened the door a crack to hear better.

"It's my Gloria." A plaintive note sounded beneath the drunken slur of words. "She's not home."

"I know." Ray looked over his shoulder at her. "It's okay. I'll be right back."

She started to reply, but Ray turned back around, quickly distracted by the drunk.

"Is she here? I can't sleep when she's not home."

Ray sighed. This was the third time in a month Sergeant Mackenzie Burke had shuffled his way over there. "She's gone, remember? She passed away. We went to the funeral."

He frowned, an expression of utter confusion. “Who are you? What are you doing at my house?”

“It’s Ray, Sarge. Ray.”

“Ray?”

“That’s right. You live around the corner. You haven’t lived here since Jimmy was born. Remember?”

“Sure, I remember. Jimmy’s my boy.”

“That’s right.”

The old man squinted up at Ray as if the name had suddenly clicked. “How’m I gonna sleep, Ray?”

Ray was keenly aware of what he was supposed to be doing—watching out for Gillian, not the remnants of what used to be his family. But he couldn’t just leave the old man wandering around. Why was it he seemed to attract all the pain in the butts in town?

Ray slung an arm around the old man’s shoulders. “How about you stay here for a while? That be okay?”

The man leaned back, gazing up at Ray as if he were a giraffe in the zoo. “Where’s Gloria, Ray?”

Ray looked away, swallowed, then came back to Burke. “We’ll find her.” Gently, he patted the man’s pockets. He not only wanted the bottle, if there was one, he wanted to make sure Mac hadn’t stuffed his .38 in one of his pockets. But he was clean, no booze, no weapon. “Come inside now.” Ray maneuvered him up the steps and through the door.

He led him to the easy chair, winding past Gillian to do it. “Keep an eye on him?” he said to her.

“Sure,” Gillian said.

Ray went into the kitchen, riffled through a bunch of papers under magnets on the fridge door, found the one he was looking for. Stared at it as if the numbers might leap off the page and whack him over the head.

He took a deep breath, grabbed the phone, and punched in the number.

It had been over a year since he'd heard Nancy's voice. Not since the funeral. She'd stood at her mother's grave holding her little boy, who wiggled to get down. She'd shushed him, told him to be still, her voice cracked and strained. She wore some awful black sack of a dress and no makeup, but there'd been a kind of peace in her eyes that had never been there when she'd been married to him.

Someone on the other end picked up. Ray braced himself.

"Hello?" Her voice was sleepy but familiar. At least it didn't send that jolt through his heart anymore.

"Nancy, it's Ray."

She yawned. "Who?"

He might have let that hurt him once. Now it just seemed funny. In a sad, pathetic way.

"Ray," he repeated, drawing out the single syllable as if that would make a more indelible impression.

"What time is it?" In the background he heard Peter asking who it was, and Nancy telling him and Peter asking what he wanted.

"I know it's late," Ray cut in. "But your father wandered over to the house again looking for your mom."

She groaned.

"I've got him here, but he's drunk. You'll have to come get him."

"Let him sleep on the sidewalk," Nancy said.

"Nance . . . come on."

"He couldn't seem to live with her when she was alive. Now she's dead, he can't live without her?"

But he didn't want to rehash old arguments. "Look, I'm

working. I can't keep him. And I can't leave him alone, either."

"You're working? Now?" One thing he didn't miss was that tone of voice. Disappointed, angry, disgusted, resigned. As if he'd fulfilled every expectation she ever had of him.

He bit down on a reply in kind. "I'll keep an eye on him 'til you get here."

"What about Jimmy? Can't you call him?"

"Jesus, Nancy. He's your father."

"Yeah, and we all know what a great dad he was, too."

"Jimmy's working, too. I just saw him."

She sighed, and it turned into another yawn. "All right," she grumbled, "Give me ten minutes."

He hung up. Figured her ten minutes would stretch to half an hour, so he started a pot of coffee.

"Everything okay?" Gillian asked from the doorway. The lunatic from the truck seemed to have vanished, and in her place was the woman who'd comforted Ruth. Someone calm and decent, despite what had been done to her, and—he saw it lurking in her eyes—someone curious.

"How is he?" He dumped a bag of coffee into the filter, slammed it home, and turned on the tap to fill the carafe.

"Snoring. Out cold."

"Good." He didn't want to deal with the pitiful version of Burke. He used to be a real son of a bitch, a cop's cop. Seeing him disintegrate like that, well...it was beyond disturbing. Ray poured the water into the coffeemaker, turned it on, waited for the inquisition.

"Couldn't help overhearing," she said. "You called the old guy Burke; on the phone you called his daughter Nancy. Then there was Detective Burke at the museum and *his* Nancy." She leaned against the wall by the counter, crossed her arms, still covered in their blood-spattered violet sleeves. “I’m thinking there’s a connection here.”

“Sherlock Holmes has nothing on you. He’s my father-in-law.”

“Your father-in-law?”

“Okay. Ex-father-in-law.”

“Like Detective Burke was your ex—”

“Brother-in-law. That’s right.”

“And Nancy’s—”

“His sister.”

“Your—?” She raised blond questioning brows.

“Ex.”

“Wow.”

He thought of the tangled web, those ties he could never seem to cut clean through. “Yeah, it’s a nice little incestuous nest we’ve built.”

She met his eyes. Said softly, “So are these the ‘circumstances’ that brought you to town?”

He admitted it. “More or less. Got no family back East. Nancy’s was here.”

Simple explanation. Cut-and-dried. As if he hadn’t talked his ass off getting Nancy to Nashville. Not to mention getting her to stay.

The coffee was almost done. Thank God. Gave him something else to talk about. “Grab a couple of cups from above the sink,” he said, and dove into the fridge for milk in case she wanted some.

He turned to find her on tiptoes, reaching for the mugs. “Hey, short stack. I got it.” He leaned over her shoulder to grab a couple, and she pivoted at the same time, turning away from the cupboard. And just like that, they were face-to-face. Her arms were braced on the counter behind her, arching her back and pushing her breasts against his chest. He smelled the spicy scent of her hair. Was suddenly keenly aware of how tiny she was. A small, fragile, female thing.

He scolded himself. That was the trick of the photographs. To make her appear vulnerable. Like she needed help. From what he'd seen so far, appearances were definitely deceiving.

He stepped back, thrust a mug at her, using it like a shield as much as anything else. She poured herself a cup, and he watched her ruin it with milk and sugar. Sipped his own black. Fifteen minutes more or less until he had to face Nancy and her big belly.

"So how come you and all your exes are so chummy?" Gillian asked.

Did she have a couple of hours? Could she spell s-i-c-k? Because it definitely bordered on the pathological. "Burke lives a couple blocks away." He stuck to the facts. "This was his house when he and Gloria first got married. He kept it, rented it out. When Nancy and I separated, I moved in here. Supposed to be temporary, but..." He shrugged.

Silence while she sipped at the coffee. "I don't suppose you have any Oreos? Health maniac like you?"

He opened a cabinet and tossed a package of cookies at her.

"See"—she grinned—"I knew you had a weakness." She bit into a cookie. "Somewhere." Carefully, she separated the top half from the rest. Scraped her teeth against the white icing.

He repressed a smile. She could have been sixteen. Small and delicate and young.

No. Somehow he doubted she'd ever been young.

Still, he couldn't help wondering about the teenage Gillian. The file he'd read had been full of her childhood.

Or at least the part connected with her mother's death. Not much on the intervening years.

He had known some of the back story on Holland Gray and her beautiful daughter. Not that the mother was a slouch in the beauty department. On cover after cover of *Vogue, Cosmo, Elle,* Holland embodied 1980s glamour. Even after her child was born, she continued to wear the supermodel crown. So there'd been great upheaval in the celebrity world—and among those who pay attention to it—when Holland abruptly withdrew to Nashville. And when she was killed, the coverage bordered on frenzy, if the mountains of articles were any indication.

One cover had stood out. He'd been fourteen when Holland Gray had died. His mother had subscribed to *People,* so he didn't know whether he remembered the cover or not. But it struck him when he saw it in the file. The orphaned Gillian, then a blond wisp of a child, innocent, trusting, hair like angel dust against the setting sun, eyes closed in sleep in a chair on her dead mother's front porch.

It had hit him then, just as it hit him now.

The first dead Gillian.

The first dead shot.

There had been many since. Many dead children, teenagers, women, all of them her. The media fury after her mother's death eventually died away, but her own work had made her famous again. Or infamous if you read the tabloids.

The Diva of Death they called her.

She caught him staring at her. "Sorry." She pushed the cookies toward him. "Did you want one?"

He shook his head. "No. Thanks."

She finished the cream, polished off the plain half. "Something on your mind, Ray?"

He nodded slowly, still thinking about that beautiful, lost child. "Your . . . work. The photographs. Why do you do them?"

Carefully, she wiped the crumbs off her hands. "Why do you think?"

"Therapy?"

She laughed. "That's right." She leaned back, crossed her arms, and studied him. An ugly gleam reflected in her eyes. "We've all got issues, don't we, Ray? Murder is mine."

"Because of your mother?"

She stiffened. "So . . . you think you know all about that."

"I read your file."

She nodded sagely. "Ah. My file. I see. Or do you mean *People,* the *Star,* and the *Enquirer*?"

"Those, too." He shrugged. "Enlighten me. How does it help, burying yourself in all that gore?"

"I told you. It's the truth. We're one of the few species that murders its own. We not only do it, we glorify it. On TV, in the movies. Only it's not glorifying. It's ugly. Horror-filled."

"And you shove our faces in it."

"You bet I do."

They stared at each other for a long moment.

Then Gillian slid a second cookie out of the package. "So, Ray, tell me . . . who's the girlfriend?"

He gave her a swift look. "Excuse me?"

"The girlfriend. In the hockey pic on the place of honor on your shelf."

He paused, silently debating whether or not to answer.

It wasn't any of her business. But saying so made more of a big deal out of it, and it wasn't. Not anymore. "That's Nancy."

She seemed to consider that. "Been divorced long?"

"Three years."

She bit into the cookie. "So... still carrying a torch?"

He scowled. "I keep the picture because of the trophy. Division championship. It's the only one I have." Hockey had been his ticket to college. It had led him to Birmingham, and the University of Alabama Chargers had led him to a burger joint on the edge of campus. Nancy had been behind the counter. Nancy with her ready hands and her eager mouth, and her Nashville family. Hockey had been the beginning and end of everything.

Gillian winked. "Ah, yeah sure, the trophy."

The doorbell rang, and he immediately tensed. His ex-wife had been quicker than he'd expected.

But it wasn't Nancy at the door.

"Where is he?" Peter Coombs asked. Instead of a shirt, he wore a pajama top stuffed into his pants. Shorter than Ray, he was a slight man, sandy-haired and sandy-eyed. Made the most unremarkable impression a man could make. But he was a fifth-grade teacher, not a cop, and that was the main attraction.

Ray stepped aside so Peter could see Burke slumped in the easy chair.

"Where's Nancy?" Ray asked.

"It's late," Peter said curtly, as if that was all the explanation Ray needed. But of course, it wasn't, because he added, "And she's pregnant."

Ray nodded. Didn't know if he was relieved or annoyed that she hadn't come. Relieved, he decided.

Together, he and Ray managed to heft Burke's weight

out of the house and down to the curb where Peter had parked his car. Burke mumbled and swore, farted once, but didn't completely wake up.

"He's getting worse," Ray said when they'd laid Burke in the backseat. "He needs someone looking out for him."

"Nancy's got her hands full with little Carson," Peter objected before her name had even been mentioned. "And now with the two new ones coming—"

"Okay, okay." Ray put up his hands in stop mode. He didn't need an inventory. "Whatever. It's just one of these days you'll be picking him up at the morgue."

"I'll talk to Jim," Peter said.

He was the only one who called him "Jim." "Yeah, you do that."

He watched Peter drive off. The husband of his wife. The father of his wife's children. Could his life get any weirder?

Then he turned back to the house and saw Gillian Gray at the door.

13

From the doorway, Gillian watched Ray and the man she'd gathered was Nancy's husband stuff that confused bloated old man into the backseat of the husband's car. Finished, Ray closed the door, then stood sentry as they disappeared into the darkness.

Then he headed back to the house.

He came in, looked her over. "Ready?" he asked. No cursing, no commentary about what had just happened. Something had to be done, and he did it. Calmly and with grace.

"You're a nice guy, aren't you, Ray?"

That made him shift in embarrassment, which amused her.

"What was I supposed to do," he said, "leave him in the street?"

"Others might have."

He shrugged. "Maybe." But he didn't sound convinced. He checked his watch. "Look, it's late. If we're going, we should go."

But the scene with Ray's ex-family had dampened Gillian's enthusiasm for partying. So instead of going downtown to close the tourist bars, she directed Ray west, into

Belle Meade, where the bronze statue of a prancing Thoroughbred and colt paid homage to the area's racing history and where the *capo di capo* of old Nashville money resided.

Like most of the homes in the area, the Gray house was set far back from the road. It sat on four wooded acres a stone's throw from the Belle Meade Country Club. Pillars with open iron gates guarded the entrance. Ray drove between them slowly.

"These gates ever close?"

She looked at the braided black bars and decorative scalloped edge. "I don't know that they can close. They've been there since 1872 or something like that. I think they're rusted in place. Like the tin man."

He grunted a reply, his eyes scanning as he drove up the curved drive that led to the house.

On either side, poplars, black walnuts, and Osage oranges lined the road. They were big trees, with heavy foliage that arched over the path in summer to create a light-dappled bower. Now, skeletal branches furred with buds reached over the drive. To Gillian they always looked like witch's fingers, poised to snatch the innocent.

Ahead, the house loomed stately and patrician, its Greek revival portico gleaming ghostly white in the moonlight. It wasn't hard to imagine the clatter of hooves and the jingle of harnesses, the open carriages that disgorged giggling women in bell-hooped skirts.

But not tonight. Tonight, the spirit of the Old South was dead, and the only vehicle pulling up to the door was working class. And there was no Scarlett inside.

Ray braked. Sat for a minute, eyeing the landscape.

"Looking for anything in particular?"

"Whatever's out there."

She followed his gaze out the window into the inky air. Did he also know about the monster? Did he expect to find him here? "Anything?"

He turned back to her. "No."

"Too bad." She lifted the handle to open the door, but he reached across and stopped her.

"I'll take you in," he said.

"It's two steps away. I'll be fine."

He opened his door. "That's what Gerhard Bruckner thought, too. His driver dropped him two yards from his house, and he was assassinated at his front door. Don't get out until I get there."

She plopped back, knowing he didn't get it and suddenly too drained to tell him. Maybe it was the scene with Sergeant Burke. Maybe it was the proximity of her own screwed-up family. Or maybe, just maybe, some deep inner quirk responded to being protected.

Out of perverse curiosity, she tested the feeling. She hadn't objected when he'd knocked her flat at the museum. Or on the walk up to his own house. Now, she sat still while he came around the truck's front end and opened her door. Docile, she let him escort her to the house. Unlocked the door without protest while he guarded her. Hand on the knob, he spoke.

"Is there an alarm system?"

She laughed. "Of course. In the closet to the right."

"What's the code?"

She turned the knob herself and entered. "I have no idea. They usually forget to turn it on."

His brows rose in surprise. "Forget?"

"Accidentally on purpose you might say. In this house, no one likes to be reminded how vulnerable we are."

She ignored his frown because now that she was inside,

the smell of roses slapped her back. As it did every time she'd been away and returned, the sharp tang hacked away at the false front of the present to reveal the bones of the past. The funeral. Standing at the bottom of the stairs while her grandmother tugged a coat on her. Scratching at the sleeves because they were too tight.

"It's cold." Genevra had fastened the top button until it choked. She had to lean close to do it, so the rose smell had overwhelmed. "We'll be outside, and you'll be glad to have it."

Gillian remembered that coat clearly. Navy blue with a velvet collar.

"Where's your room?"

The voice startled her out of the past, and she turned to the sound, looked up, almost surprised to find a tall, big-boned man standing beside her.

Ray.

"You want to see my bedroom?" She threw him a provocative smile, eager to bury those memories.

He deadpanned his response. "Yeah, short stack, I believe I do."

She took him up the winding staircase and down the carpeted hallway to her room. She remembered the first time she'd made that trip without her mother's comforting hand to guide her. The walls were mountainous, the furniture monstrous, the carpet swallowed the sound of her feet and made her feel like a ghost.

She'd felt that way for a long time. Unreal. A phantom. And then she found a way to make herself as real as anyone. Instinctively, she hugged herself, rubbing hands up and down her covered arms. That's when she noticed Ray at her shoulder, crowding her back. She stopped short, and he nearly ran into her.

"What is it?" He was immediately on his guard.

"Do you have to stand so close?"

He relaxed, but only just. "Arm's reach is SOP." And as if she were completely stupid, "Standard—"

"Operating procedure. Yeah, yeah. Okay."

When they got to her room, he pushed her aside, opened the door, and wouldn't let her in until he'd checked it out.

He gave her the okay, and she sidled past him, irritated anew with the level of vigilance. How was she supposed to reach the heart of darkness with Ray Pearce skulking around every corner?

"Can I go to sleep now?"

"First, a couple of rules," Ray said.

She threw her evening bag on the bed. It lay there glittering on the cream satin. "Do I seem like the kind of girl who follows rules?"

He leaned against a gilt-edged dresser. "I think you talk much bigger than you are."

"Not always." But she admired his refusal to take her bullshit. "Okay, lay them on me. What are these rules?"

"You do what I tell you, no questions. You don't leave the house or go anywhere without me."

She laughed. "You're kidding."

He shook his head. His face was dead sober. "Not even a little bit."

"No questions? Me?"

"Yeah, I can see where following orders will be hard. But if anything happens, it could save your life."

"Maybe. But I have other plans."

Immediately, he straightened. "What's that supposed to mean?"

"Nothing." She threw Genevra's embroidered pillows

in a corner, backtracking quickly. Never reveal too much too fast. "Look . . . let's not get all dramatic here."

"No drama. Just the truth." He gave her a pointed look. "And I hear you're big on that."

Ouch. "It's only for a few days, right?"

"That's right. I'll be back in the morning. Early. So no running out to Starbucks without me."

"I won't be up early, so sleep in if you want to."

He nodded. "I don't keep diva hours. I'll be here when you get up. That's all you need to worry about. And one more thing. Tell your grandparents to start setting the alarm. I'll need the code. And a key to the front door."

She shuffled in her purse, found hers, and tossed it to him. "You can get a copy made tomorrow. Just pull it shut. It locks from the inside."

He started to go, turned back. Looked down as though debating with himself, then up at her. "And thanks for your help. At the house. With Burke."

She nodded. "No problem."

He gave her a long, thoughtful look, then swung around and left.

She turned off the overhead light and switched on the lamp by the bed. The soft light was easier on the eyes. Reaching back, she unzipped the dress and peeled it off. Threw it in the same corner as the pillows. God, she never wanted to see that dress again.

She opened a dresser drawer, took out a ratty olive tank, and pulled it over her head. She kept a closetful of clothes here, most from high school, most shredded or frayed or washed to death, but that still fit. Gaining weight had never been her problem, and using the clothes here kept the luggage at a minimum. Little or no luggage meant she could pretend the trip home would be over almost before it had begun.

She slithered into bed, mindful of the soft pull of the six-hundred-thread count cotton Genevra always insisted on. She reached over to turn off the lamp, and in the yellow glow, her scars seemed angrier than usual. She snapped off the light and lay in bed, rubbing the raised edges of the weird shapes that danced up and down her arms.

14

Jimmy Burke was on his way home when the police band radio barked a 10-64. Dead Body. His shift was over, and a beer called from the fridge, but that and the *Today Show* were all he had waiting for him.

So he detoured left, thinking about it. A few more minutes with the guys wouldn't kill him, and besides, he was curious. The crazy at the museum was down for the count, and nothing much else of interest had happened that night. Except maybe seeing Ray again.

Which wasn't exactly on his Top Forty Things of Interest anyway. He could do without another sighting of Saint Ray. Ray of the Sacrificing Husbands.

He shook off the mood. He should go home. Grab a few hours sleep.

But he wasn't tired.

He'd stopped for dinner at Krispy Kreme, chomped down two hot ones and gulped three cups of coffee. Between the sugar and the caffeine, he was pretty wired.

And truth was, he didn't like going home much. Too quiet. The weekends when Scott was there were better, because a six-year-old can really tear the place up. But

Scott was with his mother now, and Jimmy's apartment was empty.

So he headed south, passing used car lot after used car lot. Seventy-seven in a single seven-mile stretch, a good portion with Spanish names and Spanish signs.

He'd lived in Nashville all his life, and he still remembered when Nolensville Road was staunchly redneck, covered in used furniture stores like Oldhams, with its hanging cribs and naked mattresses outside the door. Now you'd think the Rio Grande was south of the city and the whole of Mexico had waded over. Oldhams was now Garcia's, though the mattresses still hung there. A place shouting POLLO ASADO had replaced the Dairy Queen. Strange grocery stores advertised PAN DULCE and Mexican beer. Taquerias dotted both sides of the street. It made him uncomfortable.

"The trouble with you, Jimmy, is you don't like change." His ex-wife's voice screeched in his head, a little dose of whatever she'd heard lately from Dr. Phil. "Well, get used to it, because nothing and no one stays the same forever."

The woman wasn't the smartest, but she was right about that. Even the sign for the H&R Block office had SE HABLA ESPAÑOL spelled out in black letters.

Jimmy pulled into the strip of blacktop that served as a parking area in front of the store. It was already filled with patrol cars, their lights flashing in the morning. The area around the office had been blocked off, and a couple of uniforms were standing around making sure no unauthorized people got too close.

Jimmy ducked beneath the yellow police line tape and nodded to the uniform outside the office door. "Hey, Shelby, who's the DRT?" DRT meant Dead Right There, and whoever it was, they had died inside. Through the plate-glass window he saw a group of men milling around, jotting down notes, glancing at the walls, jotting more stuff down. Triangulating the body position, looked like.

"Female, midforties. Two stab wounds."

That was interesting. "Who caught it?"

"Mills."

The uniform nodded and let Jimmy pass. He stopped to slip a pair of paper covers over his shoes.

Inside, several desks had been pushed aside to clear room. In the middle of the empty space lay the body of a woman wearing a plaid skirt and a white blouse. Three bloody wounds danced down the front of it. The woman lay peacefully, her eyes closed. A knife lay just out of reach of her open hand.

"Hey, Burke!" Mills waved him over. "What are you doing here?"

"Caught the code on my way home. Thought I'd stop by, check it out." He looked down at the dead woman. "Robbery?"

"Not unless they took tax forms."

He gave the body a full 360. Her skirt was unzipped. "Rape?"

"Don't know yet. ME still has to do the kit. Maybe."

Burke looked around, taking in the scene. A man huddled in the far corner, head in his hands. Suited up for the day, prim and proper. Only the curve of his back and the droop of his head belied his true state. Burke nodded in his direction. "Who's that?"

"Neeley. Victim's boss. Found the body."

Burke knew most murders were carried out by those who knew the victim. He eyed the man closely. "He tell you a story?"

"Not much of a one." Mills flipped through pages of a

pocket notebook. "Deceased was still here when he left around seven. Stopped at Bar-b-Cutie for a pound of pork and coleslaw. Home around eight. Dinner with the wife and kids. There all night."

"You got a time of death?"

"Approximate. Maybe ten, eleven last night."

Burke looked at the body again. Something tugged at him. "I've seen this before."

Mills laughed. "What? A dead body?"

"No, this dead body."

"Go home, Burke. You're tired."

"No, there's something..." Burke wagged his finger at the air, thinking about it. He glanced around the room. A figurine on one of the desks caught his eye. He pointed to it. "What's that?"

"Cookie jar. Killer placed it on a plant stand above the body. Winnie the Pooh." Mills shook his head. "We got us a strange one."

Burke headed over. Didn't touch it. Didn't need to.

Benton James smoothed the front page of the morning's *Tennessean* across his desk and admired the point size of his headline: DEATH DIVA DAMAGED. Better than the lead, the story was spread over the coveted strip, the section just below the paper's name.

Around him, the features department was a ghost town and would be until later this afternoon. If he had any sense, he'd be home in bed, too. But he couldn't resist coming in and crowing just the teensiest little bit. After all, he'd stayed up half the night writing the story. Larson, the night managing editor, had wanted to bring in a crime reporter, but Benton was already there. An eyewitness.

Benton enjoyed being the town arbiter of good taste, but the sad truth was, there wasn't much art to critique in Nashville. One opera, once a year. The symphony. A few galleries scattered around. The occasional piece of non-professional theater. And the road shows.

That gave him enough to do, but it wasn't as if he was somewhere where art mattered. "Now, Benton," the angel voice in his head said, "where else could it matter more than in a place where there's so little of it?"

Not to be outdone, the devil voice countered, "Yes, but wouldn't it be delicious to spread a wider net?"

Benton smoothed his mustache and almost cackled as he reread what he'd written the night before. World-class artist, attacked at home. Protesters. Violence. God, could it get any better? Maybe if he was lucky, the wire services would pick it up. Maybe the *New York Times* would call.

He did cackle then, and the sound echoed in the all-but-silent space of empty cubicles. He was good. God, he was good.

He turned on his monitor and logged on. Thought about the headline as the machine warmed up. The night editor wanted to go with something simple, like ARTIST ATTACKED. Benton had talked him into something a tad more inflammatory.

While he was remembering their argument, he checked his e-mail. He ran down the list: nothing, nothing, later, nothing...he paused. The last entry was titled "Something to Interest You" and was from *MAPulley@hrblock.com.* Who the hell was MAPulley? He started to hit the delete button, but his curiosity got the better of him. He moved his mouse and clicked on the entry.

The message was a picture. He watched as it downloaded. Saw immediately what it was. The Gillian Gray photograph that had been spattered with blood last night. Well, phooey. What the hell good was that going to do him?

He closed the picture, and just as it disappeared, something caught his eye. Quickly, he reopened it. Gasped.

The dead girl in the picture was no girl. And it was definitely not Gillian Gray.

15

The morning after the museum fiasco, Gillian thought she'd sleep until noon. But when she opened her eyes, the sun outside her window was low in a blue sky, and her Nikon called to her. She threw on some clothes, grabbed her camera bag, and slung the camera around her neck.

She'd had the 35 mm since she was seventeen. It was her first camera, an aging relic that was already twenty years old when her art teacher had placed it in her hands. She remembered the first time she looked through the viewfinder. The way it sliced the world into a fraction that was both closer than the eye and more distant because the lens created a barrier between them. A barrier behind which she was safe. Behind which she could carve the world into as many segments as she wanted. Create her own borders, her own universe. A place where she, and she alone, was in control.

Outside, the air had a newly washed feel, and she tramped over the grass to the north side of the grounds where a group of flowering trees formed a small meadow. The redbuds were fading, their pink fuzz wilting like the tattered gown of an impoverished Southern belle, but the dogwoods were out in force. Oyster white and salmon pink blooms cupped upward as though welcoming strangers. From a distance they appeared benign, even friendly. But when she took a closer look, she saw that each flower consisted of four distinct petals. And each petal culminated in a clear, spiked point.

She didn't usually respond to the physical landscape, but something about the rich morning light caught her. As she framed her shots, she wondered what it would be like to place a body there among those deceiving petals. A small, thin, hanging girl, her feet bare, her hands tied, her neck broken.

Lost in the view, both inside and outside her head, she didn't hear anyone coming.

"I thought I told you not to go anywhere without me."

The masculine voice burst into the silence of the glade, and she whirled to find Ray Pearce approaching. She'd forgotten how big he was, broad-shouldered and towering. Solid against the delicate branches of buds and baby leaves. In a dark suit and tie, he looked competent and strong, but incongruous. Agent Smith among the flowers.

He stopped a few yards away as though he knew she was working and respected that. The branches of a half-pink redbud crept over his shoulder like tentacles.

She raised her camera, manually focused the lens. "I thought you didn't keep diva hours." She pressed the shutter button, committing the picture to film. Moved to grab another angle.

"I thought you weren't getting up early."

"Well, I surprised myself. But I haven't gone anywhere." She raised the camera again, found another shot, but in two steps he broke the invisible wall separating them.

"Leaving the house is going somewhere." Gently, he pushed the camera aside.

"Don't like your picture taken?"

"Not here to model."

"So you say." But she left him alone and turned back to the woods. For a moment, the scene from the night before flashed back—the chill of the blood, the thunk of ribs as Ray bodychecked her, the stony floor, unyielding as she hit the deck. "But Ruth is in custody, and Matthew Dobie hasn't set up shop at the front gates."

"He made the morning news, though."

She lowered the camera so it hung between her breasts on a leather strap. "Really?" She rarely watched the news.

"Matt Lauer and all."

A shiver hit her. She found herself clutching the camera as if it were an anchor in a roiling sea. But national news was good, wasn't it? Maybe he'd hear. Maybe he'd come for her. "Not much I can do about that," she said, reaching for calm and not quite achieving it.

"You can stay inside until I get here."

"All right. All *right.*" She was as much irritated with the necessity of his presence as she was with his insistence upon it.

He held up protesting hands. "Don't shoot the messenger."

"Fine. Whatever. Just stand over there so you're not in the light."

She spent the next hour absorbed by the glen and its denizens. Ray watched her work, a blond urchin in ancient overalls that were ripped at the knees, a black T-shirt whose long sleeves ended in frayed edges, and a paint-stained gray sweatshirt that was wrapped around her waist. Rags and tatters. Poor little rich girl.

Not that she looked like she cared much. She snapped pictures of the trees, often contorting into weird shapes to get the angle she wanted, sloshing in mud if she had to, and crouching low to get shots of things that looked like weeds to him.

He liked the way the work absorbed her. He'd had moments like that on the ice, pure, focused moments when the stick became an extension of his arm and connected with the puck like it was destiny.

He reached for that concentration now, sharpening his hearing and sight, reaching outward to maintain an uneasy vigil. No way could hc preserve a secure perimeter with the wide swathe of open ground around them. He'd have needed at least three other men for that, but Chip Gray had weighed the limits of his granddaughter's patience and settled for one. In Ray's opinion it would have been overkill anyway. Unpleasant as the assault had been the night before, it was intended to hurt feelings and make a point rather than maim. But anything was possible, so he kept a keen eye on the surroundings.

A large part of executive protection was common sense. Keep the client away from crowds, in a small, manageable space. Control the environment, and you reduce the threat. Unfortunately, you couldn't keep people locked up. They lived in a certain place, worked in a certain place. And most would only go so far to change their routine unless the danger was life-threatening and imminent. Neither one applied in this case.

So here they were. Outdoors. The small vulnerable blonde looking perfectly capable of taking care of herself, and him, towering over her, protecting her from the trees.

"Ridiculous" didn't even begin to describe it.

Until the sound of footsteps crashed through the undergrowth.

In a second, Ray's heartbeat skyrocketed and he leaped. Gillian was hunched over, aiming the camera up through branches to the sky. In one great stride, he pulled her up.

She unbalanced and screeched in surprise.

"Quiet." He looked wildly around. No place to make a clean stance—they were open on all sides—so he shoved her against a tree and blocked her view from the intruder.

She pushed against his spine. "What is it?"

"Gillian!" A shout came at a distance. "Where are you? Gillian!"

A woman's voice.

"It's Maddie." Again, she put a fist in his back. "Let me go. It's just Maddie!"

The Crane woman came flying out of the woods, black hair streaming, a witch's raven in black slacks and a black top.

"What is it?" he demanded. Behind him, Gillian was struggling, and he held her back with some effort. Something had terrified Maddie Crane, and he had no intention of letting Gillian go until he understood what. "What happened?"

Maddie bent over, braced her hands on her knees and panted. "Dead," she said finally. "Someone's . . . dead."

16

"It's a fake," Maddie said, referring to the photograph Detective Jimmy Burke had placed in the center of the ornate marble coffee table in the Grays' spacious living room. Maddie was standing over it. She reached out and touched the picture with a long, curved nail painted a purple so deep it was almost black. The picture moved slightly, and she stood back, studying the thing as if it were an insect under glass.

Silk drapes framed the windows on the east side of the house. A warm apricot color, they magnified the morning light. Ray stood in front of the window, the sun beating against his back. Across from him, Genevra Gray sat in a cream armchair. She looked plucked and drawn. It wasn't just the thin neck and sharp chin that gave her the appearance of a chicken about to be slaughtered. It was the hard stare that was both resigned and defiant.

What she was staring at was Burke. Not the photograph that lay there among them like a little grenade waiting to explode.

"It's not Gillian's," Maddie said.

Burke nodded. "We know. It's been Photoshopped." He had that line on his forehead. The one that meant he would single-mindedly pursue this no matter what. Ray looked at the white faces around the room, saw the withdrawal, and hoped Jimmy would notice and step softly. But he used to leave the deft touch to Ray. "Body's real enough," he said.

The words seemed to freeze the air even further.

Ray and Burke exchanged glances. Burke seemed to be saying, "What's wrong with these people?" and, silently, Ray told him to go slow. It was a familiar moment made uncomfortable by that familiarity. Ray looked away, and Jimmy pushed the picture toward Gillian.

"Recognize her?"

Gillian glanced at the abomination. Saw what should have been her. Was always supposed to be her.

"Miss Gray?" Burke repeated. "Have you seen this woman before?"

"Of course she hasn't," Maddie said.

Burke sent her a sharp look. "Why don't we let Miss Gray speak for herself. I think she's a big enough girl." He turned to Gillian. "Miss Gray?"

Gillian fistcd a hand. How darc hc? IIe had no right to steal fate from her. No damn right to . . . her breath clotted in her chest. Oh, God. Dead. Someone else was dead.

"Have you ever seen this woman before?" Burke demanded.

Ray watched the emotions play across Gillian's face. The wise guy suddenly stunned into silence by shock, anger. Grief. She seemed incapable of responding, and Ray felt the tug of that moment in the museum. The moment when he'd heard the deep bass warning bell keening his own demise. When he'd looked in Gillian Gray's eyes, seen the sadness below the resolution, and wanted to take it away almost as much as he wanted to run like hell.

But he hadn't run. He'd taken the bait. Like he always did.

He moved to her chair. Crouched in front of her. "Hey. Short stack," he said quietly. Waited for her to focus on him. "We need your help." Although there was no "we," and what Jimmy wanted had nothing to do with him. He wasn't there to catch the bad guys anymore. But still, for old times' sake... "Just a quick yea or nay."

It always amazed him how most people, even the toughest, responded to kindness. Gillian was no exception. She blinked, seemed to breathe again. "No," she said. "No, I don't recognize her."

"Okay." He turned toward Burke. "Who is it?"

Burke ignored him. "Are you sure?" he asked Gillian again.

She said nothing.

"Miss Gray, are you sure?"

Ray rose to his feet, blocking Gillian from Jimmy's gaze. "She's sure," he said.

"Back off, Ray. You're not the cop here," Burke said.

Ray let that one slide. But he didn't budge, and Jimmy turned to Genevra. "Mrs. Gray?"

Gillian's grandmother shook her head emphatically. "Never saw her before." She rose, a prelude to showing him out. "Now if that is all..."

But Jimmy was nothing if not persistent. Before he made detective, Ray and Jimmy and the senior Burke and some of the guys from the shift used to play pool. Jimmy wouldn't go home until he'd beaten Ray at least once. Sometimes Ray would say he was leaving early, just to watch him beg. But in the end he usually stayed. Jimmy was six years older, been a cop longer, and truth was, Ray hadn't liked disappointing him.

Now Jimmy looked from Genevra to Maddie, then back to Gillian again. "Who does your taxes, Miss Gray?"

The absurdity of the question seemed to stump her as much as it did Ray. "I'm sorry, my—?"

"Taxes. You do pay taxes, don't you?"

Genevra spoke. "All of my granddaughter's financial affairs are handled by the family firm. I can provide you with the name—"

"Ever been to H&R Block?"

"No," Genevra said. "There are trust funds. Inherited monies. It's very complicated."

"How about the name Margaret Ann Pulley?"

"No," Genevra said.

"*Miss* Gray," Burke insisted.

"No," Gillian said. "I'm sorry. No."

There was a small silence. Into it, the door slammed, and Chip Gray's voice blustered from somewhere outside the room.

"Gennie! What the hell is going on? I told you not to—" He burst into the room, red-faced. Saw Burke. Bore down on him. "Detective. We all agreed to come down to your office and sign your papers there. No need for a house call."

"It's not about the museum," Ray said.

Chip looked at him, astonished. "Well, what else could it be about?"

Silently, Maddie handed him the photo.

"What is this?" He looked down at it. His face blanched. "That's not—"

"No, sir," said Burke. "It's not your granddaughter. It's a real body. A real murder."

Chip stared at him. "Oh, my God." He sank onto the sofa.

"Scotch, anyone?" Maddie said to the room in general.

"Yeah," Gillian said. "Why don't we all get drunk?"

"It's not even noon," Genevra snapped.

"For God's sake, she isn't serious," Chip said. "Why do you never see that?"

"Excuse me," Burke said, "but do you know the woman in the picture?" He ran through his questions again, but Chip came back with the same answers. He didn't recognize the woman in the photo, he'd never used H&R Block, and he didn't know a Margaret Anne Pulley.

"Is that all, Detective?" Chip asked at last. "If so, I'll have Bertha show you out." He gave the photo back to Burke.

"For now," Burke said. "But don't leave town, Miss Gray. We may have more questions."

That roused Chip. He stood, took a billfold from his pocket. "If you want to speak to us again, get in touch with my lawyers." He removed a card, wrote something on it. "They can arrange a meeting in a more neutral setting." He handed the card to Burke, but Jimmy stepped back from taking it.

"Look, there's no call to get fussy and bring in lawyers."

Chip tucked the card into Burke's breast pocket. "This house has seen more than its share of police, and we're all aware of how you work." He led Burke out. "You ask your questions, and we answer. Over and over again. And in the end, it doesn't amount to much."

Gillian watched him go, wishing the cloud of fear he'd brought would depart with him.

But just short of the hallway, the detective dug in his heels and turned back to face the living room. "The woman in the picture," he said to Gillian. "It's supposed to be you, right? You're the victim in all your photographs?"

Gillian nodded.

"Then I'd watch my back, Miss Gray."

She met the cold certainty in his eyes head-on.

"What are you saying?" Chip demanded.

"He's saying the murder might not have anything to do with the actual victim," Ray said, "and everything to do with who she's supposed to be."

Every gaze swiveled to Gillian. She rose. Walked over to the window and crossed her arms protectively over her middle. Stared out at the terrace. Pots of pansies were strategically placed and winked yellow, purple, and white. So pert and pretty.

Behind her, Genevra emitted a strangled gasp. "Are you saying my granddaughter could be in even more danger?"

She heard her grandfather's heavy tread as he crossed the room to her. "It's all right," he soothed. "Everything's going to be all right."

"Don't treat me like a child," Genevra snapped. "Is that what you are saying, Detective? That my granddaughter could be a target for this, this...?" The word "killer" seemed stuck in her throat.

Burke rescued her. "The murderer didn't set this up accidentally. He replicated the photograph for a reason. Could be he's practicing."

"Practicing for what?"

"The real thing."

Another warbled cry.

"Detective, I think you should leave." That was Chip being firm and decisive.

And still the detective lingered. "Miss Gray, is there anyone out there who'd want to harm you?"

"There's Matthew Dobie and his crowd," Ray said.

"We're checking on that. Anyone else?"

Gillian stared out at the bright sunny day and shook her head. Because how could she say otherwise? Not in front of her grandmother, who'd spent years refusing to say anything. Not to the short, squat muscular detective who only dealt in practical, tangible realities.

How could she tell him there *was* someone out there who wanted to hurt her?

That the someone was the monster from her childhood. The bogeyman under her bed. In the closet. He was real. He was out there.

And he was coming for her.

17

The story hit the air running. Matthew Dobie made it to all three mainstream networks, as well as cable, in time for the five o'clock news. In his office on the third floor of the Gray Museum, Will Davenport stared at the TV with a sinking feeling.

"This is exactly my point," Dobie was saying in his easy, round voice. Smoothed down through years of radio work, his voice gave the overall impression of great warmth and caring. But Will heard the self-important satisfaction below the tone. "Miss Gray and her work encourage the violence she claims she wants to prevent."

They had him in a studio in front of a blue background. They cut away to *Kitchen in Suburbia,* read the Gray statement. And cut back to the reporter.

"Miss Gray's statement denies any connection to this tragedy."

Dobie shook his head sadly. "She can deny all she likes, but the truth is there in front of us."

"But isn't it an artist's job to push out boundaries? To provoke, even offend?"

"In some airy, theoretical world, perhaps. But here on the ground, a woman is dead. Can't hide from that."

Davenport clicked off the TV. Bad enough the morning *Tennessean* had splashed Benton James's Death Diva headline all over the front page. At least no one had died in the museum attack last night. Besides, no one read the paper anymore. But now this...this killing was all over the television.

He'd already fielded phone calls from two board members. Two others who usually couldn't wait to talk to him suddenly had meetings and never called him back. And the exhibit hadn't even opened.

He went to the window and stared out at the scene below. The blur of colored dots meant Matthew Dobie and his followers were still camped outside. He'd promised to ramp up attendance tomorrow for the opening. Anyone wishing to enter the museum would have to run through a gauntlet to get there.

Will cursed silently. Forget tomorrow. What was going to happen next week and next month? The anniversary celebration was supposed to be the kickoff for next year's development campaign. And from where he stood, the museum's budget was about to be as dead as the woman in the photograph.

A knock on the door.

"Can I come in?"

It was Stephanie Bower, the head curator. A short, compact woman, she had thick blond hair, which framed her blunt face. "How you holding up?"

He shrugged. "I've been better."

Grimly, "Yeah."

For a few minutes, they sat in moody silence, each staring at their hands.

Finally, Will said, "Think we should cancel?"

Shocked, Stephanie raised her head to look at Will. "Before we even open?"

In repose, Will Davenport could appear dim-witted behind his thick glasses, but once his attention turned to you and he opened his mouth, the impression disappeared. He had an elite Southern education with a BA from Davidson and an MBA from the Owen School at Vanderbilt.

Appearances aside, he was no dummy. He'd attended the top prep school in the city, started his career working for Lamar Alexander when he was governor, and still maintained a relationship with him now that Lamar had moved on to Washington. Will had contacts all over the city, and as development director, he'd used them to get the museum's endowment established. Nashville still had many of the trappings of a small town, and his name and his future were now inextricably linked to its success. Which might explain why he was motivated more by worry than confidence, and why just now, it showed.

"It's been done," Will said.

"Not by anyone as new as us."

"Better a cancellation than loss of local dollars."

"You don't know that's going to happen."

Glumly, Will shook his head. "The story made national news, Stephanie. Nashville doesn't get covered by CNN."

"Don't I know it."

Truth was, her head was on the line, too. Bringing Gillian Gray to Nashville and making her name the center of the museum's anniversary celebration had been her idea. She'd ignored Will's misgivings, pretended the lukewarm reception the Grays had given the idea was a modest attempt not to toot their own horn. She'd plowed ahead, confident the city would leap at the chance to honor one of its own. Never mind the baggage, the unsolved murder of her mother that was at the root of Gillian Gray's work, even the impact of the work itself, which forced people to confront the violence around them. Few people liked looking that closely at themselves.

But even to think the word "cancellation" shortened Stephanie's breath. In her world, it was the greatest sin. Those who bowed to censorship were ostracized and shunned. She did not want to stay in Nashville forever. She enjoyed the Gray Center and was grateful for her job, but some days she longed for real Italian food and not just the latest at Olive Garden, or real theater and not just the second coming of Cathy Rigby in *Peter Pan.* She wanted more to do on Sunday than go to church, and she ached for the sound of waves.

So no cancellation. She was not going to have that on her résumé.

"Look, this murder is not our fault. It's not Gillian Gray's fault. It sucks, but it could work for us, too." She leaned forward, trying to persuade him as much as herself.

"Well, that's a little callous," Will said.

"It's realistic. The more people hear about the show, the more they'll come. It's sick, but true. Like rubbernecking at a train wreck."

"I don't want the train wreck to be the Gray Center."

She grimaced. "Me neither. But have a little faith. Who knows? Maybe the police will catch the guy before tomorrow's opening, and this will all go away."

Will leaned back in his chair and sighed. "We live in hope."

Gillian stared at the bathroom mirror. The glass was covered in steam from her shower, and she could just make out the vague outline of a face. It was her face, but because of the haze she couldn't see it. Did it matter? She thought of Margaret Anne Pulley's face. Did it make a difference whose face was dead on the kitchen floor?

A tear skated over her cheek, and instantly she scraped it away. Jerked open the cabinet and looked inside. Toothpaste, brush. Deodorant. The products gleamed in their packaging, all fresh and newly bought for her stay. Genevra always swept away the old and repopulated it with new.

She rummaged around, thinking about who was outside the closed door. A man, fully clothed. Sitting, waiting for her to come out in one piece. Should she walk out as she was, give him an eyeful?

If the man had been Ray, now . . .

But it wasn't Ray. It was someone Ray had assigned to sit there while he was downstairs with Carlson and her grandfather and a team of security advisors. They were making what Carlson had called a "threat assessment." Which meant tramping over the grounds, opening doors, poking into closets, starting background checks, and the like.

She closed the cabinet on her grandmother's brand-new toiletries. Thought about what she knew she was going to do. Then did it.

Just above the rim was a loose tile. She felt around, carefully wiggled it out. Behind it was a small cavern. Years ago she'd hidden a pair of manicuring scissors there.

Now she brought the little tool down and gazed at it. Examined the clean point, tiny and sharp.

She couldn't say why she hadn't thrown them away long ago. Did she know there would be a moment like this one? That ten years after she stopped carving into her own body she'd be tempted again?

She clutched at the sink and closed her eyes, the scissors point cutting into her palm. She could still dredge up the excitement, the satisfaction of the pain. When she thought she would explode, she'd etch a line in her skin, and the blood would leach the rage.

She'd probably be dead by now if the camera hadn't saved her. If she hadn't learned to show that rage on film.

In her head she repeated the mantra she'd learned so long ago she'd forgotten where.

It isn't my fault. It isn't my fault.

But the words didn't stick.

A knock on the door made her jump. The scissors clattered into the sink.

"Miss Gray?"

She swallowed. She was sweating in the heat. "Yes?"

"They're asking for you downstairs."

"Be right there."

She looked at the scars on her arm. At the metal point that glittered against the porcelain bowl. It took great strength, but slowly she picked up the scissors. Forced herself to put them back in their hiding place. Her hands were shaking, but she managed to set the tile in place.

Then she slipped on her bathrobe and went to get dressed.

18

Ray leaned against the sideboard in the dining room and watched Carlson work Chip Gray. The two men were standing over charts and papers on the dining room table, and if he didn't know before, Ray knew now why Carlson owned the company. Because he could sell the hell out of it.

Gillian entered, barefoot and encased in tattered jeans slung low on her hips. The house was warm from the afternoon sun, but sleeves covered her arms from shoulder to wrist. Her shirt, tight enough to outline a pair of small, lush breasts, was cropped to reveal a line of skin that winked in and out as she moved.

Against the formality of the room, the clothes seemed as much a "screw you" as anything else about her. She brushed past him, leaving the smell of soap and shampoo in her wake. Nothing floral and girly, but spicy and sharp. Sexy. Another way of thumbing her nose at the grandparents. Or him. Either way, the bare skin and the fragrance reeled him in, more strands in the sticky web around him.

She cut him a small, private look, as though she knew exactly what he was feeling and why, then padded to her grandfather like a jungle cat creeping up on its prey.

"We'll get the gate off its hinges and set up a remote opener—you really should have done that years ago—with a camera system. We'll put motion detectors here." Carlson was pointing to a rough map of the estate. "Install cameras here and here. We'll have to cut down some trees, of course. Rewire the house. Refit the windows for more efficient electronic alarms—"

"This is ridiculous," Gillian said. "You're suggesting permanent changes. Turning everything into a prison camp. They could catch whoever it is tonight, and this will all be wasted effort."

Chip's aging broad body stiffened as he rose from bending over the table. "We're not relying on the police for your safety."

"You don't even use the security system you have."

An indignant flush tainted Chip's cheeks. "That will have to change."

"I'm just saying that all this"—Gillian waved an arm to indicate Carlson's reams of paper—"is unnecessary."

Ray agreed. And though Carlson was salivating over the job, Ray voiced his concurrence. "Solution is simple." Keeping his expression neutral, he looked straight at her. "Get on a plane and go back to New York."

She raised her chin. "The police said not to."

He crossed his arms. Shrugged. "The hell with the police. They can ask. But they can't hold you here."

But there was something in her face, some hard determination. The hell with the police was right. She *wanted* to stay.

Before he could probe why, Chip waved Ray's observation away. "We don't want her to leave. We've made that clear. Whoever this lunatic is, he could follow her. At least if she's here, we can keep an eye on her."

"Then the security net we're recommending is crucial," said Carlson. "Including at least a two-man team, double that if you can afford it."

"I'm not walking around with four bodyguards," she said to Carlson. And to her grandfather, "And you're not cutting down trees and installing video cameras. I won't let you."

"It's not up to you," Chip said. "Your grandmother—"

"Will be a nervous wreck no matter what."

"Gillian, I'm not going to argue with you—"

"Well, you can't force me—"

"I have another idea," Ray said, silencing them both. He peeled himself off the sideboard, turned to Carlson, knowing he was about to burst his boss's bubble. Not to mention his own. "We can put her in a hotel. Confined space. Easy to guard. Off-duty PD as stationary guard. One man to handle security inside and in transit."

It was a simple solution, as elegant as a wraparound against the opposing goalie. And just as tricky.

"But we'd feel better if she was here," Chip said with a plaintive note.

Ray looked into the older man's eyes. He hadn't noticed how rheumy they were. Saw the loss and the fear. The slight tremble around his mouth.

"She'll be safer somewhere else," he said gently. "Everyone knows this place. And even if we got started on a security perimeter today, it would take the better part of a week to install all the equipment. In the meantime, your granddaughter would be vulnerable."

Chip sank into a dining room chair and nodded.

"Look, fix the gates and use the alarm you have until we can set up something more sophisticated," Ray said.

"And let us leave a car here. Two men to keep an eye on things."

Chip sighed and shook his head. "I don't know—"

"A small precaution," Ray said. "Just in case. They'll stay out of sight. Won't bother you."

Gillian put a hand on her grandfather's shoulder. "It'll be okay."

He grunted. "Tell that to your grandmother."

Ray booked them into the Lowe's across from Vanderbilt. It was halfway between the house in Belle Meade and downtown, was in a heavily trafficked area that didn't attract too many strays, and he had no trouble getting a two-bedroom suite with a connecting room for him. He made the reservation in his name and paid for it with his own credit card. One of the top ten commandments in security was never let the clients go public with their whereabouts.

He left Carlson on guard at the house while he went to grab some clothes and check in. Twenty minutes later, he came back with keys, and Carlson left.

He found Gillian and Maddie upstairs, packing. Or rather, Gillian was standing in front of her bedroom window, brooding on the view, and Maddie was flinging clothes into a battered duffel.

"There isn't a single piece of clothing here that doesn't have holes in it," she said. "Why don't we just buy what you need at the hotel?"

"Because the clothes in hotels are for people like Genevra."

Ray crossed to Gillian. "Stay away from the windows."

She startled, whirled, saw who it was. “Jesus, Ray. Don’t sneak up on me like that.”

He drew the curtains closed. “Don’t drift off. Pay attention to your surroundings.”

“My surroundings? I’m in my own bedroom, for crying out loud.”

“In front of an open window.”

“If someone is trying to get at me, it won’t be with a sniper rifle. Not if that picture of Detective Burke’s says anything.”

“You like being a target?”

She and Maddie exchanged glances. There was something in Maddie’s face. Something challenging and know-it-all. As if she were saying, see, someone else knows your craziness.

Then, as if to change the subject, she held up a scrap of cloth. Unfurled it. A T-shirt, so thin he could practically see through it. “This is from tenth grade,” she said.

Gillian gasped. “It is.” She swiped it out of Maddie’s hands. “I forgot I had it.” She buried her face in the cloth, like a kid with a favorite teddy bear.

“Here,” Ray said, and held out a keycard to Maddie. “If you’re sure you’re staying.”

Gillian looked up from the shirt. “She’s sure.”

“Be better for you to leave town,” Ray said to Maddie, making the argument one last time. “Less to worry about.”

Gillian bounced off the bed, dropped the T-shirt over the duffel. “She’s not going home. I need her here.” Gillian put an arm around Maddie, who frowned and stepped away, picked up the T-shirt, and folded it into the bag.

“You just want someone to eat the cheese off the pizza while you snarf all the pepperoni,” Maddie said.

Gillian smiled. "Don't forget the chili fries." She looked at Ray. "Maddie's a sucker for chili fries. And all the little things they put in the minibar."

"We're not going on vacation," Ray said.

"You take your pleasure where you can," Gillian said.

Maddie sighed and clawed the hair back from her forehead with those sharp purple-black nails. Ray could hear the scrape of the tips on her scalp. "You don't need me," she said quietly. "I've got things to do back at the studio."

"What things?"

"Things, stuff. Business."

"I'll let you take me shopping," Gillian said.

Maddie quirked an unimpressed brow.

"I'll let you watch Ray while he's asleep."

"The hell you will," Ray said.

Maddie pursed her lips, crossed her arms, and cocked a bony hip. "You really know what buttons to push." She looked over at Ray. "You're lucky you're so cute." She stabbed a long-nailed finger at Gillian. "But I'm holding you to the shopping."

Gillian grinned. She zipped the duffel and threw it at Maddie. "I'll meet you over there."

Maddie caught the duffel and staggered. "Meet me? Why? Where are you going?"

"I've got something to do."

"What?" Ray and Maddie both said at the same time.

"An appointment."

"No, you don't," Maddie said firmly. "I don't have you scheduled for anything until tomorrow."

"Set it myself."

"Gillian—" Maddie's voice held a warning note.

Ray looked between the two women. "What? What's going on?"

"You're going fishing, aren't you?" Maddie said, and the way she said it didn't make it sound like fun.

"No one's going fishing," Ray said.

"Not *fishing,* fishing," Maddie said, still gazing hard at Gillian. "Not for fish at least."

"Okay." Ray held up two hands. "Would someone please tell me what the hell you're talking about?"

"We're talking about murder," Maddie said. "Gillian's going fishing for a killer."

19

The fishing expedition proved to be a trip to visit Harley Samuels. Detective Harley Samuels, retired. The same Detective Samuels who had been a vet when Ray had joined up. The one who'd retired the year Ray left the job. And the one who'd led the investigation into Holland Gray's death.

They went in Ray's pickup, and he drove. Should he have waited for an armored car and driver? Debatable. Armored cars could stop a bullet. Sometimes. But everyone in protective services knew about Leaman Hunt, who was killed in an armored car when a round slipped through a rubber window grommet around the bullet-resistant glass. Freak accident, maybe. But also a cautionary tale. Protection was relative. No matter how heavy the armor, how strong the glass, there was always a weapon that could pierce it if the bad guy wanted to passionately enough.

Plus, armored cars tended to draw attention to themselves. Ray came down on the side of blending in, especially in this instance, where a public appearance and crowds weren't going to be an issue. Besides, getting a car and driver would have taken hours, and Gillian was halfway out the door.

So he shucked his suit coat, rolled up his sleeves, loosened his tie, and drove her to Center Hill Lake while Maddie took their bags to the hotel. On the way out, he stopped by her room, offered to drop her off, but she declined.

"I have a couple of things to do," she told him.

Her room was a smaller version of Gillian's, cramped but equally dolled up in gilded mirrors, rose wallpaper, and curlicue furniture. An open suitcase lay on the bed. She was packing.

He wandered in, checked the view from the window. A good drop, facing the wooded slope on the north. "How'd you know where she was going?" he asked, curious about the relationship between the two women.

She shrugged. "I've known her since we were fifteen. We were roommates at Hadley."

"Hadley?"

"Boarding school in Pennsylvania." She struck a pose. "I was the smart but poor scholarship student. She was the troubled rich girl. Very Frances Hodgson Burnett."

He quirked an eyebrow at her.

"*The Secret Garden, A Little Princess.* You know, Shirley Temple...?" She bent over the suitcase, whipped her black hair over her shoulder, and tossed him a look. "You need to spend more time on the Turner Classic Movie Channel."

"Yeah, Shirley Temple or *Monday Night Football.* Tough choice." He paused. "So. High school girlfriends."

"We published a newsletter called *Sneer.* We didn't like anyone."

"Except each other."

"Misery loves company."

"And you've been keeping company a long time."

She straightened. Shot him a pointed look. "So?"

He shrugged. “I’m not friends with any of the guys I knew in high school.”

She laughed, but it was cool and knowing. “How many of the guys you knew in high school offered you this?” She waved an arm, indicating the luxurious room.

Maddie still remembered the first time she visited Nashville during Christmas vacation, the year after she’d met Gillian. The sheer size of the Gray house had awed her. The way the rooms echoed when you walked through them. The huge bathroom, which she had all to herself, the tiny, rose-scented soap and soft, monogrammed hand towels. She’d been what—sixteen—and impressed. Shaken. Not only because it was a far cry from the tiny row house she lived in with her parents and three brothers in Juniper, West Virginia. Not even because no one came home with sweat and coal dust blackening their faces. Because it was all so big and plush and spacious. She hadn’t known real people could live that way.

“Gillian gave me a job and a lifestyle,” she told Ray. “What’s wrong with that?”

“Nothing.”

His silent perusal made her narrow her eyes. “You think I’m a mooch?”

“I think you shouldn’t care what I think.” He wandered toward the bed and the suitcase on it, but she quickly stepped in front of him.

“I don’t,” she said.

He looked over her shoulder, but she closed the lid before he could see what was in it. Gave him a pointed look to mind his own business, but he didn’t take the hint.

“Never wanted to set out on your own?”

The suitcase was vintage Roberto Cavalli and had cost a small fortune. She leaned, one-handed, on the top, enjoyed the creamy, soft leather. "And if I did? Who'd make sure Gillian didn't carry out one of her pictures for real?"

"Someone else. Gillian herself."

She hefted the suitcase off the bed and set it on the floor. "And what would become of poor little me?"

Their eyes met briefly, his expression veiled and reserved, but with suspicion lurking behind it. A small chill ran up her back. What did he know? How could he know anything?

Before her panic set in, he lightly tossed a set of car keys in the air and caught them. "Sure you don't want me to drop you at the hotel?"

"Oh, yeah, cowboy." She smiled. "Real sure."

Ray thought about that conversation as he wound his way around Center Hill Lake, looking for Harley Samuels's cabin. Thought about Maddie Crane's suitcase and what she might be hiding there. And about the bonds we create. The invisible ones we don't even know are there and the ones we carefully construct to keep others weak. Dependent. Either way, those ties constrict and suffocate the way a boa constrictor does. Eventually they swallow you whole.

"You ever think about letting Maddie go?"

In the seat beside him, Gillian shrugged. "Why should I? She's my friend."

"You pay her enough to say so."

She laughed. "Is that what you think?"

"It's what she told me."

She shook her head, still amused. "It's what she tells everyone, Ray. It's her way. Especially after someone accuses her of living off me." She shot a sly glance his way. "You did accuse her, didn't you?"

He didn't reply, but silence was answer enough.

"Uh-huh. You know, she stood by me during some of the roughest times of my life. Now she needs me, and I'm not cutting her loose."

He mulled that over. But he knew from hard experience that trust was a fragile thing, too often misplaced. "She seems to think it's the other way around. That you need her."

"I do," Gillian said, if a bit defensively. "We have a good time."

"The sneer sisters."

"She told you about that?"

"High school can be so much fun."

"Yeah, if you get them before they get you."

It struck Gillian how true that was for all her life. She looked out the window at the passing landscape. The lake was an Army Corps of Engineers wonder in the middle of the Cumberland Mountains. Four rivers spilled into it, and there were still hundreds of miles of undeveloped shorefront. To most it was a wooded paradise, but every time she got close enough, she felt the same apprehension. She knew what was waiting at the water's edge.

She'd wanted to drive herself. She always drove. It was part of the ritual. Whenever she came home, she'd see Harley. As if somehow, in the space of time between her last visit and the current one, something would have changed. Some new evidence. A new theory. Harley had married, had a couple of kids, divorced, retired. And still she came. Year after year at first, then less frequently, but even when it became clear there would never be anything new, she came. She outgrew hope, but not the trip to see Harley.

And now the ritual had become compulsory.

So she wanted to drive. But Ray had just looked at her. He'd come from Maddie's room, and they'd met in the hallway, both marching toward the stairs. He'd automatically slowed his longer strides to keep pace with her, but the minute she mentioned getting the keys to one of her grandparents' cars, he stopped. Swung his head toward her like a bull in a field who intended to keep intruders out.

"Can you corner left doing sixty-five? Do you know what to look for in an ambush? How to avoid a stopper? How to get out of the kill zone?" He waited a requisite beat. "I'll drive," he said.

And so for the first time, she didn't go alone. She bounced along in a strange pickup with a strange man beside her. And thought about another first. The first visit with a new murder.

Harley met them at the battered mailbox, where a gravel drive kissed the road. Hands shoved in his pockets, he rocked back and forth on his heels while they parked and got out of the car. Harley wasn't what she'd call a neat man, and retirement had tilted him even more toward slovenly. Couple of days' worth of stubble. An apple-shaped beer belly. A pair of red suspenders holding up his rumpled khakis.

She started to introduce them, but Harley was ahead of her.

"I remember you. Ray Pearce, right?" He and Ray shook hands like old friends. "Ole Sergeant Burke's son-in-law."

"Ex-son-in-law, but yes."

"Ex? Hell, sorry to hear that, son." He gave Ray a chagrined smile. "But it happens to the best of us."

Ray nodded stiffly. Didn't seem eager to comment on

the longevity of the modern marriage or his own contribution to the divorce rate.

Harley didn't seem to mind. "Working cold cases?"

"Not exactly."

He gave Ray a long look. "Seem to recall you made detective." He clapped Ray on the back. Had to reach up to do it. "You were young for it, too. But smart. I'll give you that."

Ray shifted, a flush seeping up his neck. "Appreciate you saying so." He cleared his throat. "But I'm not on the job anymore."

"You're not . . ." Harley faltered. Looked from Ray to her. The look clearly asked what he was doing there, then.

"He's with me," she said. As if that weren't obvious.

They started toward the house, a small cabin recessed into the woods. Through the trees she could just catch a glimpse of sun sparkling off water.

As usual, Ray hung back, guarding her rear. And as usual, he practically stripped her shoes off. But she was getting used to him now. To the awareness of his body behind her. Tall. Big-shouldered.

Harley leaned in. Whispered, "Boyfriend?"

She shook her head. "Bodyguard."

Inside, the house always smelled the same. Stale fried things and bait. It slammed her back through all the years and all the visits. The time he taught her to fish. The time she finished his jigsaw puzzle.

She looked to the corner now, saw the card table was right where it always was. A half-finished puzzle covered the surface.

"You don't change much, do you, Harley?" It was one of the things she liked about him. He was constant. A steady orb around which her crazy world spun.

"Should I?" He put an arm around her shoulder. Squeezed. "How about a beer?"

She nodded, and he disappeared into the kitchen. While he was gone, she took stock of the rest of the room. The beat-up brown couch with its puffy pillows sat across the way. An indentation on the left cushion showed where Harley liked to sit. In front of the sofa was the same battered coffee table that had been there for years. On top of the table, like always, was the deep, white Dillard's box.

Her heart lurched when she saw it, just as it always did. And as always, she tried hard to repress the flutter. Glanced out the window toward the lake and the serene water.

Harley came back with two bottles. Ray refused his, but Gillian twisted the cap off hers.

She and Harley clinked bottles. Drank. "Time was, I'd be offering you a Coke," Harley said.

Gillian smiled. "Time was, I'd be sneaking the beer."

Harley laughed good-naturedly, and Ray peeked out one of the windows.

"I'm going to have a look around." He eyed Harley. "You okay in here?"

Harley shot him an amused but tolerant glance. "I think I can handle it."

Ray slipped out the door, and Harley watched him go.

"Those boys don't like an unfamiliar setting," he said. He seemed to ponder that for a moment. Pondering Ray, she suspected, and the choices he'd made.

Then, as if he couldn't figure it out and wouldn't try, he sighed. Eased into the couch. Patted the cushion beside him. "So, baby girl. Catch me up." He nodded toward the door Ray had just exited. "You in trouble again?"

Harley didn't take the paper, and he didn't have a television. The radio was always tuned to music, jazz mostly. Not much for the news anymore, he always said. Privileges of rank, or lack thereof. So Gillian had to recount for him the assault at the museum and the replicant murder.

"It's him," she said, the beer forgotten, her voice low and unwavering. "He's out there. He's doing it again."

Harley held up his hands. "Now hold on. Let's not jump to conclusions."

She pulled the Dillard's box toward her. "There has to be something we missed. Something that would help catch him."

Harley sighed. "Honey, you've been saying that for over twenty years." He looked away. "I know I failed you," he said softly, "failed your family, but after all this time I don't think—"

She shook her head wildly, as if the movement could block out the sound of his words. "No, don't say it."

Harley laid a hand over the top of the box. "Can't we skip this part of the visit? Just this once? It's so hurtful to you. Breaks my heart to watch. And it ain't going to change anything."

Gillian thought about it. Her heart was already thumping, the sickness she'd feel when she opened the box was just below the surface, waiting to spring. What a relief not to look. Not to deal. Not to remember.

Then the image of the recently murdered woman crowded out her own pain. "Sorry, Harley."

Slowly she lifted the top off the box.

20

When Ray returned, he found Gillian and Harley on the couch, huddled over a mess of papers. The top of an empty gift box lay forgotten on the floor; the box itself sat askew on the couch next to Gillian.

The two made a cozy picture with their heads bent. The old man, like a big, fat teddy bear, and in the shadow of his rotund form, the sprite of a woman.

Ray felt reasonably comfortable that they were safe here. The cabin was isolated enough, and he had seen no tracks leading in or out except their own. He'd hear a boat coming easy. Hear any kind of vehicle. Worse came to worst, he'd mapped out an escape route through the woods, then moved the truck to make it more accessible. But he wanted to get going before dark. Carlson had sent someone over to the hotel, and while Ray was outside, he'd received the security checklist on his BlackBerry. Everything looked good, but he wouldn't feel right until he'd checked it out himself.

"How much longer—" He stopped short when Gillian looked up from the paper she held in her hand. His benign first impression vanished. Tears streaked her pretty angel face. She looked broken. Tortured.

"What the—" He turned on Harley. "What's going on?" He freed the thing from Gillian's fingers.

"It's okay." She scraped at her face. But the words and movement came from a distance because all he could see was the photograph in his hand.

The crime-scene photograph.

The kitchen, the body on the floor. The blood.

It was a lousy picture. A black-and-white photocopy, much used. The upper right-hand corner was missing, and the whole thing looked like it had been crumpled then smoothed out again.

But there was no mistaking what it was.

The kitchen was less perfect, less pristine. An ordinary room with a spotted linoleum floor. No strange, eerie light came through an unseen window. The victim wasn't a schoolgirl, but she was young enough, even in death.

He tore his gaze away and looked at Harley. Harley stared right back at him, no apology in his eyes.

"You were the lead?" Ray asked.

"That's right."

Ray picked through scattered papers. Saw familiar forms, reports. "You got the whole file here? All the case-work?"

"Every last note, statement, evidence report."

Ray swallowed panic. He glanced at Gillian's haunted face and knew there was nothing he could do to fix it.

He turned on Harley. "Are you crazy?"

"Shut up, Ray," Gillian said. "You can't talk to him like that."

"He has no business showing this stuff to you."

"No business? Who the hell's business is it if not mine?"

"It's tearing you apart."

"So what? The price of justice."

But it wasn't a price he was easy about paying. Especially if it meant he had to watch. "Let's go. We're leaving."

She stood her ground. "Like hell we are."

Harley stepped between them. "Hey, baby girl, why don't you take your walk around the lake? Me and Ray can have a few words."

"I'm not going anywhere," Gillian said.

"She can't go walking alone out there," Ray said.

At which, her face set, her chin hardened. "I can do whatever I damn well please." And despite her declaration to the contrary, she pivoted and charged out.

"Hey!" Ray took off after her, but Harley got in his way.

"Let her go. You can keep an eye on her through the kitchen window."

"Christ," Ray muttered. But Harley was right. He could see her clearly. At least, the back view. Spine straight, shoulders rigid. She looked lost in front of the wide expanse of lake. Dwarfed by the trees.

"Don't be so hard on her," Harley said softly.

Hard on her? The man should crawl inside his skull and look around. All Ray wanted to do was race out there and make it right. Do whatever it took to make the bad stuff go away. The urge crept over him like a cold sweat. That's all he ever wanted to do. When would he learn he was no good at it? He could keep someone alive, but making them happy was magic he could never work.

"No one should have to see pictures of her own mother's murder," he said.

"Better than pretending it never happened."

"Pretending? What do you mean? That woman doesn't know how to pretend."

"But the cold bitch up at the Gray house does." Harley

shoved his hands in his pockets. Rocked a bit. "After the funeral, it was like her daughter had never lived, let alone died. Subject closed with a big ole padlock."

Ray shook his head. "I've seen Mrs. Gray. Even the sight of a uniform gets her going. She's neither forgiven nor forgotten."

"Maybe. But she don't talk about it neither." Harley raised a questioning brow. "You ever hear her mention her daughter? Mention the murder? Even say the word?"

Ray thought back. Slowly shook his head.

"Gillian came to me when she was, oh, maybe thirteen. A pure mess. Little bottle of rage all stoppered up. You ever see what fury can do if it don't have a way of exploding? You were a cop. You saw the drugs, shoplifting, the joy rides and vandalism."

Ray nodded. Everyone who rode a patrol car saw kids out of control.

"What happens if you don't do any of those things? Where does the anger go? She had no one to talk to about what had happened. Family wouldn't even send her to counseling. Refused to admit there was anything wrong. But she's had problems, son... you couldn't begin to imagine."

Ray didn't have to. Whatever it was, he could sense it coming off her like an aura. It's what drew him and repelled him at the same time. Torn souls in need of mending.

"So I let her come to me," the older man said. "She needed a friend." He looked out the window to where Gillian stood at the shore. She took something from her pocket. A camera. A tiny camera. "She needed the truth. I gave it to her. I do it every time she comes home."

Ray sank against the refrigerator. The cold metal burned into his back.

"She tell you about the new murder?"

"She did."

"You think there's a connection?"

"I think it's mighty strange. But a connection after all these years? I don't know."

Somehow Ray was still holding on to the crime-scene photograph. He looked down at it. Holland Gray's body was twisted at the waist, as though half of her had tried to get away. She wore a dress with some kind of design—in the rumpled black-and-white photocopy he couldn't tell the color or discern the pattern. The best view would have been the bodice, but the chest wounds had bled out and covered the front of her dress with blood. A lot of blood.

He couldn't help recalling her face as it had been on the cover of *Vogue.* Sultry and mysterious, with a hint of mischief in her smile. Lively, vibrant. All of which was absent from the death's-head he gazed at now, with its bloodless pallor and vacant stare.

"Cause of death?"

"Two stab wounds to the chest. Sicko used a kitchen knife. We wondered if maybe she tried to defend herself, and he took it away from her."

"Rape?"

"With a vengeance. She was all tore up inside."

"She know her attacker?"

Harley shook his head. "No signs of a break-in, but we couldn't find a single link to anyone she knew. She hadn't gone to school here and so didn't have a whole lot of friends. Didn't bar hop, do the party scene. House was a little isolated thing in southwest Nashville off Highway 100. She lived quiet with her kid."

"What about back in New York? Or LA? Success always breeds jealousy."

He shrugged. “Everyone had solid alibis. Couldn’t find a motive for a paid contract. Never looked like a pro anyway. Looked like someone took advantage of a lone woman, then lost control and killed her.”

“Random?”

“That’s my bet, though we couldn’t prove it. And not for lack of trying. We pulled in the exterminator, the meter reader, the garbage collectors. Deliverymen. Repairmen. Anyone we knew of who had business at the house.”

“What about DNA?”

“We did that later, when it became available. Couldn’t track down every last one, but those we did weren’t a match.”

Ray thought it over. The conclusion seemed clear. “Maybe someone left town and just came back.”

Harley nodded thoughtfully. “Maybe. Mighty big coincidence, though.”

Ray looked down at the picture of Holland Gray, then back up at Harley. Coincidence wasn’t something that sat easy with him either.

“The thing is, that little girl out there”—Harley nodded toward the lake and Gillian—“she’s counting on it. And I mean with every breath. I were you, I’d find this guy quick. Or she will. And that’s not something I want to see.”

21

Gillian heard the screen door slam, but she didn't need the sound to tell her Ray had stepped outside. Without turning around, she could feel his weighted presence behind her, hovering, shielding. Thick and close. Closer than she wanted anyone to come.

"It's pretty out here," he said, and moved up beside her.

She looked through the tiny Canon she'd slipped into her pocket before she left. Now she fixed her shot on the lake. It was wide and deep, the water calm. Bowled above it, the sky was perfectly blue and peaceful. It set her teeth on edge.

"Ever seen a drowning victim?" She lowered the digital camera. Felt his big body beside her but didn't look at him.

A moment of silence, then, "No."

"I haven't done a drowned woman." She calculated what it would be like to have your head held under water. The choking panic, the fire in the lungs, the inevitable gulp for air that killed. The water looked so inviting yet could be so deadly.

"What do you think?" She held up the camera, scrolled through the pictures she'd shot. Watched him examine them. When he finally looked away, there was a hint of sadness in his eyes. "I think you can't handle pretty. Not without turning it into something else."

"Something real, you mean."

"Something ugly." He looked out over the landscape. "It's just a lake, Gillian. Water. Trees. The only death here is what you bring to it."

She respected his innocence, misplaced though it was. He'd been a cop. He should know better. "There's death everywhere. Even in the pretty places."

"Only if you're looking for it."

"Or it's looking for you." She held his gaze a moment, but only just. There was something in his face, a wanting, a caring, that sadness again. Sudden tears welled up, and she averted her eyes, horrified that he might see.

But once again he was kind. Kinder than she expected. He neither laughed nor sympathized with her emotion. Gave no indication that he'd witnessed it.

"You know what?" He exhaled. A deep breath as though getting rid of that intense moment between them. "You think too much. You should get a real job. Pick tobacco. Haul bricks. You'd be too tired to think."

She shot him a small, wry smile. "Lucky me, I'm rich. I don't need a real job."

He murmured a resigned sigh. "Well, come on, rich girl. We gotta go."

He indicated for her to precede him, and they walked to the pickup.

Harley met them outside. "Don't be a stranger," he said to her.

"See ya around." She gave him a peck on the cheek. And then Ray made sure she got inside the truck before taking his place behind the wheel. He turned the engine over, she waved once to Harley, and they were gone.

Another trip over. Another visit to the shrine ended.

She leaned back against the seat and closed her eyes. She could sleep for a week. A month.

It always hit her like this. The huge black dread on the way there, like an anvil over her head. Then the massive black hole on the way back. Drained. Empty.

"You talk to Harley about the new murder?"

"We talked."

"And?"

"We didn't solve anything if that's what you're asking."

"You agree with him that there's no connection?"

"I didn't say that."

She turned her head. Looked over at him. God, she needed an ally right now. "Then you think there could be a link?"

"I didn't say that either." He shot her a glance, and whatever hope she'd been brewing vaporized fast. "Doesn't matter anyway." He gazed back on the road. "I'm here to keep you in one piece, not to catch the bad guy. That's someone else's job."

"It used to be yours."

"Past tense, short stack."

Carefully, she said, "Do you miss it?"

He thought it over. "Sometimes." He shot her a glance, and she could tell he was debating how much to admit. He shrugged. "Yeah, I miss it."

"So why not go back?"

He was silent a little too long. "It's complicated."

"What isn't?"

He shrugged.

"Are we talking circumstances again?"

Another shrug.

"The same circumstances that brought you to Nashville?"

He gave her a short, tight smile. "You asking for my life story?"

"You know mine."

Music suddenly erupted in the truck. Gillian dove for her purse to the strains of the Clash singing "I fought the law, and the law won," and found her cell phone. It was Maddie.

"Still fishing?" she asked.

"On our way home," Gillian told her.

"Still alive?"

"Bullets bounce off me."

"It's not bullets I'm worried about. It's the memories."

Gillian looked out at the passing landscape. "Yeah, okay, so maybe they dig a little deeper. But I'll manage."

"Well, I got something to ease your pain."

"Shot of Novocain?"

"Bag of Cheetos."

"Yum. Cream sodas, too?"

"Would I let you down?"

"Only if a man's involved."

"Speaking of which—Lassie still with you?"

Gillian looked over at Ray. "Still here."

"Tell him to bark for me."

Gillian laughed. Turned to Ray. "It's Maddie," she said. "Wants you to bark for her."

He raised a single disbelieving, disapproving brow, then returned to concentrating on the road.

"Sorry," Gillian said to Maddie. "Not going to happen."

"Oh, geez, and I was so hoping."

"So I'll see you in about an hour?"

"There's one hitch. That Detective Burke called. You

didn't show up at the hoosegow to sign your statement about the museum thing."

"Hoosegow?"

"I'm working on my vocabulary."

"Okay, we'll make a detour. I wouldn't mind talking to him myself."

Matthew Dobie sat behind his desk in the mobile headquarters of Citizens for American Values—a trailer parked in a lot between a pawnshop and a liquor store on Charlotte Avenue. There was a knock on the door, and a young man stepped in.

"The woman's here, sir," he said.

The young man was part of Dobie's vanguard. Dobie couldn't recall the name at the moment. Davis, maybe. Or Dallas. Something with a "D." Not that it mattered. The vanguard did their duty, protected him and his work. Names were unimportant.

What mattered was they were all tall, well-muscled white men, perfect American specimens. If he could find them, even a little pretty. He liked good-looking men. Liked the curve of a wide shoulder coming down from a thick neck. The tight skin, the power.

Dobie encouraged them to exercise and avoid sugar and processed foods. It was all a matter of discipline. Of control. Of keeping the doors locked and barred against the baser urges. He was proud of his young men. He liked to watch them go through their paces in the morning. Group calisthenics, a run. A phalanx of beauty, like galloping stallions.

This one seemed exceptional, and Dobie couldn't help but take a moment to admire him, his fair hair skinned to the nub, chiseled jaw, Cary Grant cleft in his chin. But like all the others, his eyes were blank, waiting for orders, waiting for Matthew Dobie to fill them with direction.

He gestured "come forward" with a wave of his hand, and the nameless man—Davis or Dallas—stepped back and let Ruth Gellico enter.

Dobie rose, put on his warmest smile. "Come in, please. You must be exhausted. Here, sit. Sit." He nodded to the guard, who led her to a chair. She sank into it, a pale, washed-out dishrag.

"Can I get you something to eat, Ruth?"

The woman shook her head. "I'd just like to go home."

She still wore the clothes she'd been arrested in, the black-and-white waitstaff outfit. Splotches of red spattered her shirt. And she smelled from her time in jail.

"Of course you do," Dobie said. He dismissed the young man with a silent nod, and Davis or Dallas disappeared through the door. "Of course. And you will. I promise. I'll see to it myself. I'll even pay your bus ticket."

Tears sprang to the poor woman's eyes. "Thank you, sir," she whispered. "You've been so kind. You've paid my bail, everything. I don't know what to say."

But Matthew Dobie did. Ruth Gellico had worked out well. Better than he could have imagined. She'd generated the headlines he needed, kept the media attention focused. The world was falling into a devil's pit. Whoring and killing was sport, and everyone wanted a piece of the action.

"It is I who should be thanking you, Ruth." He patted her hand. "For your heroic deed. We all owe you a debt of gratitude. You're a brave woman," he said sympathetically. Always be sympathetic. "A very brave woman."

22

The familiar stench hit Ray the minute he walked through the door of the downtown police headquarters. Puke and disinfectant, the perfume of the criminal justice system.

"Nice," Gillian said, clearly meaning the opposite. "You miss this?"

"Never been to night court?" He nodded over his shoulder to a door in the corner by the front of the building.

"Haven't had that supreme pleasure."

"Oh, well, and here I was thinking you'd done everything."

A black-skinned woman in a flowing orange robe came through the night court door accompanied by two small children dressed American style in jeans. They ran ahead, and she snapped at them in a language too exotic for Ray to place. Off to the side, two men and a woman were in a heated discussion in Spanish. Lounging against a wall was a lanky guy with a Unabomber beard. Skinny, pants drooping, layers of shirts under a shapeless coat. He smiled as Ray escorted Gillian past. One of his front teeth was missing.

Outside the glass front doors over Gillian's shoulders,

more people congregated. Sitting on the concrete benches. Smoking. Waving court papers at each other.

He kept his hand on Gillian's back, weaving her toward the watch, who grinned behind his bulletproof glass window.

"Look what the cat dragged in. Hey, Ray. What the hell you doing here? Wife let you out?"

Ray looked over the watch's shoulder at the familiar room behind him. Rows of desks, a few cops milling about. He geared himself up for what was coming, like crossing an open field in full view of the enemy.

"This is Gillian Gray. She's here for Burke."

They got their temporary IDs, and the watch buzzed the door open. "Third desk on the—"

"I remember," Ray said.

He walked Gillian to Burke's desk, enduring the ribbing.

"Hey, look—it's the wife lover."

"How's the missus?"

"Nice suit. Wife pick that out?"

"Complicated," Gillian murmured.

"Very," he answered.

He threaded his way through the laughter to Jimmy's desk just as his ex-brother-in-law came from the break room with a mug of coffee. Ray didn't have to see the mug to recognize it. He'd given it to Jimmy one Christmas: HOMICIDE. OUR DAY BEGINS WHEN YOURS ENDS.

Ray had called ahead, so it wasn't as if the visit was a surprise. But still Jimmy gave him the cold stare, sipping coffee like he was playing bad cop as he sat in the swivel chair behind his desk.

"Have a seat, Miss Gray."

He didn't offer one to Ray, which was fine, because

Ray wanted to stand anyway. Better view of the room. Not that Gillian was in danger in a room full of cops, but standing was what he was used to.

"I've got your statement here." Jimmy fished through a mess of papers. Ray laughed to himself. Jimmy never could find anything on his desk. Everything changed, yet nothing did.

"Betty!" Jimmy barked across the room to the squad secretary. "Where's that Gray statement?"

"On your desk, James," she called. She was a round, jolly-faced woman, brown-skinned, with a ready smile. She saw Ray and turned it on. Then rose and hurried over.

"Why, Ray Pearce. What are you doing here?"

"He's with me," Gillian said. There was something in her face. Some teasing mischief Ray didn't think he was going to like.

Betty raised a brow and a white-toothed smile split her face. "Well, that's nice."

"Yeah, moving on is the best thing," Gillian said a little too loudly. "He looks great, doesn't he?"

Betty examined him. "I believe he does look great." She winked.

"Don't you have reports to type?" Jimmy snapped.

"Not for you," Betty said archly. "Good to see you, Ray." She patted his arm and returned to her desk in the corner.

Gillian gave him a sly smile, which Ray refused to commiserate with. "You find that statement yet?" he asked Jimmy.

Jimmy pulled something out of a pile triumphantly. "Got it."

He settled Gillian in one of the interview rooms to go

over her statement. Ray stood outside the door as Jimmy came out. He glanced at Ray, started to say something, then didn't. So Ray did.

"How's your dad?" he asked.

"Better." Jimmy looked away. "Spoke to Peter. Thanks for what you did the other night."

Ray smiled, shook his head at the other man's grudging tone. "Hey—Jimmy. Don't go all mushy on me."

"Look, I said thank you." Jimmy opened the door, stuck his head inside. "You let me know if you need anything," he said, and came back out. "Bring her back when she's finished." He turned to walk away, but Ray spoke.

"Is he going to be all right?"

"Who?"

"Your dad."

Ray gave him an irritated look. "He's going to be fine."

"You talk to Nancy about assisted living? Maybe some kind of home health care?"

"He's not sick."

"He's not well either."

Jimmy's jaw tightened. "He's my father, Ray, not yours. Not anymore. Appreciate what you did. Don't need your help or advice. Don't want it."

"Look, I'm just—"

"What are you doing here, Ray?"

Ray deadpanned him. "Trying to reach past your inner asshole to the real James R. Burke."

Jimmy gave him a barely tolerant look. "No, not here, in this building. Here. In Nashville. Why are you still here?" He said it as if it was the puzzle of the ages. "Nothing's keeping you. No family. No connections. Why the hell haven't you just"—he waved a hand—"blown away?"

Ray shifted his feet. Those were questions he didn't like asking let alone answering. "It's none of your business. And I didn't come here to talk about—"

"You never did know when to cut your losses," Jimmy said. He shook his head and took off.

Ray called after him. "You remember Harley Samuels?"

The other man slowed. Turned. "Yeah, sure. What about him?"

Ray went through the cold case, describing what he'd seen in the Holland Gray file. During the recitation, Jimmy slowly walked back until the two of them were once again toe-to-toe outside the closed interview room.

"You're saying there's a connection?" Jimmy asked.

"It's a possibility. Holland Gray's murderer was never found."

Jimmy looked at him for a short, heavy beat. "Okay. Thanks. I'll check it out."

Ray stared. "That's it?"

"What do you mean?"

"I was hoping you'd share the case notes."

"You're not a cop anymore. I can't do that."

"Yeah, you can. If you want to. You interview Dobie? What did he say? Alibi out? Did you check out news footage of the crowd outside the museum? Run faces through the system?"

The smaller man gazed at him, hard and silent, and Ray could see he'd get nowhere.

Calmly, Ray said, "You're a prick, you know that?"

"You're a quitter, you know that?"

"I just quit my job, Jimmy. Not my marriage. Can't say the same for you."

"Yeah? Well at least I still got my badge."

"Right. Your badge."

"Better than nothing. Which is what you got."

Jimmy walked, and Ray fought to quell the anger shooting through him. By the time Gillian came out a few minutes later, he had himself more or less under control.

He escorted her back to Jimmy's desk, where she laid the statement on top of a pile of papers.

"Signed, sealed, and delivered," she said.

"Good," Jimmy said. "And just so you know, assailant made bail."

"Damn," Ray muttered. "How?"

"Dobie."

Ray thought about this. "She working for him?"

"Says not. Can't prove it one way or the other."

"What do you know about her?"

"Originally from Ohio. No priors. Not even a traffic ticket. Younger sister murdered when they were kids. Got involved with Dobie's group a couple of years ago. Managed to sneak in with the waitstaff at the museum party."

Gillian grabbed the chair in front of Jimmy's desk. Sat. Waved a dismissive hand in front of her. "Doesn't matter."

"If you want to prevent more incidents, it does," Ray said.

"It was a prank. Some fake blood. There are more important things to worry about," she said.

Ray had a feeling he knew where she was going. "Don't bother," he said.

She ignored him. Put all her attention on Jimmy. "The man who murdered my mother. He's still out there."

"Yeah, Ray already mentioned that."

She shot Ray a swift look, then back at Jimmy. "And?"

"And I'll look into it," Jimmy said.

She frowned. "That's not good enough."

"It's the best you'll get," Ray said.

She leaned in toward Jimmy, an intense expression on her face. “He’s out there. He’s doing it again.”

“Maybe. I said I’d check it out. I will.”

“You better do more than check it out. This department screwed up once; don’t make the same mistake again.” She scrawled a phone number in the corner of a report on his desk. “Call Harley Samuels.”

Jimmy stared her down Dirty Harry style, but she didn’t back off. “Do it.”

“Yes, ma’am. Soon as you have a lieutenant’s patch on your shoulder, I’ll jump to do anything you say.”

23

Ray phoned hotel security on the way back, alerted them that Ruth Gellico had made bond. Arranged to have a guy on the hotel doors keep an eye out for her. A guard named Mallory was already stationed outside the suite.

When he and Gillian tumbled in, Maddie was elegantly sprawled on the floor of the suite's living room facing the television, surrounded by cellophane snack bags and six-packs of soft drinks.

Ray's room wasn't part of the suite proper but had a connecting door. He headed for it. "Let me know if you want to go anywhere," he said to Gillian.

"I will." She held up two fingers. "Scout's honor." And he took that for what it was worth. Not much.

He turned to Maddie. Still dressed in expensive black, she looked out of place amid the garish colors of the junk food bags. "Keep an eye on her," he said.

She saluted lightly. "You betcha, Sarge."

But to make sure, he crossed to the suite's main door and spoke to the guard—loud enough so both women heard him. "Miss Gray goes nowhere without an escort."

"Understood." Mallory was a young guy, but his uniform was pressed, his manner professional and competent.

"I get the feeling you don't trust me," Gillian said when he'd closed the door. She dipped into one of the bags and crunched on an orange Cheeto, looking at him all wide-eyed and innocent.

"Just covering my bases." He plunged into his own room.

"Or his ass," he heard Maddie murmur behind him. "He does have a nice one."

"Very nice," Gillian agreed.

They giggled, and the sound reminded him they'd been friends since high school.

While he was organizing the move to the hotel, he'd arranged with Carlson to have Gillian's file sent over. Now he shucked his tie, throwing it over the chair at the desk, stretched out on the bed, and took out the coffee table book of her photographs.

In the room beyond, he could hear Maddie and Gillian still giggling like schoolgirls. But here, death stalked in weird, eerily lit photographs of ordinary places. A child's bedroom. A paneled basement. All elaborately staged with precise, everyday details. A clown's head night-light. A metal TV tray painted with flowers.

And dead bodies. An entire book haunted by fragile, glassy-eyed dead women.

He turned the page. Dusk in a backyard rimmed with a white picket fence. The wheel of a pink tricycle to the left. A pale blue kiddie pool under a tree. Draped over the edge, a green garden hose was filling the pool with water. But the hose had been forgotten, and the water had risen and spilled over the ground into light-bathed puddles. Above the pool, like a ballet dancer frozen in moonbeams, a blond urchin hung from a rope.

His heart clutched at the photograph's beauty and sadness. He thought about the trip to Harley Samuels and the crime-scene photographs. Unbidden, a reluctant respect rose up. What Gillian had done took great courage. Denial was highly valued by most people, but she refused to look away. Refused to deny her own pain. There was something brave about that. About reliving her tragedy over and over until she understood it. Until she could explain it to the world. Brave and dangerous. Because you never knew what you might find when you dug that deep.

Himself, he was big on blinders. On not asking the hard question. Like the one Jimmy had asked earlier.

Because who wanted to face failure every day in the mirror? Who wanted to admit that staying might not be the virtue it seemed, but only a vain, foolish grasping at the only life he had?

He closed the book, shutting those thoughts with it. Best leave the introspection to those who could afford it. He lay back, placed his gun on top of the book, his hand wrapped around it, ready, if necessary. Then he closed his eyes. Breathed in through his nose to the count of four, then out through his mouth to the same count.

He woke a few hours later, his inner alarm not letting him sleep too long. The place was quiet, dark. He got up, padded to the door, and stood in the doorway where he could check the suite's spacious living room. In the dim light of a corner lamp the remains of bags and drinks were scattered on the floor like ash after a fire. One of the bedroom doors was closed, the other half-open.

He peeked into Gillian's room, expecting to see her asleep. But the light from the living room showed an empty bed.

"Gillian?" He stepped in farther, checked the bathroom. Also empty. "Gillian!"

The sound of his voice echoed in the stillness. A tight, wary feeling gripped his chest.

Wheeling around, he strode back out and knocked sharply on Maddie's door. "Maddie?" No answer. He shoved it open. She also wasn't there.

He pivoted, headed straight for the door. Wrenched it open. Fear flooded full force. The guard, Mallory, was gone, too.

Gun drawn, he raced to the elevator, stabbed the down button but couldn't wait for it to arrive. He bolted the few feet to the exit door, yanked it open, and flew down the stairs. Dug for his cell phone, fingers punching in numbers as his legs hammered over the steps.

He thought his heart would stop by the time hotel security answered the phone.

"Ruth Gellico," he shouted. "Is she here? Did your men spot her?"

The man on the other end assured him that the woman hadn't entered the hotel.

"Miss Gray's missing. So is the guard at the door." A picture of the dead woman, the real dead woman, swam into focus. She had Gillian's face. A picture of a picture of a picture. Dead. All dead.

"She's fine," the security guy said. "Better than fine, and the cameras don't lie. You got yourself a handful. Check the lobby bar."

He burst through the final door into the lobby. Saw the shock on the faces of the clerks behind the registration desk and realized his gun was drawn and aimed at them.

He held up a hand, pulled back the weapon, but didn't stow it. The bar was around the corner, and he sped there.

A burst of noise ricocheted around him. It came from a clutch of people, mostly men, gathered around a tiny blonde in the center. The guard was in the circle, laughing with them.

Ray stopped short, fear turning swiftly to fury. Holstering his weapon, he elbowed his way through the crowd to the woman at the center. "What the hell do you think you're doing?"

"Whoa," said someone in the crowd. "Slow down, man."

Gillian smiled. "It's all right. He gets paid to be that way."

He turned to Mallory. "You're supposed to be watching the door."

"You said not to let her go anywhere unescorted." The guard shrugged. "And she was going."

"Get back to your post," he snapped, and the younger man nodded and backed away.

"Hey—don't take it out on him," Gillian said with a giggle. "Wasn't his fault."

"Think I don't know that?" He took her by the arm. "Let's go."

She grabbed her drink from the bar and held it high, as if to toast with it. "Good time's over, boys. Daddy's here."

A few snickers, which he ignored, and a couple of protests, which he also ignored. He pulled her through the group and toward the lobby.

"You're supposed to be hiding out. Keeping low."

She stumbled beside him. He knew she was struggling to keep up, and he didn't care.

"Not my style," she said.

"Not your style? Jesus, what do you think this is—an art show?"

"Come on, Ray, don't be that way." They were almost out the door, but she dug in her heels. Held up her glass. "Have a drink with me."

"I don't drink."

"Seriously?" She peered up at him, shielding her eyes as if gazing into the sun. "I don't know if I trust a man who doesn't drink."

"The idea was to bring you someplace safe, where no one could get to you. Not fling yourself around in public where everyone could."

"I know what the idea was. And I'm as safe as I want to be. I had Mallory watching out for me."

"He's supposed to be on the—"

"—And Maddie." She nodded to a corner, where Maddie sat in the shadows like a spider, quietly nursing a drink and a stranger, who leaned in and nibbled her neck. She stared at Ray, ignoring the neck biter.

Ray turned angry eyes on Gillian. "You were supposed to let me know if you wanted to go somewhere."

"You were asleep. Guy's gotta sleep, Ray."

"And you—you don't sleep?"

"Not after a visit with Harley," she said quietly.

She raised defiant eyes at him, but he could see the grief underneath. He muttered a curse. "Okay," he said, "but if you want to drink, do it back at the room."

"Too quiet there." She plopped down in a chair at one of the small bar tables. "Sit." She patted the chair beside her. "Tell me why you won't have a drink with me."

He ground his jaw, gazed around. He'd already noted all the entrances and exits; now he made sure he noted every face in the room.

"Your job is to go where I go," Gillian said, "not tell me where. And I'm staying."

He blew out a large breath and reluctantly took a seat with a good view of the space. Now that he was settling in, the room was starting to get to him, as all bars did. The smell of booze, the clink of ice, the overloud laughter.

"So, tell me all your secrets, Ray."

He swung his glance over to her, then back out to the room. One of the guys from the crowd, a dark-haired, overgrown frat-boy type, kept looking in Gillian's direction. He had a hungry, possessive expression in his face that Ray didn't like. "I don't have any secrets."

"Everyone has secrets." She leaned in, touched her fingertips to his wrist. The place where they landed burned. "If you don't drink, how do you relax?"

"I don't get tense."

She laughed. "Yeah, right."

He gave her a tight smile. "I breathe."

She looked at him.

"I do breathing exercises. In and out to a count of four. Brings down your heart rate. Relaxes you."

She gazed at him over the rim of the glass. "How very Yoda of you."

The man at the bar made his move, and Ray snapped to his feet, blocking his route to Gillian. "On your way, pal."

He was big but loose-jowled, a football player gone to seed. He'd eased the striped tie around his neck so it didn't dig into the flesh, but the buttons of his blue shirt strained against his middle. "Only if that's what the lady wants."

"I'm telling you what the lady wants."

The man's eyes narrowed. "She doesn't need a mouthpiece."

"The hell she doesn't."

Suddenly, Gillian was between them.

"Don't go getting all macho on me," she said to Ray. And to the frat boy, "Thanks, but I'm heading up. Another time."

And like that, she did what he'd asked her to do in the first place. She walked out.

24

Ray followed, hurrying to catch up. Seemed like he was always catching up. To her mood and her motives if not to herself, and it pissed him off.

Which is why he stabbed the call button, and when the elevator came, why he held her back with a less-than-gentle arm until he checked it out. When he declared it safe, he let her slip in. She slouched against the wall, crossing her arms under her breasts. The movement outlined them against the taut T-shirt and also hiked it up so a band of soft skin showed above her hip-slung jeans. Something tightened down around Ray's groin, and he looked away.

"You know, if you're not going to let me have company, you're going to have to provide it yourself." Her voice was low and husky, and when he turned at last, she was eyeing him in a sexy, predatory way.

"What's that supposed to mean?"

"You know what it means."

He did, but he didn't want to. No, that wasn't it. He wanted to. Christ, he wanted to. But he couldn't. For a thousand reasons, not all of them professional. "Forget it."

"I don't spend the night after Harley alone." She said

it like it was a rule that couldn't be broken, but he didn't abide by her rules.

"You won't. I'll be right outside your door."

"I don't want you outside."

"You don't want me, period."

The ends of her mouth curled in a small, sly smile. "Oh, Ray, that is so not true."

He ignored the smile and the heat it generated. "You want a warm body, any body. Not me. Frat boy down there would have done just fine."

"Oh, he would've done. But not fine." She moved toward him. "Not like you." She ran a hand down his arm, rubbed the skin on his palm. Moved to his hip and his thigh.

He stood frozen, unable to resist that hand. The press of her fingers sent the blood racing through him, and he hardened faster than he would have believed possible.

And she knew it. She swayed toward him, her breasts pressed against his arm, her hips grinding into him, her mouth open, inviting.

Just then, the elevator stopped. The door opened.

It broke the spell, thank God, and Ray pushed back, then hauled her out.

She laughed. "Saved by the bell, sweetheart."

He tugged her down the hallway. Mallory rose as they approached.

"You want to sleep with me tonight, baby?" she said to Mallory. "Ray here isn't interested." Her gaze flicked down to that telltale spot and back up, amused. "Well... he's interested, but..."

Mallory grinned, but Ray gave him a lethal look, and he wiped the smile off. He opened the door, and Ray pushed Gillian inside. She went straight to the window, a huge wall of glass that overlooked the city. Lights twinkled in the black vista, outlining the shape of structures. The Batman Building, designed for BellSouth in the shape of a phone in its cradle but bearing the distinct shape of the superhero, glowed blue against the shadows. Her hands pressed the pane as if she were drinking in the night, a blond vampire draining the darkness. A perfect target.

"You never listen, do you?" Ray reached for the cord to pull the drapes shut.

"I listen," Gillian said, stopping his hand. "I just don't do what you want." She pulled him closer. "Come here. Look at this." She nodded in the direction of the city lights. "See that? That's the Pinnacle on top of the Sheraton. My mother took me there once. She dressed me up in pink tulle and velvet, and we sat at a window table. The restaurant rotated so you could see the city in all directions." He followed her gaze, saw the circular hat of flashing lights on top of the hotel. "She was excited to show me this marvel, this moving room. She smiled and clapped her hands and pointed out the sights. But what I remember most is that dress." Her voice was dreamy, nostalgic. The ghost of a smile played around her lips. "All little girls should be princesses for their mothers at least once."

She lingered on the view but removed her hand from his. It hurt him to do it, because it felt like he was covering up the one good memory she'd had all day, but he pulled the drapes, and they slowly swished closed, concealing the scene.

Her eyes overbright with emotion, she turned away, blinked, then laughed with embarrassment. "Whew," she said, blowing out a breath, "look at me getting all sentimental, when all I really want to do is take you to bed." She grabbed his hand and, walking backward, pulled him into her bedroom.

"I thought we'd been over this."

She made a face. "Yeah, but if you won't sleep with me, you can at least tell me a story so I can go to sleep."

"I don't know any stories."

"Yeah, you do. Once upon a time, there was a guy named Ray. He had a strange job catching strange guys. A job he liked. But then something happened. Something he called... circumstances." They were inside the room now, and before he knew what was happening, she reached for the hem of her shirt and pulled it up over her head.

The room was dark, lit only from the overflow of the living area, but he could still make out the full, generous shape of her breasts. "Jesus." He turned his back. "You gotta warn me when you do that."

"Next time," she said, but he heard the tease in her voice and the hint of a promise she had no intention of keeping.

He cleared his throat. "I'll be outside."

She sighed. "Okay, Ray, you do that. I'll let you know when it's safe."

He retreated to the living room, closing the door behind him. He was aching with the fight inside himself. Touch her, don't touch her. Burn or burn hotter. It felt like the same battle he'd been waging since he clapped eyes on her.

Seconds later she opened the door and stood there, curving around the doorway like a pole dancer. A flimsy robe had replaced the jeans, revealing a scrap of black lace that hugged her breasts and matched the barely there panties. "Aren't you going to tuck me in?"

He stared at her, at the innocent eyes and fluff of gold hair that looked so angelic and the body that was so wickedly not. "Not if my life depended on it," he managed to choke out.

She laughed. Dropped the pose. "Oh, all right." She came toward him, her legs swinging in and out of the robe, the black lace coming and going. And coming again. "You are not a confidence booster, you know that?"

"I don't think confidence is something you need a boost in."

She held the sides of the robe out, waggling them and displaying herself. "Last chance. Free night of sex, no strings attached."

He reached around her, found the robe's tie, and brought it to the front, using it to rein her in close. "There are always strings." He watched her watching him as he knotted the belt. Her mouth was soft and bruised-looking, open and waiting for him to bend down and taste it. Her breasts brushed against his arms as he tied the belt tight, and he felt a shudder go through her as well as him, a shivery current bouncing from one to the other.

He swallowed. There was too much heat between them, too much feeling. He remembered his promise to himself not to get involved, the words "ten days" echoing foolishly in his head.

Then he looked at her, the ache and want almost strong enough to make him do something about it. A ripple of apprehension replaced the electricity, distress she must have felt, too, because when she met his gaze, the amusement and play had vanished from her face. She was dead sober.

"You're right." His hands were frozen on the belt, and she disengaged herself and stepped back. "You're a nice guy, Ray, and that's deadly. Nice guys want the house, the picket fence. The wife and kids."

He didn't know whether or not to be insulted, or regretful, or just relieved for the air between them. He retreated to the bar, a mirrored counter set against one wall and shimmering with soft lights. "Maybe. Once," he said.

"But oh, those circumstances, right?" She sat on the arm of the couch and dangled her feet, watching him the way a cat does, intent, fixed. "So tell me about them. I'll stay here, far, far away, and you can tell me the entire heartbreaking saga."

"I think you should go to bed. It's late."

"I told you, I won't sleep tonight." She eyed him. "Not without a little help. And we've already decided that's not going to happen. So...tell me a story. I like sad stories." She shot him a mischievous smile. "But I bet you already knew that." She slipped onto the couch proper, stretched out, and lay back against the armrest. "Once upon a time, there was a man named Ray. And Ray fell in love with an evil witch named Nancy." She circled a hand in the air, indicating him to continue.

"Not a witch."

"No?" She closed her eyes and crossed her hands over her chest like a corpse laid out for viewing. "What, then?"

It was uncanny to see her like that. Dead even in life. To distract himself, he answered her. "A girl who spent her life around cops. And didn't want to marry another one."

"So why did she?"

And suddenly he was telling her the whole depressing tale. The ballad of Nancy and Ray.

25

He told her how he'd promised Nancy he was going to law school. How he'd talked her into coming home to Nashville, where he could go at night. How they had a big cop wedding with law enforcement all over the place.

"Even the crooks took the day off," he said, quoting her father.

But then he needed a job to pay for law school, so the sarge pulled some strings and got him working security for TJ Maxx. But it was shitty hours, lousy pay. Worse than cops made, if she could believe it. Chasing skinny little teenagers all over the parking lot. Nancy's father, her brother were both cops. Joining up was a natural. And it was temporary. He swore it up and down. Just until he got that law degree.

"But Ray, he liked being a cop," Gillian said, her voice sleepy.

He paused. Recalled that familiar smell from today. Envisioned the squad room, the case meetings, the reports, the court appearances. The feeling that he was doing something decent, something important. Keeping the wolves away from the sheep. "Yeah, he liked it."

"People don't usually quit the things they enjoy."

And then he was making his confession, telling Gillian how he went from three classes in law school to two classes to no classes. How the temporary became permanent, and how Nancy . . . well, "unhappy" wasn't the word for it. Fights, threats, misery. She got pregnant and swore she'd stay; then she lost the baby, and it seemed as if nothing could hold her.

And then one day, he looked around. His partner was divorced, most of the guys he knew were divorced. They drank beer by themselves, played pool by themselves, sat at home and got drunk alone. Then there was Bob Denton. Same job as Ray, but been married two, maybe three times. Couple of kids out in California he never saw. Lived in a crappy little apartment in Antioch. One night after shift, he went out, had a drink with the guys like he did every night, went home, shot the back of his head off.

Ray mimed the action. "Bam, just like that."

Gillian unfolded herself and sat up. She looked at him.

"The only people who showed up at the funeral were other cops."

He still remembered how scared he'd been. How sick inside to think of himself so alone.

"So you quit."

"You can always get a new job. Not so easy to replace your family."

Gillian thought about all the exes in his life. "Then where's your happy ending?"

He laughed, a self-deprecating twist of his mouth. "Yeah, funny thing that. Six months after I quit, Nancy left."

"See? I told you she was a witch."

"Not a witch. She just didn't want to be married to me anymore."

"Oh, I find that hard to believe," she teased.

"Well . . . you met Peter."

"That nebbish who came to your house?"

"She'd been sleeping with him for months. She was pregnant. And this time, it sure as hell wasn't mine."

Gillian watched him struggle with the admission. With the embarrassment and the anger. She remembered the viciousness of the ribbing today. Who gives up his career for love? Most men would say wives were a dime a dozen. Hell, even she'd say it. Give up the thing she believed in most? Never. Who would ask that of anyone they truly loved?

Then again, how would she know? She'd never been put to the test. Never loved that hard, never let it mean that much. That kind of love wasn't in the cards. Not for her. She wasn't planning on living long enough.

26

Morning came faster than Gillian expected. She woke on the couch, exactly where she'd fallen asleep the night before. Only someone had slipped a blanket over her. It was warm under the blanket, and soft. She didn't have to strain too much to figure out who'd covered her.

She sat up slowly, her neck stiff from the headrest. Ray was asleep in a chair at the door, his hands wrapped around his gun. Her steadfast sentry, making sure she couldn't escape. She stretched, watched him sleep for a few minutes. The picture made her smile a little. And yearn. What would it have been like to be with him last night? To feel that hard, muscled body wrapped around hers? Would she have felt safe? Protected? Was that even possible?

Of course, he'd been right. She would have been using him. And guys like Ray, the nice ones, the decent ones, they deserved more.

He looked peaceful in sleep. Peaceful but strong. A rock of a man, like a sculpture. She tiptoed off the couch and found her camera. The lighting sucked, but that might be a good thing. If she could manipulate the shadows, she could sculpt his face even more.

But she hadn't clicked off many shots when he suddenly spoke, his eyes still closed. "That better not be you trying to sneak around me." His voice was deep and firm, and it sank into her like the sun after a cold night.

She kept the camera focused, watched him through the lens. "And if it is?"

He cracked open one eye. "I'll have to shoot you."

"With a camera?"

He straightened. "I make no promises."

She lowered the camera, and they faced each other. She found herself grinning. "Morning."

"Back at you." He stood, holstered the weapon, and opened the suite door. "Problems?" he said to Mallory, who was still outside.

"All clear," the guard said. "Got a replacement coming? I'm off in fifteen."

"He'll be here. Tell him to check in; then you can go."

Gillian called for coffee, and ten minutes after the changing of the guard, it arrived, and she was drowning herself in caffeine and sugar.

Ray came out of his room, fresh from a shower wearing khakis and a long-sleeved white shirt, both of which he filled out nicely. Too nicely. She dipped her gaze away from his long, muscular legs and focused on her coffee. Felt Ray's eyes on her as she doctored her cup.

"What?"

He shrugged and wandered over. "Nothing."

"Come on. Why are you looking at me like that?"

"Not at you, short stack, at your coffee." He poured himself a cup and took a sip.

"What's wrong with my coffee?"

"Nothing if you're five and like milk shakes."

She scoffed at his own cup. "Oh, let me guess, big strong man likes it black?"

"And tough little cookie likes it all sugared up."

Well, hell, who was he calling little?

"Better than the pencil shavings you drink."

He tried to look insulted. "Pencil shavings?"

"You heard me. Like someone steeped the dregs of a pencil sharpener in hot water."

Now he did look insulted. "This is pure ambrosia. The way God meant coffee to be drunk."

She grunted. "Well, then, maybe me and God have a little talking to do."

He laughed, and it nearly stopped her breath the way the smile lit up his face. "Now that's an argument I'd like to hear," he said.

She grinned back at him. "Don't think I'd win?"

"Frankly, I wouldn't take any bets."

She gulped the coffee, letting the hot, sweet drink warm her whole body. Or maybe it wasn't the coffee.

He poured himself another cup, gazed at her with a soft light in his eyes. "So... we should go over your schedule. Your plans for today."

"Plans?"

"Yeah. Plans. The show at the museum opens to the public today. You *planning* on being there?"

Oh, poor guy. Just when she thought he got her, inside and out. "I never plan," she told him. He looked at her, and she tossed off his skepticism. "I don't."

He sat back in his chair, examining her. "You're a big important artist. People like you always have a schedule to keep."

"People like me?"

"Celebrities."

"Oh, them."

"So... the museum. You going today?"

"I think I've had enough red guck thrown at me. So, no, probably not. But who knows? I don't have a calendar or one of those berry things. Like I said, I don't plan. I don't look ahead."

She waited for him to ask why, was already parsing out the required explanation, the "live in the moment" crap she pawned off on most people. But he didn't ask.

Didn't need to know? Didn't want to know? Either way, it irritated her.

"Aren't you going to ask me why?"

"I already know why," he said quietly, his look deep, his face sober with wisdom.

She stared at him, suddenly spooked by his silent insight. No one knew that much about her.

"Short-term memory loss," he said after a long moment, then lost the battle to keep his face straight.

She threw a pack of sugar at him.

"Because you're weird, that's why," he said, fending off the packet. "What about meetings, gallery openings, stuff like that?"

"Maddie handles it."

"Maddie."

"Yeah, Maddie. Remember her?"

"Fine. I'll talk to Maddie." He rose and walked toward her door.

"She won't be there," Gillian sang out.

"Why not?"

"She just won't."

He paused, turned to her. "How do you know?"

She didn't want to get into this with him. Some instinct told her this was something he definitely wouldn't understand. Especially after their . . . disagreement . . . the night before. "I just do."

He leaned against the wall beside Maddie's door. "What's the big mystery?"

"No mystery."

"So..."

She sighed. He wanted it, she'd give it to him. "I told you, I never sleep alone after Harley."

Understanding dawned on his face. And it wasn't pretty. "So she, what, she stays away? Facilitates your evening?" He crossed his arms, narrowed his eyes. "Does she line the men up, too?"

"Jesus, did it look like I needed help lining them up? No, I do the choosing. And last night, stupid me, I chose you."

"Well, you weren't alone. Not for a minute."

"Yeah, I noticed," she said dryly. "Me and my blankie. Maddie understands, okay? Something you don't."

"Oh, I understand just fine," he snapped, and plunged into Maddie's room. "She keep an appointment book?"

She heard him crashing around. "I don't think she's going to appreciate you mucking around in her things," she called from where she was sitting.

He didn't answer. She listened, and suddenly only stillness came back at her. "Ray?" She frowned down at her milky coffee, waiting for him to say something or come back to the living room. Neither happened.

Curious, she left her coffee and went into Maddie's room. Ray was standing over Maddie's open suitcase on the bed. A bunch of papers were clenched in his fists, and he was scowling at them.

"What is it? What's the matter?"

He tore through the pages. "I knew she was hiding something."

"For God's sake, what?"

She ripped a sheaf of paper out of his hand, and the block letters screamed up at her:

YOU WON'T FORGET ME.
I WON'T LET YOU.
FREAK.
YOU'RE ALREADY DEAD.

She looked through the others. There were five, no, six of them, all with similar threatening themes. A bolt of something—half fear, half excitement—stabbed her. "Where did you find these?"

"Maddie's suitcase. A little hate mail from your so-called friend."

"Don't be ridiculous. Maddie would never—"

"Never what?"

They whirled in time to find Maddie in the doorway.

27

Maddie gave Ray an aloof stare. "Never come into your room when you're not there and snoop through your personal things?"

He watched her slink in. She looked like she'd had a hard night, her normally immaculate black hair now mussed and a little knotted on one side, her makeup smeared. Seemed Gillian wasn't the only one who didn't sleep alone.

"Yeah, you're right," Maddie said. "I wouldn't."

"Did you write these?" Ray demanded.

She looked from him to Gillian and back again. "What do you think?" Something indefinable crossed her face. Indecision? Guilt? Ray was taking no chances.

"I think it's possible."

She snorted and came farther into the room. "You would."

Gillian looked down at the pages she was holding. "Maddie, what are these?"

"Nothing. They're nothing."

"The hell they are," Ray said. "Those are threats. Did you send them?"

Gillian said, "Shut up, Ray. Of course she didn't.

They're from him, aren't they?" Her voice was low and keyed up.

"Him?" Ray asked. "Who is 'him'?"

"The big bad bogeyman," Maddie said, and snatched the papers out of Gillian's hand.

"Wait—let me see that!"

Maddie started to rip up the messages. Both Ray and Gillian jumped at her.

"Don't!"

Ray got there first. "This is evidence. It could lead us to the killer."

Maddie laughed. "I don't think so."

Ray peered at her closely. "You're pretty certain. What do you know about it?"

"Nothing," she said calmly, and when Ray continued gazing at her, "All right. I confess. I did it." She held out her hands to be cuffed. "Arrest me, Officer."

"Why didn't you show these to me?" Gillian asked.

"Why?" She gave a mirthless laugh. "Take a look at yourself. You're practically strapping on your six-gun."

"That's not your call," Gillian said. "You don't make decisions for me."

Maddie shrugged. "Why not? I'm the one picking up the pieces."

Gillian opened her mouth to respond, then didn't. There was a pinprick of hurt in her eyes, and an equal measure in Maddie's. She softened, reached out.

"Gillian—"

"You should have let me see them."

Maddie's face hardened, and she threw up her hands. Busied herself slamming the suitcase shut and flinging it in a corner.

Ray waved the paper in the air. "These are Internet messages."

"From my Web site," Gillian said.

"You have a Web site?"

"Deadshots.com," Gillian said, pointing to the Web site address at the bottom. "Maddie runs it for me."

Maddie. It always came back to Maddie. She ran Gillian's career, her schedule. What else did she run?

"Don't look at me like that, watcher boy."

"You could have manufactured this."

"I could have, but I didn't."

"Stop it." Gillian got between them, turned to Ray. "Why would Maddie do something like that?"

"Keep you scared. Give you a reason to let her keep hanging on."

"She's my friend. I don't need a reason," Gillian said.

"Her position would be a hell of a lot more secure if you had one."

"They're not from Maddie," Gillian said emphatically. "Don't you see? They're from the killer." Excitement made her voice breathy. "My mother's killer."

That was a leap Ray wasn't ready to take. "We don't know that."

"I do. Who else would send them?"

"I don't know. Let's see what Maddie thinks. She seems to run everything around here." Ray swung his head to look at Maddie. Her face was stony, her lips pressed into a grim line. "Who else, Maddie? If not you, or Holland Gray's killer, who else is there?"

Maddie looked from him to Gillian, struggling with some decision. Then her mouth softened and she gazed down at her hands. "We've been getting them..." She paused, then looked back up at Gillian, almost pleading for understanding. "We've been getting them on and off for the last six months."

Gillian gasped. "And you didn't tell me?"

"There are others like this?" Ray asked.

She breathed out the admission. "Yes."

"All in the last six months?"

Maddie nodded and avoided Gillian's eyes. Gillian sank onto the bed, refusal to believe in every line of her body.

Ray looked between the two of them. "What happened six months ago?" No one answered, and he repeated the question, a little louder and more insistent. *"What happened six months ago?"*

But Gillian only looked at Maddie and said, "You think it's Kenny?"

Maddie said nothing, but knowledge was there in her eyes.

"He's vicious enough," Gillian muttered.

"Who the hell is Kenny?" Ray asked.

"And jealous," she added.

"Who the hell is Kenny?"

The two women looked at him. "Kenny Post, rock-and-roll star," Gillian said. "Well, no, hardly a star, is he, Maddie? You ever hear of Black Roach?" she asked Ray.

"No."

"Yeah, most people haven't. Which is why Kenny is also a drunk, cheat, and all-around scumbag," Gillian said.

"Her ex-boyfriend," Maddie clarified.

"Violent and jealous ex-boyfriend," Gillian said.

Ray stared. No one had mentioned an ex-boyfriend during the threat assessment.

"Where's your computer? I want to check this out."

Maddie picked up a briefcase and hauled out a laptop. "So, you believe me now?"

"I didn't say that. But I want to see the messages for myself."

She stopped in midgesture, the machine half in and half out of the case. "You can't."

"Why the hell not?"

Maddie flushed. "I deleted them."

"You what?" Ray roared. "Why?"

"Maddie!" Gillian groaned.

A pause, a beat, in which Maddie lost her infamous composure. She stuttered. Seemed to search desperately for an explanation.

"Why, Maddie?" Ray persisted.

"I didn't want Gillian to see them!" she burst out at last. "Okay?"

"Or they were never there in the first place, and you created them yourself," Ray said.

"So we're back to that?"

"Stop it," Gillian said to Ray.

Maddie turned a hot gaze on Gillian. "I don't need you to defend me." And to Ray, "Yeah, you're right. I wrote them, then hid them for six months."

"Not very well, since I found them," Ray said.

"You didn't 'find' them; you hunted them down. And you had to go in my room and through my suitcase to do it. Find anything else you like, Ray? Silk undies?" She waved a pair under his nose, which he grabbed and threw back on the bed.

"And, remember, we only have your word on the six months."

"Back off, Ray," Gillian said.

"And what the hell is wrong with my word? It's been good enough—"

"Not for me."

"I didn't—"

"Back off!" In the wake of Gillian's raised voice, silence descended. "She didn't do this," Gillian said at last. "Maybe it's Kenny; maybe it's someone else. But it isn't Maddie."

"Friendship and love are the easiest things to manipulate," said Ray.

"What is that," said Gillian, "Confucius? We're not talking about you, here, Ray. Or Nancy, or whatever sad misery you made of your life."

That hit like a missile, straight to his heart. But he shook it off, taking refuge in frigid calm. "That's right, Gillian, we're talking about you. You and *your* witch."

"You know what?" Maddie jerked open a drawer, grabbed some clothes, and banged it shut. "I need a shower. And so do you," she said to Gillian. "You're scheduled for the Art House this morning." The Art House was the biggest visual arts educator in Nashville, with classes for kindergartners up through adults in every media.

"Shit," said Gillian, "I forgot."

"If you'd check the schedule every once in a while—"

"I know, I know." Gillian sent Maddie an unrepentant grin. "Life in the fast lane."

"And wear something outrageous. You have dinner with Grandmaw and Pappy this evening."

A shadow passed over Gillian's face. She looked decidedly unhappy about that.

No more than him. He hated surprises, especially piled on. "You're supposed to tell me if you've got something scheduled."

"I did tell you," Maddie said coolly.

"In time to check out the sites."

"Look, I always do a gig at the Art House when I'm in town," Gillian said. "I sponsor a photography scholarship."

Ray didn't like the sound of that. Anything routine was public knowledge and could be tracked. "What do you mean, always?"

"Just what it sounds like," Maddie said, and gestured to the bedroom door. "Now—do you mind?"

Ray clamped down on his jaw and gestured to her computer. "Do you?"

She gave him a cheerless laugh. "Be my guest." And swept into the bathroom, slamming the door behind her.

Ray grabbed Gillian's arm and led her out of Maddie's room. "I want her gone," he said to Gillian.

"Go to hell."

"I don't trust her. I can't protect you like this."

"Tough luck, baby, because I'm not sending her away." And she, too, strode off, slamming her bedroom door behind her.

Shut out and frustrated, Ray clenched his fists, looked around for something to throw. Or punch. But he did neither. Seething with manufactured calm, he made himself breathe instead. In and out to a steady count until the calm was real enough.

Because the threat was, whether Gillian wanted to acknowledge the danger or not. And it could be coming from the people closest to her.

Maddie leaned against the closed bathroom door. Beneath her clothes, she was sweating. She didn't need the mirror to know she looked horrible, because she felt horrible. Sick and swirly and anxious.

She remembered those bitches at Hadley calling her the coal miner's daughter, and how many times Gillian had stood up for her. They'd thumbed their noses at the snobs and to hell with everyone else.

And now?

She tossed the clothes she'd grabbed from the drawer on the toilet, leaving the cell phone she snagged beneath them in her hand. For an instant, she stared at it as if it might howl at her. Then she closed her eyes and punched in a number.

The call rang and was answered. Maddie identified herself and her reason for calling. Five minutes later, she got the assurance she'd been seeking, but it didn't make her feel better. Didn't make her trust that they wouldn't be caught. They were skirting too close to the edge. Someone was bound to slip up.

28

While Gillian was getting ready, Ray called the office and had them check the databases for Kenny Post. He also asked them to find a photo and scan whatever crowd footage of the museum party they could get to see if Post was there. If the threats were from him, and he was in Nashville, protection would rise to a whole new level.

In the meantime, they would check with contacts in New York and see if they could track him down. Finally, he asked someone to pick up Maddie's laptop. There were ways of retrieving deleted messages off the hard drive, and Carlson kept two IT experts on staff. If Maddie created those threats, they'd find out.

"And send someone over to the Art House now," he said at last. "Miss Gray has an appointment, and I want to make sure we have exit strategies in place, just in case."

Then he called Jimmy. He wasn't there, but he left a message about Gillian's ex.

While he waited for more definitive information on Kenny Post, he used Maddie's computer to check out the basics for himself.

Reviewers called Black Roach's music "head-pounding," "brutal," and "aggressive," and touted Kenny Post as the band's Sid Vicious–inspired front man. A picture showed him tall and lanky, with ripped jeans and heavy, motorcycle boots. He had greasy dark hair, wore a goatee and a sneer. Past the reviews, there were also some blotter reports, one an incident in SoHo where he'd ripped apart a bar and was hauled off by the cops. Another in Chicago, where he attacked a hotel room.

Bad news all around.

Bad enough to want Gillian dead?

"Been reading up on your boy," Ray said to Gillian when she came out of her room. She wore a tiny jean skirt that cupped her ass, a floaty, see-through blouse that hid and revealed her breasts, and black boots with fuck-me heels that added a good four inches to her petite frame. Tough, vulnerable, and sexy all at the same time. A silent groan of self-pity went off inside Ray.

"He's not my boy anymore," she said, pouring herself another cup of coffee and sitting on a stool by the counter. She crossed her legs, the skirt riding high on her thighs, and Ray looked away.

"Sounds like a real heartbreaker."

She laughed without smiling. "Well, he did like to break things."

"You, for instance?"

She paused in the action of stirring sugar into her coffee and looked at him questioningly.

"He ever hit you?" he said bluntly.

She returned to doctoring her coffee. "Once or twice. When he was drunk. Then again, I got in a few good ones, too. And keep the lectures to yourself."

"I didn't say anything."

"I heard you anyway." She lifted her cup, looked at him

over the rim. "Look, he's gone," she said. "Been gone. Just like all the rest."

"The rest?"

"All the loves of my life."

A rope of something like jealousy tightened inside him. "You were in love with him?"

She shrugged. Hid behind her coffee cup. "He passed the time."

Had she ever been in love with anyone? Ever taken any relationship seriously? More important, had anyone ever been in love with her? Really cared about her?

He thought of Genevra's harsh bite and Chip's acquiescence to it. Of his own white-knight refusal of her body. He should fuck her and get it over with. If he believed her, it would have meant nothing to her, and it might let him breathe again.

But he didn't believe her. More fool him.

"Where is he now?"

"I don't keep track. But if he's not on tour, he'd be at his apartment. If he's on tour, you can call the booking agent to find out where." She gave him the address and the relevant phone numbers.

An hour later, he had Kenny Post's arrest record in front of him, but no one had been able to track him down in New York. He wasn't at his apartment, and his booking agent had nothing scheduled and no idea where he might be. Neither, it seemed, did the rest of the band. Kenny Post had disappeared.

Ray wasn't taking chances. He ordered a car and driver, and the hell with blending in.

Once again, Maddie refused a ride.

"Whatever," he said, glad to keep as much distance between the two women as possible. But Gillian had other ideas.

"How are you going to get there?" Gillian asked Maddie. "Come on, don't be crazy."

"That's your department," Maddie said, grabbing a coat and her briefcase.

"So don't drive me over the edge," Gillian said. "You're coming with us."

"Fine," Ray said, "whatever. Just let's go." He waited for Maddie to precede him, then Gillian; then he took his place behind her. They got down to the lobby and the front door, where the car was waiting.

But between them and the vehicle was a mob of reporters and photographers. They caught sight of Gillian through the glass doors and went wild. Only hotel security kept them from storming the lobby.

"Jesus," Ray said. Without another word, he wheeled about, taking Gillian away from the door. "Back entrance!" He spoke into the ear mike and heard the squeal of tires as the limo took off. "Come on." He pushed Gillian ahead, speeding through the lobby, Maddie running beside them.

"See, this is why I told you to stay in your room last night." Ray steered her around a corner. "Tabloids pay good money for information. One of your friends from the bar cashed in."

"Or one of the maids." She flicked a disparaging look at him, and he tugged her forward. "Hey—you picked the hotel."

They dashed through the lobby and waited by the door for the car to go around the building. By the time it arrived, some of the paparazzi had found them. Ray took Gillian's arm and held it as he shoved his way through, blocking her face from the cameras.

He saw her and Maddie into the limo, then got in beside the driver. While he was sliding in, Gillian pulled one of her insanely brainless stunts.

She rolled down the window.

Every camera clicked; reporters shoved and jostled to get a statement from her.

"Hey, Gillian! Over here!"

"You going to the museum today, Gillian?"

"What do you think of the Death Diva murder?"

"Kill anyone today?"

Inside, Ray went red in the face, blood pressure shooting skyward. "What the fuck are you doing?" he shouted at Gillian. "Go!" he said to the driver. "Go! Go! And roll up the damn window!"

The black-tinted glass slid up, and Gillian sat back, a smirk on her face.

"Are you crazy?" Ray said.

"You know I am."

"Maybe she sent those letters to herself," Maddie said, double-teaming him.

That was it. The last straw. "You know what? You want to sneer and laugh and hang yourself, go ahead. But I'll be damned if I put myself on the line while you do it. I'll get you to your appointment; then you're on your own, just like you want to be."

29

Gillian cruised the Art House hallway, carefully examining the photographs on display. Around her, a swarm of children followed, chattering and skipping to keep up.

She stopped at one interesting shot of a downtown corner. The photographer had captured the edge of a building, half in and out of shadow, creating a knife-blade effect. "Who did this?"

A hand shot up. It belonged to a small boy with chocolate skin. He had a huge smile on his face, but he couldn't stand still and swayed back and forth.

"What did you like about it?" she asked him.

He grinned at her but didn't say anything.

Gillian tried again. "What made you take this picture?"

"I like the sun," he said finally. One hand swooped diagonally in a sharp down stroke. "I like the way it cut the building." Then he laughed, and the other children giggled.

Gillian laughed, too. "I like the way it cuts the building, too," she told him.

Maddie stood off to the side, leaving Gillian with the kids and their teacher. And the man-who-should-be-Ray.

Gillian remembered him from the museum but forgot his name. Landon? Landsdown? Out of the corner of her eye, she saw him, impassive, watchful. He was smaller than Ray. A bland, insurance salesman face. Nothing that made her want to put him in front of her lens. He could have been anyone. Nameless, faceless. A stranger.

Landowe. That was his name. She rolled it around in her head. Landowe, push a plow. Eat a cow. Raise a sow.

Jesus. What was with the farm imagery? But she knew.

Guilt nicked her. Maybe she shouldn't have pushed things at the hotel. She should have been meek and obedient and hidden from the press.

Yeah, right. Exposing herself was not only habit, but it was also necessary. How could the killer find her if he didn't know where she was?

She stopped in front of a picture of balloons crashing into the sun. "This is fun." She eyed the sheer colors and the sun's rays spreading out behind them.

"That's Marcy's," one of the kids said, and the others agreed, pointing out a slim redhead with Pippi Longstocking braids who hid behind the other children.

"She's shy," several of the children shouted.

Shy was never Gillian's problem, and Ray could just like it or lump it.

Lump it, looked like, since Landowe was here.

The kids were pulling at her skirt, vying for attention, and she smiled absently and stared at the pictures on the wall. Some of them were quite good, but she couldn't concentrate. Not with thoughts of Ray boring a hole through her head.

God, he was a pain in the ass.

But the new guy didn't get her blood humming the way Ray did.

Well, too bad. She had a plan, and if you got in the way of the plan, so long, Marianne.

She tried to focus on the next picture. A black-and-white shot of a hood ornament on an old Ford truck.

"My daddy's truck," a tiny voice in the crowd said.

"That's Dewayne's truck," another voice echoed.

At least she wouldn't have to deal with the tension between Maddie and Ray. Now all she had to worry about was the monster. And how long before he came after her.

Ray got a ride back to the hotel with the guy who brought down Landowe. Carlson wasn't happy with him, but at this point who the hell cared?

Now he pulled out of the hotel lot and swung right on West End. The office was in the other direction, but he needed time to cool down, get his breathing going again. So he just drove. Maybe he'd keep on driving. Head down the Trace, get the hell out of Dodge. That had been the plan all along, so why didn't he just get it done?

The day was cool, but the sun was doing its duty and struggling through the clouds. Everywhere the pink redbuds were fading, and the dogwoods were going strong. Pansies and iris dotted the Kroger lot in Belle Meade, as if their bright color could make up for the concrete and exhaust.

Ten minutes down, the road split, and he went left onto Highway 100 where he could pick up the Natchez Trace. But that meant he'd have to go through Bellevue, land of condos and midlevel subdivisions. Land of husbands and wives and children not his own. Land of Nancy and Peter. A little self-torture. Just what he needed.

But there was something else down Highway 100. A

picture of Gillian's face rose in his head, but he shoved it away. She wasn't his problem anymore.

To get his mind off her and the rest of his exes, he pulled into a strip mall, got out of the car, and headed to Starbucks. But his luck was so far gone it was playing in Cleveland. He stopped short. Across the lot, Nancy was struggling with a load of packages and a toddler. And her huge belly was getting in the way of both.

Shit. He froze. Stay or go? Story of his life.

He started to pivot away, but before he could make his move, she looked up and saw him. Right straight in the face, bull's-eye.

Holding up a package, she waved tentatively. "Well, hey, Ray. What are you up to? Playing hooky?"

Oh, man, what were the odds? "Sort of." He crossed over, relieved her of a couple of packages. "You okay?" he asked because he didn't know what else to say.

"Fine."

Her dark hair was pulled into a ponytail, and her face was scrubbed clean of makeup. Her washday look, she used to tell him, and add, "But, hey, you want to do the laundry, I'll get all dolled up."

Why did he remember these things? It killed him that the details of her life were still floating around in his head.

"Who's that?" The little boy whose hand she was clutching looked up at him. He was fair-haired like his father, but he had Nancy's green eyes. A pang Ray refused to acknowledge went through him.

"That's Ray," she told him, ruffling his hair. "Say hi."

But the boy only continued to stare at him, making Ray feel like an exhibit at the zoo.

"So...," Ray said, searching for something, "you look good."

She laughed. “No, I don’t.” She rubbed her protruding belly with a satisfied air and quirked her brows conspiratorially. “Four more weeks.”

“I heard twins.”

She nodded. A giggle escaped. “Can you believe it?” It was a cliché to say all pregnant women glowed, but he couldn’t think of a better word to describe the look on her face.

“Congratulations.”

“Thanks.”

“You look…” He cleared his throat, the admission sticking there. “…very happy.”

She thought about it. Her smile widened, taking over her whole face. “I guess I am.”

They gazed at each other, and the uncomfortable moment stretched. Should he mention her father? That he’d seen Jimmy? Since she wasn’t a fan of the sarge, and since his last encounter with Jimmy hadn’t exactly been friendly, mentioning either seemed as awkward as the silence.

“Well, we should go,” she said at last, then waited expectantly.

“Oh,” Ray said like a boob. “Here.” He handed her back her packages.

“See you.” Nancy waved.

“Sure.” Ray waved back, knowing it wasn’t likely.

He slipped into Starbucks and ordered his coffee. Like he needed more acid inside him.

His drink came, and he practically swallowed it whole. Fuck it. So Nancy never looked that happy when she was with him. So what? Let Peter worry about her happiness now. Ray didn’t have the knack. Even his mother had been a sad sack—right until the minute she’d wrapped her car around that tree. Nothing he did ever put a smile on her gin-soaked soul.

He took what was left of the coffee back with him to the truck. Turned left out of the lot and continued south toward the Trace. Except now he knew he was taking a little detour.

Highway 100 had once been a two-lane country road that led through farmland. He and Nancy used to drive out here to the Loveless Café for fried chicken and biscuits, and she'd tell him that when she was a kid, the place where he'd stopped for coffee had been the last outpost of midcentury civilization. Beyond it was all grass and farms. He wondered what they'd grown. Tobacco? Dairy cows? Horses, maybe.

Whatever it was, the farms were mostly gone, and miles of blacktop lapped the pavement. As ubiquitous as fields must once have been, another Kroger shopping center sprang up a few miles farther on, this one with an Ace Hardware and the ever-present nail place. But twenty years ago he would have been in the middle of nowhere. Which is exactly what Holland Gray must have wanted when she moved there.

He recalled the address from the file at Harley's and slowed as he approached it.

The cozy little home sat on a hill on the outermost edge of Davidson County. A split-rail fence lined the drive leading up. Two white clapboard outbuildings dotted the grassy knoll. The house itself had a tidy front porch with dollhouse trim. A couple of old rockers sat on the porch, but whether or not they were the same rockers Gillian had slept in on the cover of *People,* he couldn't say. A sturdy stone chimney meant a fireplace inside. A real one, not the ersatz kind with the gas logs.

Ray understood how Holland could have fallen in love with this sweetheart of a home. Just the kind of romantic little farmhouse a woman in the mood to nest would love.

But was she in the mood to nest? Her parents had a huge mansion in Belle Meade. Why had she come all the way out here and buried herself? Press reports had her giving up the fast life for her child, but Gillian had been six or seven when Holland renounced the celebrity world. Why the sudden change?

He slowed, pulled over to stop. He could imagine Holland with her small blond angel of a daughter. A refugee from the bar scene, the fashion shoots, the celebrity treadmill. Twenty years ago the house could have been a refuge. A sanctuary. But nestled among the rolling Tennessee hills, it would also have been isolated from the world. Which would have made it easy for the killer to creep up unnoticed by anyone. Holland could have screamed, and no one would have heard her. And her murderer could have escaped down any one of the twisting offshoots that wound around the hills.

He slipped the crime-scene photograph out of his pocket. This morning, he'd found it in the shirt he'd worn to Harley's. He didn't remember pocketing it, so he must have done it absently, not even thinking. Today, he'd done it on purpose, though at the time he didn't know he'd be here, staring at the front door of Holland Gray's pretty tomb.

He stared at the photo, something nagging at him. Something to do with the house? He was tempted to get out and knock on the door. See if the current occupants would let him in. He had an overwhelming urge to view the back, the place where the killer might have slipped in, the kitchen with its linoleum floor where Holland Gray had died.

Would he see something no one else had? Find some unnoticed connection between what happened then and what was happening now? And why did he even care? He was done with Gillian.

His cell phone rang. "Ray, it's Jimmy. Where's your client?"

"My client? You mean Gillian?"

"Yeah, you got any other clients? I thought you guys took it easy and worked one at a time."

Ray let the barb pass. He could have said Gillian wasn't his client anymore, but then Jimmy would have just hung up. "Why? What happened?"

"That reporter at the *Tennessean,* Benton James?"

"What about him?"

"He got another photograph."

30

Gillian stared out the limousine window on the way back from the Art House. The black glass tinted the landscape dark and shadowed.

Someone had died. Someone else. Not Gillian, never her. Just another imitation.

Once again, a photograph had been staged and sent. Someone had described it to the new guy, and he in turn had described it to Gillian. The den with TV on, the cookies and milk on the floor, the body, lying half on, half off a game of solitaire. The smear of blood over the ace of spades from the raw and bloody slit across the young girl's throat.

After School.

Gillian remembered the photograph well. The complicated shoot, the effort to get every detail absolutely correct in its ordinariness.

Especially the victim's open and staring eyes.

I see you, she'd wanted them to say. Come whisper your name in my ear.

But he'd whispered his name in someone else's ear.

A runaway. A natural blonde. And young. So young. Landowe had said fifteen or sixteen.

Tears clogged the back of Gillian's throat, but she hung on, dry-eyed and alone. They'd rushed her out of the Art House so fast, they'd even left Maddie behind.

And the new guy, Eat-a-Cow, refused to answer her questions.

The driver pulled up to a back door, and she stumbled out of the car. The new guy crowded her from behind, holding her arm, guiding her inside the hotel like a dog herding sheep.

"Back off," she told him.

"This is standard—"

"Yeah, I know." She shrugged her arm away. "Back off anyway."

The new guy's jaw tightened, but he took a half step back. Gillian picked up her pace, and, by some miracle, the elevator was open and waiting when she got there. She dove in just as it closed, leaving Landowe behind.

"Miss Gray!" The cry came as a muffled roar through the door and what sounded like . . . a kick? Well, good for you, Push-a-Plow.

Not that she'd rid herself of him for long. He was probably huffing up the stairs that very moment, and knowing her luck, he'd be right there when the door opened at her floor.

But Landowe didn't greet her when the elevator opened.

Ray did.

She gasped, then cursed silently for letting him take her by surprise.

"Miss me?" He made the question a goad and a come-on at the same time, nodding for her to exit.

She slipped past, not looking at him. What was that emotion buffeting her—excitement? Happiness? She didn't want to feel that good about seeing anyone. Not now. Not ever. Especially not Ray Pearce.

"Sure I did. Like a bad cold."

Just then, Landowe jolted through the exit door to the stairs. He was breathing heavily.

"Miss Gray," he panted, leaning over his knees. "Don't... don't do that again."

Ray gave him an understanding pat on the back. "Take a break. I've got her." Like she was a wild horse they were trying to corral.

Landowe nodded, and they left him in the hallway.

Inside the suite, Ray turned to her. "Burke's on his way over, so brace yourself." He said it flatly, no censure for what she'd done, no explanations for why he returned.

He was right. There were too many more important things to think about. Recriminations could wait. She had to focus on murder, on correcting the wheel of fate. Turning it to face her instead of those other poor innocents.

She sank onto a barstool, suddenly weary.

"There's something else," he said.

She looked up. Saw the bad news forming behind his eyes.

"While we were checking out Maddie's computer, we found another message on your Web site."

She played with an empty coffee cup, dread building. "What did it say?"

He hesitated, then said quietly, "'I make it real.'"

She caught his gaze. Meaning crashed around her.

"He's creating an actual death." She squeezed her nails into her palm to keep from screaming. "I just... shoot pictures."

"Looks like it."

A cold, gray wave shook her. That bastard was using

her. Using her the way every critic of her work predicted—to create more death and violence. She leaned over the bar, scrambling for a glass, a cup, a ledge, something to keep her from falling.

What she found was Ray. A strong hand at her back, steadying her. "It's okay," he said softly.

"The hell it is."

He was silent.

"You still think it's Maddie?" she said at last.

"Maybe," he conceded.

"She was with me at the school. Your pal Landowe saw her with his own eyes the whole time we were there."

"She wasn't with you last night after you left the bar. And that's when the message was sent." He paused. She could tell she wasn't going to like what came next. "Look, there's no sign of Post yet. Which is why we have to get you out of this hotel. Too many people know where you are."

She didn't like it. "I don't think so."

Ray stared at her. "You're kidding. You're going to give me a hard time about this?"

Another confrontation brewing. Normally, she'd say bring it on. Except she knew what she knew and didn't want to argue about it.

She peered at him closely. "What are you doing here exactly? I thought you quit."

Ray left the bar, crossed to the wall of window. Hands shoved in his pockets, he gazed at the closed drapes. He didn't want to analyze why he was back here. Why he was staring into those troubled violet eyes once more. But running into Nancy, then seeing the house that symbolized the core of Gillian's personal tragedy...

He remembered the day campus police had arrived at

his dorm room. That had been shock enough, but beyond that half-second reaction, he'd known, bone deep, that something terrible had happened. They took him inside, made him sit on the narrow, twin bed. While the dread churned inside him, another voice laughed and told him he was getting worked up over nothing. It was probably a parking ticket, or something to do with the hockey team. Then, with the kind of impersonal compassion that soldiers and cops have for complete strangers whose lives they are about to change, they told him that his mother had wrecked her car and herself, and they were sorry for his loss.

He'd had misgivings about going away to school in the first place. Vague unease that he couldn't verbalize. But Birmingham had given him a free ride in exchange for playing hockey—an offer he couldn't afford to turn down.

But after the police patted his shoulder and left him numb and speechless, he'd been alone in his room, staring at *An Introduction to Political Science.* And he finally understood what he'd been afraid of. That leaving meant taking his eyes off her. And who knew what would happen if he wasn't watching?

"You've got two dead bodies on your tail," he said at last. "Why make it a third?"

Gillian came up beside him, and he felt her there, small and vulnerable. "So," she said, "you're sticking around? I don't know how I feel about that." Her mouth twisted wryly at the corners, the first sign of a smile since his return.

"One condition," he said.

"Why are there always conditions with you?"

"Send Maddie home. She's one more body to look out for."

"I need her."

"No, you don't."

"Well, she needs me."

"Fine, I won't argue that."

"I'm not going to let her think that I blame her in any way—"

"Look, forget blame. Just think about this. What if the killer comes after you and misses? What if he gets Maddie instead?"

He watched the message hit home. Followed up before she could marshal an argument. "I can send Landowe to pick her up at the Art House. They can take her directly to the airport. You can have her bags shipped."

"Are you kidding? I'm not shipping her off like a package. She comes here, I explain it to her, and we say goodbye. Like real people."

Gillian might have plenty of faults, but disloyalty wasn't one of them. "Okay." He held up a palm. "All right. I'll have Landowe bring her back here."

31

Burke showed up at the hotel before Maddie did. The guard let him in, and he pushed past Ray to the living area where he laid a heavy black binder on the coffee table. He looked like he hadn't slept much. Given the circumstances, two murders, clearly serialized, who could blame him?

"Any line on Kenny Post yet?" Ray asked.

"We got BOLOs out for him, here and in New York. Hopefully we'll find him."

"It's not him," Gillian said.

Burke cast a sharp glance her way. "What makes you say that?"

"Because it's someone who's been here before. Kenny didn't know anything about my mother until I told him. He's too young anyway."

"You still think the murders are connected?"

"Of course."

Burke eyed her, thinking it over.

"Did you call Harley Samuels?" she asked.

"I did."

"And?"

"Look, I can't give you the details of our investigation.

But if anything comes up that you need to know or you can help us with, I'll be sure to tell you."

She glared at him. "You arrogant—"

"People in glass houses—"

"Thanks," Ray said, interrupting the gathering storm. He looked at Burke. Dead people he was great with. But the living… "Appreciate whatever you can tell us."

Somewhat mollified, Burke said, "Take a look at this." He slid a photograph onto the table. A teenager with overteased blond hair and too much makeup. "Dawn Farrell," he said. "Our second victim. Ever seen her before?"

Gillian studied the picture. "No." She spoke coldly, but her throat caught on the word. She cleared it. "Never."

"Where were you last night?"

Her eyes flashed. "Me? Why the hell do you want to know where I—"

"She was here under guard," Ray said quickly. "And downstairs in the bar. Also under guard."

"No one approached you who seemed…" Burke shook his head and shrugged. "I don't know…strange? Obsessed with your work?"

"We were drinking, Detective. Not discussing art."

"What about the other one. Your assistant—Madeleine Crane."

Gillian's face grew stubborn. "She was with me."

"Not quite," Ray said quietly, and Burke turned to him. "She and Gillian were together until about midnight. Then Gillian came up here, and Maddie stayed at the bar. We didn't see her until this morning."

"Was she alone?" Burke asked.

"You've seen her," Gillian said tartly. "Do you think a woman like that has to spend a night alone if she doesn't want to?"

"We don't know," Ray said, underscoring the words and giving Gillian a subtle but firm signal not to misrepresent what actually happened. "She was with someone at the bar when I escorted Miss Gray upstairs. She was alone when she walked into the suite this morning."

"Who was she with at the bar? Did you know him?"

Gillian shrugged. "No."

Burke tapped a finger on the coffee table, thinking. "Okay." He rose. "I'll talk to the bartenders, ask around. See if we can find Miss Crane's mystery man."

"Look—Maddie has nothing to do with these murders."

"I didn't say she did. But she's your personal assistant, isn't she? And she kept important information from us. So I'd like to talk to her."

Ray checked his watch. "She should be here any minute." And as if she'd timed it to his words, Maddie strolled in.

She scanned the room, gave Ray a cool glance, then turned to Burke. "Detective. Nice to see you again."

"I'd like to ask you a few questions."

"I'm sure you would."

"You don't have to answer," Gillian said.

"What's a little interrogation between friends?" She glanced at Burke. "Are you my friend, Detective?"

Burke looked flustered, but not enough to sideline him. "Why didn't you tell anyone about the threats?" he asked.

She hesitated, then sighed. "Look, I didn't take them seriously. And I thought they would upset Gillian. My job is to be a buffer between her and whatever distracts her from her work. The messages were a definite distraction."

Burke turned to Gillian. "And you buy that?"

"Absolutely. Maddie is extremely overprotective."

"I can be quite suffocating, actually," Maddie said.

Burke looked between the two of them. From the expression on his face, he didn't know if they were telling the truth or putting him on. A little of both, Ray thought.

"And where were you last night?"

"I told you," Gillian said. "She was with someone. Sorry, Maddie," she murmured.

"I was in the hotel." Maddie gave Burke the room number, neither embarrassed nor hesitant about her one-night stand.

"Can anyone back that up?"

"I ordered room service. You can check the time with them. And I was there when it was delivered. I'm sure you can also verify that."

No names, though. Like Gillian said, Maddie was protective.

Burke's gaze lingered on her. "Okay, I'll get on it." He rose and turned to Gillian. "In the meantime, you let me know if anything or anyone suspicious happens, or if you remember anything that might be helpful."

"I'll walk you out," Ray said, and accompanied him to the elevator.

"Look, Ray, you can't pump me for information I don't want to give."

Ray acknowledged this with a slight nod of his head. "Can you tell me about the victim?"

Burke sighed. "Runaway. Got a mother in Portland with a string of bad boyfriends. Girl ran away a couple of times. Got her on a shoplifting charge last year. Juvie returned her to the family. She took off again, about six weeks ago. Girls on Dickerson Road said she turned the occasional trick to pay for food."

"You have a profiler on this?"

"We do now."

"Show him this." He took out the crime-scene photograph he'd taken from Harley. "Look at the placement of the body, the wounds."

"Where the hell'd you get this?"

"Shut up and listen. I drove out to the house today. Where Holland Gray was killed. Pretty little farmhouse out past Pasquo almost to the county line. I was looking at the house and at the photo, and something was bothering me. But I didn't figure it out until just now. Killer stabbed her twice. Here"—he pointed to the picture, then to the left of his breastbone—"and here." Again, he put his finger on the body in the photo, then pointed to the same place on his own stomach.

"So?"

"So get hold of a copy of Gillian's photograph. The girl in the photograph has three stab wounds, not two."

Burke looked interested for the first time.

"The first murder, the picture you showed us at the Gray's. How many times did the killer stick her?"

"Twice."

"That's right. Twice. Just like Holland Gray."

"Jesus Christ."

"So if the killer was re-creating the photograph, why was his re-creation closer to the original murder?"

32

By early evening, Carleco had cleared Maddie's computer. Although it took one suspicion off Ray's list, no one could guarantee she hadn't sent those messages from some other machine.

Burke had also called. Seems most of Maddie's whereabouts the night before had been confirmed. She'd left the bar shortly after Gillian, though no one remembered seeing her leave with anyone. She'd booked a separate room, been given the key, and evidently stayed there. Alone. She'd ordered room service for one, and the person who delivered it saw no evidence of a roommate with her. So why hadn't she said so?

When asked, she said, "It's no one's business who I sleep with or don't. When I sleep with them, or don't. Or why."

Hardly a satisfying answer. Which left Ray still wanting her out of the way.

Luckily, her own safety was the best argument for doing so, and Gillian bought it. She closeted herself in Maddie's room, and though he didn't know what she said, when they came out around six, Maddie had her suitcase with her.

Ray was standing in front of the TV, gazing intently at the picture instead of Maddie's closed bedroom door. Long lines at the Gray doubled and tripled around themselves as people waited to be among the first to see the controversial dead shots. Off to the side, protesters still carried placards and banners, harassing the line, but they weren't keeping anyone away.

"I guess what they say is true," Gillian said, watching a reporter stick a microphone in the face of a woman in line.

"No such thing as bad publicity," Ray said, completing her thought.

He switched off the set and, without being asked, relieved Maddie of her suitcase. He told the guard outside to call for a bellhop and a cab, and alerted Landowe she was ready to be escorted out.

Maddie eyed him, and he faced her, doubts still circling. The fact that she was leaving was a check in the pro column. "Look," he said, albeit reluctantly, "suspicion goes with the territory."

"Is that supposed to be an apology?"

"Of a sort."

She pursed her lips, thought it over. Glanced at Gillian as though weighing her options for and against forgiveness.

Gillian held up her hands. "Don't look at me. You're on your own here."

Maddie turned back to Ray. "I'll think about it," she said, and swept past him. At the doorway she turned, gave Gillian a rueful smile. "Take care of yourself, goofball."

"I will."

"I mean it."

"I know you do."

She cut Ray one last glance and turned to go. "He does have a nice ass," she said over her shoulder. And then she disappeared down the hallway.

Landowe put Maddie in the back of a cab, where she sat quietly and let herself be driven to the airport. She even let the cabdriver unload her suitcase once they arrived. She paid him and tipped generously. If the police came snooping around, she wanted him to remember her.

A baggage handler approached her. "Check your bags, ma'am?"

"No, thank you."

She wheeled her own suitcase through the glass doors into the building. Passed the crowded check-in lines for Southwest, and followed the signs for "baggage area," then "transportation." Stepping onto the escalator, she rode two levels down, then exited the building and walked to the taxi stand.

The first cab in line pulled up. The driver—a Sikh in turban and beard—swung her suitcase into the trunk while she got into the back.

When he returned, she gave him the name of a downtown hotel not too far from Gillian's. If she had to, Maddie could walk between the two. And knowing what she knew, she might have to.

The cab slid away from the curb, and Maddie sank against the seat and closed her eyes. She wasn't going to let Ray Pearce chase her out of town. Not when she had so much riding on what happened there.

33

An hour after Maddie left, Ray put Gillian in the limo and took her to the Grays' for dinner.

A growing crowd of protesters and paparazzi had gathered outside the estate gates, which had been lifted off their rusted hinges and reconfigured on new ones that would allow the gates to close. The two men Carlson had placed at the estate had requested backup, so in addition, Ray brought Landowe along.

For once, Gillian seemed to welcome the extra protection.

The limo crawled through the photographers and placard carriers to the slowly opening gates. A couple of paparazzi slipped inside the property, and Landowe jumped out to round them up while others on the security team held the rest of the crowd back.

Meanwhile, the limo crept forward to the entrance, and Ray escorted Gillian inside. A maid showed them into the living room, where Chip presided over a bar cart, and Genevra gave Gillian a disapproving once-over, lingering on the thigh-high skirt and the knife-blade bootheels.

"Streetwalking today?" Genevra asked.

Gillian grinned. "Not in four-inch heels."

Ray sensed a heightened awareness in the room, as if everyone knew chaos reigned just outside the walls, but no one wanted to acknowledge it. He took up his position at the doorway, where he could keep an eye on the room as well as the hall.

Gillian followed, grabbed on to his arm, and held fast. "Ray is joining us for dinner," she announced.

He stared at her. "I don't think so."

"Of course you are. Genevra's dinners are legendary."

"The man is working, Gillian," Chip said.

"He can't protect you and cut his duck at the same time," Genevra added.

"Oh, you'd be surprised. Ray can do anything."

He looked from the gleam of amusement in Gillian's eyes to her grandparents. "Will you excuse us?" He pulled her out of the room. "This why you didn't kick when I brought Landowe?"

"He can stand guard duty for one meal."

Could his hands actually meet around her neck? Were two hands even necessary?

"Look, I need the distraction," Gillian said. "Otherwise, it's going to be question, lecture, question, lecture all night."

"Nothing like the bodyguard sitting down to a cozy meal with the whole family to deflect attention off you."

She shrugged. "Food's good." She grinned. "Come on, Ray, help me out. Call Landowe on your Jack Bauer radio and tell him to take up his post here."

Ray should have demurred. Not only was dining with his client unprofessional, but also getting caught in the Gray cross fire wasn't his idea of a pleasant evening. But he had a few questions that only the Grays could answer. And it wasn't likely he'd get a better chance to ask them.

Which is why he came to be seated across from Gillian at the Gray's eighteenth-century walnut dining table, while Landowe stood guard at the room's entrance.

"Everything all right?" Chip asked Ray in a lowered voice. And then with a fast look at his wife, "We understand there's been another—"

"Charles," Genevra barked.

Ray took the measure of the moment: Murder and mayhem did not make for appropriate dinner conversation. So he left out all the detail. "Everything is under control."

"Well, except for the second murder, that is," Gillian said, undermining the silent pact he'd just made with her grandparents.

"We will not discuss it at the table," Genevra said.

"She was, what, sixteen? Or was it fifteen? Which was it, Ray? Fifteen or sixteen?"

"Sixteen," Ray said curtly. "The duck is delicious, Mrs. Gray."

"We have it sent from a farm outside Jackson," Genevra said.

"They hack the necks off first," Gillian said. "At least, I think they hack the necks off first." She turned to her grandmother. "Do they hack the necks off, or do you take care of that personally?"

Ray remembered Harley's words about Mrs. Gray and her refusal to talk about her daughter's murder or admit there might be anything wrong with her granddaughter. That damn cold bitch, Harley had called her. Ray cut a glance at her. Cold, yes. But there was also something in her face Ray recognized. Defiance. A refusal to give in. Not unlike someone else at the table.

"I do it personally." Genevra gave Gillian a direct look. "If you want a job done right..." Calmly, she put a forkful of duck in her mouth. It was deftly done, graceful and dainty. Her mouth closed around it, and she chewed. Swallowed. Laid the fork down. "I thought you'd like to know that the art auction is going well. We've had a wonderful response and hope to raise quite a lot of money for the new hospital wing."

Gotta admire the way she declined to rise to Gillian's bait.

Ray did some mental dancing. The art auction was the charity event at the end of next week.

"Genevra's the event chair," Chip explained to Ray. "She's done a remarkable job, too."

"Even I donated something," Gillian said. "*Big Date.* Have you seen it?"

Ray thought back to the coffee table book. Couldn't place it.

"Blonde in a tub of bloody water. Lots of lotions and soaps lying around."

Oh, yeah. That one.

A beat. The two Grays looked momentarily horror-struck.

"Just kidding." Gillian smirked.

"I asked for the flowers," Genevra said.

"And that's what I sent."

Chip cleared his throat. "Where are you from, Ray?"

Here it came. Deflection time. "Originally? Long Island."

Genevra asked, "Do you still have family there?"

"My mother died when I was in college."

"And your father?" Leave it to Gillian to ask the question he didn't want to answer.

"Out of the picture," Ray said at last. "The less said the better."

Gillian brightened. "Really? I had no idea we had so much in common."

Ray sensed another level of tension in the room. It intrigued him. In all the file information Ray had read, Gillian's father had never been mentioned. Not even his identity. Briefly he pondered using the short silence to ask his questions, but it felt like piling on. And Genevra spoke first.

"How long have you been in Nashville?"

Her effort to change the subject did not go unchallenged. "We all have fathers," Gillian said. "Not everyone has a father no one talks about."

"There's little to say," Genevra snapped. "Your father is dead."

"How convenient for me," Gillian said.

Ray looked between the two women. Clearly a sore subject.

"More club soda?" Chip asked Ray, whose glass was already full.

"I'm fine."

Chip held up his own glass. "You don't drink?"

"No, sir." He didn't explain. These people were already burdened with their own pasts. They didn't need his as well. "I went to college in Birmingham," Ray said instead. "Played hockey for the Chargers. You played football, didn't you? Vanderbilt?"

"Quarterback." Chip beamed. He plunged into a story about being selected SEC Player of the Year, and the conversation moved to safer ground.

Dessert was served in the library, a room with polished wood and studded leather. Shelves of books lined one wall. An ancient globe sat on a stand in one corner, a grandfather clock in another. In the shuffle between locations, Ray excused himself to talk to Landowe.

The night appeared quiet, the estate as well. "Some of the protesters have drifted off," Landowe told him. "But a few of the 'razzi are still there."

"Everything else set?"

"Just give the word."

Gillian appeared and glided over to Landowe. "Can I get you anything? Cigarette? Scotch?" She put her arm through his and leaned in. "A little weed?"

Landowe shot Ray a fast glance. "No, thank you."

"Good." She grinned and let him go. "Because I was kidding about the weed."

Ray ignored her shenanigans. "Need a break?" he asked Landowe.

"I'm fine."

He took Gillian by the arm and escorted her back to the library. "Leave Landowe alone."

"He's a grown-up. He can take care of himself." She thrust a coffee cup at him. One of those dainty china things that feel like they'd break in your hand. "Black as coal," she said, "and tastes the same. Just the way you like it."

He sampled the hot liquid. It was good and strong.

A maid was serving some kind of cake. He refused a piece. Wondered how many times the Grays had sat down to dinner in their own home with the help.

In deference to that rarity, and to the fact that he felt more in control, he remained standing. The room was quiet, the tick of the grandfather clock filling the silence. Gillian's grandparents were braced on matching leather armchairs that were deep enough to have been thrones. They appeared armored and protected, and that was the best position they'd been in all night. He took his shot.

"I went for a ride today," he said to no one in particular. "Out Highway 100."

Three pairs of eyes suddenly focused on him.

"I saw the house." No one asked what house he was talking about. "If Holland moved there today, she would be in the middle of suburban sprawl. But back then, she was in the middle of nowhere. Remote. Cut off. Made me wonder."

"We aren't going to talk about this." Genevra's face was sharp enough to kill.

"Wonder what?" Gillian asked.

He turned to her. "Wonder why she left this beautiful house. Her family. The safety net she had right here."

"Safety net?" Gillian muttered. "Cage more likely."

Gillian was focused on him, so she didn't see the tiny flinch in her grandmother's face.

Genevra set her coffee cup on the arm of her chair. "Holland was always wild. Never listened to anyone."

"But she came here to get away from the wild side," Ray said. "At least, that's what the press reported." He ignored the scowl on Gillian's face, the dagger stares from Chip and Genevra. He shrugged. "The media rarely gets anything right, so..." Ray lifted his free hand. "I wondered if there was some other reason she came home."

"She came home for me." Gillian's eyes glittered. "To give me something better than a drugged-out party life."

Ray sipped his coffee again. "Well, she'd had you for, what—six, seven years? She didn't seem to care about her celebrity lifestyle in all that time. Why the sudden change of heart?"

Genevra rose, overturning her cup and saucer. The cup landed on the rug, but the saucer hit the strip between the rug and the hardwood floor, and shattered.

A moment of silence, as if the broken china represented everything wrong in the room. One violent act that smashed the world into pieces.

Chip leaped to his feet and called for the maid. The uniformed woman who'd served dinner scurried in, threw up her hands, and scurried back out again. She ran back with a dish towel and proceeded to mop up the mess while everyone looked on stoically.

The subject of Holland Gray was lost in the commotion, and when Ray looked up, Gillian was gone.

34

He found her upstairs in her bedroom, Landowe at the door.

"It's okay," Ray told him. "I'll take it from here. Get the limo ready."

Landowe left, and Ray slipped into the room. Gillian was bending over a thick scrapbook. He leaned against the door and watched her ignore him.

"You ever go back to your mother's house?"

"No."

He quirked his brows skeptically. "Not like you not to confront your demons head-on."

Her head snapped up. She scowled at him. "I don't need to go back to remember it. To see it." She held his glance a moment. "Okay, so I'm chicken. Everyone's allowed one small yellow streak."

But he wouldn't call her reticence cowardice. It was a way of keeping her distance so she could re-create the reality in her photographs. Manipulate the memories. Objectify them, maybe. Dull the impact and make them easier to live with.

He moved into the room, sat on the edge of the bed. "I wouldn't call it small. I'd call it barely visible."

He'd spoken gently but her eyes glared. "Why all the questions about my mother anyway?"

"Just wondering," he said mildly, not a little surprised at her disapproval.

"It upset my grandparents." Not to mention her.

"So let me get this straight. It's okay for you to upset them, but they're off-limits to anyone else?"

"Maybe," she said grudgingly. "Something like that."

"Why, Gillian Gray." He clapped a hand to his chest in mock astonishment. "You do have a heart."

"Very funny."

He nodded toward the scrapbook. "What's this?"

She opened the book. The top of the spine had separated from the binding because the book was so fat. "My grandmother still thinks she kept this from me, but I've known about it since I was eleven." Slowly, she turned the pages.

Articles about Holland mixed with magazine pages and photographs. Holland as a teenager in sale circulars for local department stores that no longer existed. Later, in catalogs for Bergdorf and Neiman Marcus. And still later, in the *New York Times* style section and *Women's Wear Daily.* He'd seen some of the covers in the file, the public stuff, but the book contained private things as well. Keepsakes. A broken bra strap from a Valentino show in Rome. An invitation to Fashion Week in Paris. Photographs of friends and colleagues.

"See what a liar my grandmother is?" Gillian said. "She pretends she hated my mother, but she kept every last scrap Holland saved."

Ray fingered the yellowed newspaper articles, the faded pictures of Fashion Week and the old Polaroids of photo shoots. "How many times have you looked through this?"

"Thousands?" She gave a little self-deprecating laugh. "A lot. I used to go through the book and pick my father out from the pictures."

She showed him a behind-the-scene photo of a fashion shoot. Holland was in front of a glittery backdrop. A sandy-haired man straddled a camera on a tripod. "I liked his long hair."

She flipped another few pages, came to another candid shot of Holland, this one with her hair in rollers, laughing in a chair in front of a makeup mirror. A man with a hairdryer stood over her. "Or maybe it's the hairdresser."

"You know who they are?"

She shook her head. "Not their names."

"How about your father?"

"Oh, his name I know. It's dead."

"Your father's name is—"

"Dead. At least, that's all I ever got from anyone about him. Mommy, who's my daddy? Your daddy's dead, sweetie. Grandmother, who's my daddy? Your daddy's dead, dear." She shrugged.

"Didn't you ever try to find out?"

"Oh, yeah, sure. Who wouldn't? But after several tens of thousands, I decided dead was as good a name as any. I mean, what's the point? He couldn't sweep in and take me away anyway." Wistfully, she ran her finger over her mother's face in the photograph. "I like her like this. No makeup, hair in curlers. Laughing. She was so pretty."

Ray watched the sadness seep into her face. Gently, he reached over and closed the book. "We should go."

"Yeah. Enough wallowing." Hauling the overstuffed book into her arms, Gillian crept down to her grandmother's room.

Inside the room, the rose smell invaded her senses. It

was strongest here, where her grandmother kept her *Jardin de la Vie* cream on a vanity in one corner.

Left of the vanity a closet covered the wall. She opened it, stretched on tiptoes to stow the book high on a shelf behind a row of hatboxes Genevra rarely opened. "Wasn't easy doing this when I was eleven."

An arm reached over her head and pushed the book easily into place.

She came down from the balls of her feet. "You're a handy guy to have around."

"You're welcome."

They walked toward the stairs. Gillian shot him a curious glance, then looked away. "So... your father's dead, too?"

"Probably not. Cockroaches never die."

She was taken aback by the strong words. "Whoa. What'd he do?"

"Stole money from the company he worked for. Got arrested. Blew town while he was on bail. Never called. Never wrote. Never caught."

"Ah. Not much."

While Gillian was saying good-bye, Ray checked his phone. Landowe had sent a text message that he was on his way, and Burke had asked him to call. He punched in his former brother-in-law's number.

"We traced the last Web site message," Jimmy said. "It was sent from the first victim's machine—a computer in the H&R Block office." So, not Maddie. "And we found a new one. Text messaged from Dawn Farrell's cell phone." He repeated the content, and Ray's stomach clenched.

"Prints?"

"No."

Nothing to track back to the killer. "He's not taking any chances, is he?"

"You keep a close watch on her," Burke said, and disconnected.

A few minutes later, Gillian came out of the library. She looked around. "Where's Landowe?"

"With the limo." Ray nodded to the back of the house. "Come on."

"Uh—the door's the other way." She pointed to the front. "Where are we going?"

"You're big on adventure. Wait and see."

He took her around to the back, where Chip's driver had the Land Rover waiting.

"Get in," Ray said, hovering over the passenger side until she complied. He came around, slid behind the wheel, turned the engine on, and took off.

"Chip gave you the keys? He never lets anyone drive this car."

"His driver, Eugene, gave me the keys. Chip gave me permission." He rounded the bend that led to the front of the house and the drive through the gates.

"Where's the limo?"

"Probably on its way back to the hotel by now."

"A decoy?"

"A decoy."

Suspicious, Gillian glanced at him, a vague feeling of uneasiness sweeping over her. "But you know I like my notoriety."

"Uh-huh." Then he turned west, away from the hotel.

"You taking me out, Ray?"

"That's right."

But she didn't think so. And short of jumping out of a moving car, she had no recourse but to take the ride.

Resentment brewing, she stared out at the night until they passed the turnoff to Highway 100.

Ray stole a glance at her. Did she have memories of the road? If so, she didn't say.

Ten minutes later, he turned into River Bend Estates.

"Didn't think there were any clubs here," Gillian said.

"Private club," Ray told her, and pulled up to a house at the end of a cul-de-sac. It was ordinary enough, stone and wood with decent landscaping, but nothing that stood out. A small iron stand held a lamp aloft, lighting the stone path to the door. Ray escorted her up it.

"What are you doing, Ray?"

"Keeping you safe."

"I'll be safe at the hotel."

"You and I, we have different definitions of that word."

He would have let her unlock the door again, but he wasn't sure she would do it. Instead, he reached over her, inserted the key, turned the lock, and opened the door himself. She didn't budge, and he gave her a gentle push inside.

35

Ray closed the door, and Gillian turned to him, violet eyes flashing. "You are one slick dude."

"You wouldn't have left the hotel otherwise."

"Isn't this considered kidnapping?"

"We arranged it with Chip, so your family knows all about it."

Her mouth came down in a hard line. "Give me the car keys," she said.

"I don't think so."

"This is ridiculous. You're not a cop anymore, and you can't keep me here."

"I can try."

"I'll call a cab."

"No phone."

She glared at him, then dove into her purse.

"It's not there," he said mildly. "I left it back at your grandparents'."

"You're kidding."

"Had to get you out of the public eye. Security company owns the house. It's a bridge site. Temporary safe house when we need a place to regroup."

"I don't need to regroup."

"While you were messing with your grandmother's head, your Web site received another message."

She stilled.

"Killer did a little editing."

She raised a single questioning brow.

"Took out the 'I'," Ray said. "Added the words 'with me.' "

She put it together. "Make it real... with me. With me. He wants me to join him? Kill someone together?"

"Or be his next victim."

Acknowledgment crossed her face, acceptance tinged with eagerness. It scared him. "So," he said, looking around. The walls didn't seem strong enough to hold her in. "Regroup. Some of your stuff is already here." He gestured inward. "You should have everything you need."

She eyed him, seemed to debate how much to protest, then sighed. "Fine."

He paused. That was too easy. "Fine?"

"Fine. Fine!" She stormed around, threw her arms up in the air. More like what he expected. "We're here. Fine." She threw her purse on the couch. Flopped down beside it.

"There's food. I had them get you that puffy cheese stuff you like so much."

"What a guy." She looked around. "This it? Just me and my keeper? Oh, and mustn't forget, snacks."

"Landowe is outside."

"I suppose he has a phone."

"He's not going to call you a cab."

"God, no. Of course not."

"Glad you're being such a sport about this." She gave him an evil look. "Come on. I'll show you the rest of the house." He led her down the hallway and opened the first door on the right. A bedroom. Her suitcase was on the bed. "You're in here."

"And you?"

He gestured vaguely. "I'll be around."

Gillian let the vagueness slide. Truth was, all she really cared about were those keys. And getting back out where the monster could find her.

She glanced at Ray, at his sleek, long body, the hard-edged face, and her fingers curled instinctively, wanting to touch. Okay, so maybe the monster wasn't all she cared about. She hadn't missed the sidelong looks Ray had been giving her all day. Like he wanted to take his eyes off her but couldn't quite manage it. And his white shirt, wrinkled now, yes, but still clinging to his broad shoulders, offsetting his powerful neck... She wasn't the only one having trouble keeping her gaze to herself.

All of which was beside the point. The point being those keys.

She sidled up to him, moving in closer. "Around where?" She had to tilt her head up. God, he was big. So big.

"Wherever." He swallowed, the Adam's apple in his throat bobbing hugely. "Around. Don't worry about it."

She put her hands on his waist, felt him go rigid. "I'm not worried."

"Good. Because I wouldn't want you to be."

His mouth was close enough if she stood on tiptoe, but his pocket was closer. He was staring down at her. Dazed. Distracted. She forced herself to remember what she was supposed to be doing and that she might not get another chance. In the time it took to draw a single breath, she lunged for the pocket where she'd seen him stash the keys.

But he was quicker and a lot less distracted than she'd imagined. His hand shot out and clasped her wrist. "Oh, no, you don't."

She refused to give up. Her fingers fished around, felt the metallic shape of the keys, and though her wrist was imprisoned, she managed to close her fingers around them even as he pulled her hand out of his pocket.

She hadn't counted on his other hand, though, which quickly closed in on the keys and snatched them away from her.

"Give me those!" She grabbed for them, and he held them over her head.

"Not on your life."

She jumped, swatting at his hand, which he easily jerked out of reach. Stumbling, she landed against him. Pushed and shoved and used the moment to swipe at the keys again.

An irritated look crossed his face. "That's enough. Stop it."

"Make me."

"You're kidding." He laughed, which made her more angry, and she glowered at him, daring him silently.

He gave a tiny shrug, moved, and, before she knew how, he'd pinned her back against the wall. She struggled, but he held her effortlessly, her hands trapped over her head.

"Let me go," she growled.

"No."

Her back was arched, her breasts extended, and he was looking. Not just looking. He was riveted. Rapt. Her nipples hardened and burst through the thin fabric of her bra as though his eyes were drawing them up and out.

"Let me go!"

Instead, he bent down and captured her mouth. He

wasn't gentle about it either, but she didn't want or need gentleness. A bolt of pure energy ripped through her. Her knees rocked, and without warning, a groan escaped.

"Still want to leave?" he whispered, and kissed her again.

She fought to loose his hold, but not to escape, never to escape. Only to touch him. She wanted desperately to feel his strong, solid body beneath her hands. And when he pulled back for an instant, she darted her head forward and grabbed his mouth, drinking in his lips and his tongue. He groaned, softened, and let her go to wrap his arms around her.

And she snatched the keys out of his hands and dodged away.

He shouted and ran after her. Pounded down the hall. The next thing she knew, she was on the floor. Like the first time at the museum, his big body trapping her beneath him. But this time, God this time. His breath was in her hair, his mouth at her ear, and the hard length of him against her hip. She couldn't help herself. Keys fisted in her hands, she rotated around so she could wrap her arms around his neck. Somehow she forgot about running. Her hands, had they been full of something? Something besides his shoulders and his muscled arms? Eagerly, her fingers ran over that white shirt, jerking it out of his pants, fumbling with the buttons, then ripping them apart. Suddenly he was free of it. His skin, his powerful chest, everything open to her.

He parted her shirt, and cold air hit her own bare chest, but his frantic mouth warmed her. Her breasts, still sheathed in black net and lace, her belly, and lower, God lower. She raised her hips, and he shoved up her skirt, ripped off the black thong she wore underneath. Too fevered to take off shoes and boots. Just his zipper. God, open up for me, babe. And then he was inside her.

"Ray," she moaned. "Ray, God."

They were on the floor in a pool of fire, and he was doing what she'd wanted him to do for days. Half-naked, half-clothed, thick with the charged heat of passion.

"Going somewhere?" he said, panting.

She nicked his lip; he bit back. "Wherever you take me."

She gasped as he thrust inside her again and again, hard. So hard. She spread her legs, the heels of her boots digging into his back. His body was touching her, stroking, taking her higher—and suddenly she was flying, screaming, and he swallowed her scream in his mouth, chugging her name as he came inside her.

And then there was only silence. The quaking aftermath of what they'd done.

Into the quiet, Ray jerked and pulled away from her. His earpiece had been dislodged, and he scrambled to find it and turn it on. "What?" He spoke into it quickly without putting it on. "No, no, we're fine. No, stay there." He cleared his throat. "No, everything's fine. We're good here." He straightened his clothes, stood, zipped up.

The gesture sent a shudder of heat through her, and she couldn't resist. Not bothering to shed her blouse or cover herself up, breasts tight against the lace of her bra, one strap dangling, she crawled over to him. Wound her way up his leg until she was kneeling in front of him. Her hands reached for the zipper. "Uh, I'll let you know." He slapped her away, but she came back. He gasped as she touched him. "Nothing. No, we're good."

"Oh, no, we're not," she murmured. "We are bad, Ray. Very, very bad." And she smiled to see he was hard again.

She freed him. Licked him. The hand without the radio

grasped the top of her head. Begging her to stop, urging her to continue. "Okay," he said into the mike, his voice straining. "Okay. Later." Then he groaned, giving voice to what he'd been repressing, and his fingers tightened on her head as she took him full in her mouth. "Jesus Christ."

He collapsed against the wall, his hand still fused to the top of her head, his sex sliding in and out of her mouth. She tasted all of him, the hard, massive length, the arrow tip. He leaped against her tongue, and she teased him again. He moaned, and she gently ran her teeth up and down him.

All at once, he shuddered violently, then wrenched away. He kicked off his shoes, stepped out of his khakis, and, swooping down, lifted her up as though she were a doll. She wrapped her legs around him, and he impaled himself in her, his tongue now where his cock had been, and his cock...God, she could feel him clear up to her womb. She grunted with wet, loose pleasure, feeling the sting of ecstasy carry her away again. New, fresh, as if she hadn't just done this ten minutes ago. As if she'd never done this. Not with him, not with anyone. She was climbing that hill, reaching for that fierce, special place where the sun was bright and warm, and darkness couldn't touch her. But before she could arrive, he was moving, going somewhere else. She whimpered a protest, but he took her with him, still buried deep inside her, and they tumbled into a bedroom and onto the bed.

The fall disengaged them, and she crawled on top of him, wanting the warmth back, the heat of him inside her. She slid home, moaning with the feel of it. Desperate for his fingers, for the brand of his palm, she wrenched off her shirt and bra, and his hands cradled her liberated breasts. He caressed the tips, leaned up to kiss them. She arched back, rode him deep and fast, and when they came, they collapsed together, folding in on each other like trees in a hurricane.

It felt like a year before she could breathe normally again. A century before the world came back, and she saw she was sprawled across him. That his hand was in her hair, on her bare back and shoulder, and finally, finally, her naked arms.

She stilled, ever so slightly.

"What the—" He finished the question by rolling her over. There was a lamp on the beside table, and he snapped it on. Gillian covered her eyes with the back of one hand, but she felt his fingers roaming up and down her arms. Felt his eyes, seeing for the first time, burning with questions. She braced. Waited. Marshaled all her explanations.

And then he did what no one had ever done. He pulled her to him, cradled her in his arm, and asked nothing. Nothing at all.

36

Hours later, Ray woke to find Gillian naked and bending over him, her little camera in his face. "Jesus, what are you doing?" He pushed her arm away.

"What's it look like I'm doing?" She clicked another picture, crawled over the sheets and his legs to a new position, and clicked once more. "I'm memorializing you. Don't you want to be remembered for all time?"

"Not without my clothes on I don't. Cut it out." She sighed, dropped the camera. "Come here," he said, pulling her against him. "God, you're freezing." He rubbed up and down those thin, mutilated arms, trying to warm her.

She raised the camera in front of them both, and before he could dodge, she clicked the picture. Her arm dropped, and the hand holding the camera hit the bed with a small thud.

"Don't you want to know?" she said at last.

She lay against his shoulder, and he traced the odd-shaped scars, ugly flaps of skin that looked like knife wounds or burns or—he let himself face it silently—torture. Some kind of sick torture. But nowhere in any file or record had there been any indication that she'd been abused. Was this Kenny Post's work? But the marks were old, faded, embedded in scar tissue. Whoever hurt her had done it long ago. He pictured the angelic child she'd been, and a fierce rage gripped him.

He let out a long breath, struggling to keep the fury bottled. "Yeah, sure I do," he said. "But it's your story to offer when you're ready."

"Why don't you ask?"

"Ask what? What happened to you? I can see what happened. Who did it? Christ, I don't think I want to know. Not sure I could keep"—he fisted a hand—"keep from hunting him down and killing him."

"Her," she said quietly. "Killing her."

"What?"

"And you won't have to do much hunting."

A shock wave hit him. Her grandmother? My God, no wonder Holland took her daughter away. No wonder Gillian hated Genevra Gray so much.

"Look, you don't have to go back there," he said rapidly, making it a vow. "Ever."

But instead of snuggling close, she pulled back, propped her head on her hand and looked at him. "Back where?"

"To Belle Meade. Your grandmother. I won't let her hurt you again."

She did the oddest thing. She laughed. Traced a finger down his nose. "Oh, Ray." She sighed. "What am I going to do with you?"

"Just stay close. Let me keep you safe."

"That's sweet. So very sweet. So very Ray. You're a sweet man, Ray—when you're not being a pain in the ass—a nice man."

He knocked her hand away. "You know what I've figured out? When you're sneering, you care the most."

Their gazes locked.

"Well, you're a child of the Age of Psychobabble," she said coolly. "Don't you know you can run, but you can't hide? Not if the horror is inside yourself."

"What are you talking about?"

"Genevra didn't put those scars on my arms, Ray."

"But you said 'her.' Who else—God, Maddie?"

She shook her head. "One more wrong guess, and you lose the minicamper and the vacation package." Her eyes never left his face.

And he saw it. Right there in the depths of the violet haze. Saw it. Got it. And it cracked his world.

"Oh, my God." The rage seeped away, replaced by a sadness so deep he could have drowned in it. "My God." Tears tightened the back of his throat.

"Hey—you going to get all weepy on me, do it somewhere else."

"Fuck you, Gray." He swiped at his eyes.

"Or we could choose that option again."

Like a rattlesnake striking, he darted up and over so fast she was on her back and trapped against the bed before she knew he was coming.

"You fucking did that to yourself? You carved yourself up like a piece of meat?"

"What if I did?"

He stared at her with total disbelief. "What if you did? Oh, my God." Then he pulled her up and into his arms. "My God." He held her tight, kissed her neck, her cheek, her lips. "Why wasn't anyone there? Why didn't anyone take care of you?"

"It's all right," she said, holding him, comforting him, which was ironic, but nice. "It was a long time ago."

She remembered other reactions to those scars. Some

guys were turned off, some turned on. Some guys couldn't wait to hear every gory detail. The first time Kenny had seen them, he'd wanted to add a new one. "To remember our first time. We'll do it together," he'd said.

No one had gotten this worked up, though. At least, not for her sake. For the child she'd once been. Or never been. So she let Ray's concern wash over her without further comment. She sank into the power of his compassion. Felt those strong arms around her like a shield. A wall of safety that no one and nothing could breach.

He held her tight, kissed her tenderly, and, God help her, she liked it. Liked it a lot. Too much. She could get so used to this. To having him around to keep the monster at bay.

She pushed at him. "Enough. Stop. You're suffocating me."

He stared at her, long enough for her face to heat and his eyes to chill over. "You seemed to enjoy it just fine a little while ago."

"That was then."

Abruptly, he let her go. "Fine." He swung off the bed. "You want your space? Whatever." Went in search of his clothes. Or his sanity.

Or hers.

Alone now, she curled into herself, burrowed beneath the covers. Stared at the scars. The dark triangles where she'd pressed a hot iron into her skin, the crude hunks of slashed flesh that were supposed to be her own initial twined around her mother's. The twisted *H,* the awkward *G.* All the other attempts to keep from screaming.

She'd stopped cutting when she picked up the camera. Learned how to focus her anger and channel it outward. But still, the pall of destiny never left. It was with her now, in this room, when she looked at Ray and saw what he wanted from her.

Happiness. Hope. Safety.

Things she never thought about. Never planned for. Never expected.

Not if she was going to face the black evil still walking free. Still killing. Still coming after her.

37

Genevra Gray belted the silk charmeuse robe around her and sat at the little vanity her mother had insisted she have. Macey Holland wanted her daughter to have her own bedroom, too, but as a young bride, Genevra had thought that too old-fashioned. The compromise was her small dressing area with the mirrored vanity.

She sat there now, more than fifty years after resolving that dispute with her mother, and reached for the *Jardin de la Vie* hand cream. Genevra had bought her first jar on her honeymoon and used the rose-scented lotion ever since, even when she had to have it shipped directly from Paris.

She smoothed the cream over her hands. She'd always been proud of her hands, of her long, thin fingers. Now the knuckles stood out, the joints misshapen by arthritis.

She sighed. She'd been brought up to expect expensive things. Pretty things. The Hollands had been royalty in their small Alabama town, her father the mayor and the banker, and Genevra had presumed she would become a queen.

And she wasn't far wrong. She attended Vanderbilt, was recruited for Kappa Alpha Theta, the most prestigious sorority on campus. Elected to homecoming court as a freshman, she found her true calling two years later as the wife of one of the most handsome and popular men on campus, with a family that reached back five generations in Nashville. Her wedding was the social event of the season, and she expected her life to continue as it had begun. Privileged. Entitled. Blessed.

But it took her three painful years to conceive and two miscarriages before her daughter was born. And something went wrong, so there were no more children after that.

But Holland was so beautiful she seemed to make up for everything. As if God and the universe were apologizing for all that came before. Even today, Genevra remembered the silky feel of her baby daughter's fine hair. She had her mother's famous blue eyes and fair coloring, her trim, lithe shape, and her father's height. And though Genevra was somewhat dismayed to see her daughter's face and body in the newspaper and Sunday circulars, she was also secretly proud.

Until Holland moved to New York and her face began to appear on magazines and television. She had no time to come home, and when Chip and Genevra went north, little time to spend with them. They were astonished and disgusted by the noise, the vulgarity, the ever-present drugs and sex.

Genevra shouldn't have been surprised when Holland became pregnant, but she was. Unmarried, she refused to reveal the father's name. Genevra shuddered, recalling the enormous embarrassment, her friends' sidelong looks, the cruelty cloaked in kindness.

But she weathered it. As she'd weathered earlier disappointments. By reminding herself that this was not what God intended for her, and soon He would rectify His mistake. So when Holland came home at last, Genevra knew she'd been right. She'd been chosen, and God didn't forget His special ones.

Until He did, she thought with a bitter laugh, and oh, how He did. With a slash of His hard, brutal whip.

She didn't want to think about that awful time. Some days she'd felt as though she would dry up, turn into a husk, crumble into dust, and blow away.

Yet no matter how much she yearned otherwise, she woke every day. Woke to the same nightmare, a black dream she was forced to vanquish by denying it existed. In the end, the battle had hardened her. Robbed her of softness until every smile was brittle now.

Genevra noticed the door of her closet ajar and realized Gillian had been there. The girl thought she was fooling her, but Genevra always knew when Gillian had been in her room. It was a sad little game they'd played for years. Genevra couldn't bear to see what was in that book, couldn't bear to face the loss, to see the evidence of how twisted and off-kilter her life had become. But she'd saved it for Gillian. It was her granddaughter's right to know her mother. Genevra just couldn't introduce her.

So Gillian sneaked in to look at the book, and Genevra pretended she didn't know.

Just as she pretended her golden life had continued. And that her granddaughter with the hard outer shell wasn't fragile as lace beneath.

Chip came in. "Didn't know you were still awake."

She looked at her husband. His once-broad chest had widened and sunk, his tanned, handsome face was merely florid now. How old they had become. "Just getting ready."

He tottered off to do the same, but the sight of him brought back memories of the man Gillian had brought to dinner. Also tall, broad-shouldered, and strong like Chip had been.

"Chip." Her husband stopped in the doorway of the bathroom and turned. She rarely called him Chip anymore. It was ridiculous. You don't call a man nearing eighty Chip. But there it was, suddenly, on the tip of her tongue and the roof of her mouth, a reminder of better days. "We must do something about that man."

He didn't ask, "What man?" or "To whom are you referring, dear?" He came back slowly, watching her. "He's kept her safe so far."

She looked at him in the mirror, and their eyes locked. He understood as well as she that there were many ways of staying safe, and asking the wrong questions wasn't one.

Charles patted her shoulder. "All right. I'll see to it in the morning."

He kissed the top of her head, a gesture meant to reassure her. She squeezed the hand that rested on her shoulder. Her way of pretending that she was.

Ray closed the bedroom door on Gillian, heard noise and voices coming from the living room. His clothes were scattered in the hallway, and he quickly picked them up, deciphering identities. Landowe, for sure. Someone else.

Instantly, he knew why they were there, knew what had happened. He looked toward the bedroom, knocked the back of his head against the wall. Closed his eyes. Half of him felt shame; the other half would do it all over again. Neither felt right. And either way, he had to face the two men. He slid into his slacks and shrugged into the shirt. Fastened the bottom three buttons, but left the rest undone because the buttons were gone. A ripple of heat washed over him, remembering how they'd disappeared.

Landowe was in the front room, all right. The other guy was Coleman. A big mucker with a shaved head that Carlson usually saved for more muscular work. Landowe must have been unable to dredge up anyone else.

The two men were watching television. Women in bikinis playing beach volleyball. A half-eaten pizza sat on the coffee table in front of them. They looked at him, then back at the TV. Heat crawled up Ray's face.

"Lose something, Ray?" Coleman asked. He flipped a couple of tiny objects at Ray, and they landed on his chest, bounced off and onto the carpet, where they stared up at him like two white eyes. Buttons. "Can't watch her if you're fucking her."

"Sorry, Ray," Landowe said. "You didn't answer my last transmission."

Ray nodded. Christ. How many times had he heard this cliché? Sleeping with your client was one of the job's biggest pitfalls, but never in a million years would he have predicted he'd fall into it.

At least they'd been discreet. Hadn't burst into the room and embarrassed Gillian. Then again, why would they? Discretion was part of the job. At any rate when it came to the clients.

Coleman picked up a slice of pizza and bit into it. "So, Ray, was it worth it?" He nodded in the general direction of the bedrooms. "Little thing like that." He smacked his lips. "Bet she was nice and tight."

Ray had Coleman by the throat before he knew he was doing it.

"What the f—" The rest was garbled in a choking cough.

"Shut the fuck up!"

"Let go, you fucking asshole!"

"Ray! Ray! Jesus."

Landowe hauled him away, and, breathing heavily, Ray stared at Coleman, who was red-faced and ugly.

"Get out of here," Landowe said, throwing Ray his ear mike, which he must have found on the floor in the hallway with the rest of his gear. "Go on. Carlson will want you front and center first thing in the morning."

"I'm not leaving like this."

Landowe looked flummoxed. "Like what?"

"He wants to say good-bye." Coleman snorted. "Jesus, Pearce, I've heard about you and your women. That cunt in there's got you panty-whipped, too."

Ray rushed Coleman again, and Landowe got in his way. "Enough! Back off. Back off, Ray! Stand the fuck down!"

Landowe's fist was in his chest. Ray nodded, and Landowe let him go. "We'll explain it to her," he said. "Get out of here."

Ray looked around. He was all twisted up, and he had to get clear. Think about what had happened. What it meant. Couldn't do that with Gillian around. Hell, he could hardly breathe when she was around. Bottom line, the two men were right. He couldn't protect her if he was emotionally involved.

"You keep your eye on her," he said at last. "And I mean close."

"We'll see if we can get as close as you," Coleman said.

"Shut up, Coleman," Landowe said, and everyone stayed in place until Ray edged to the door.

He stumbled out of the house into the night. It was

cool, but he needed the chill. Needed a swift, hard slap in the face. Sleeping with your client was bad enough. Falling in love with her was even worse.

Hearing the tumult, Gillian dashed out of the bedroom. Had he come? Had he finally come for her? The thought that he had and that she'd left Ray to face him alone sent her streaking out of the room.

But before she got to the living room, she realized who Ray was fighting with. Landowe and some other guy. And they weren't fighting over the killer.

Asshole, she thought. Who's he calling a cunt? She could damn well sleep with whoever she pleased, and they could go fuck themselves if they didn't like it. She started forward to say so, but the front door opened and slammed shut, and Ray was gone.

Well, that was a sucker punch. She thought he'd have more fight in him. More stick-around. Flattening against the wall, she suddenly felt adrift and cold. She rubbed up and down her arms, remembering the feel of Ray warming her. His mouth on hers, his body inside. The slick, naked feel of him. Suddenly she didn't need to warm up. She was already hot.

She growled. Well, hell, she couldn't have that. Couldn't pine away. Not for Ray, not for anyone. He was gone. Good, fine. She had a mission to accomplish. A stalker to stalk.

Silently, she retreated to the bedroom, pulled on her clothes, but left the boots off. Stiletto heels weren't exactly made for escape.

The bedroom came with its own bath, and she poked her head in. Toilet, tub, and shower combo with a striped curtain enclosure. She peeked behind the curtain. Cut into the wall was a small window, with a rotating handle for opening and closing.

She grabbed the little armchair from the corner of the bedroom, piled her boots on the seat, and tiptoed into the bathroom with it. Flinging open the curtain, she set the chair in the tub, hopped up for a better view. She examined the window's width. Looked like it would be a tight fit, but she might make it.

She opened the window as far as it would go, letting in the night air. She was prying off the screen when a knock sounded on her door. Her heart thudded.

Damn.

She jumped down, wrenched the curtain closed. Another knock. "Miss Gray?"

"Just a minute!"

In a rapid flutter, she unbuttoned her shirt.

"Everything all right, Miss Gray?" She recognized Landowe's voice through the door.

"Ray?" She took an extra second to muss her hair, then cracked open the door. "Oh, Landowe," she said sleepily. She made sure he saw her open shirt, then leisurely pulled the sides together to semicover her breasts. Landowe averted his eyes, looking predictably uncomfortable and distracted.

"Everything okay? I thought I heard—"

"Everything's perfect, except for the sleep I'm not getting." She faked a yawn. "Can we do the bed check in the morning?"

"Yes, ma'am." Landowe turned to go, and she couldn't resist calling after him.

"Tell Ray to get his butt in here."

Landowe turned, opened his mouth to reply.

"I don't know if you've noticed," she said sweetly, before he could, "but he has a nice butt." She closed the door on his embarrassed "Yes, ma'am," and quickly returned to the bathroom.

It took her half an hour to get the screen off, but when she finally did, she tossed her boots out the window, hoping she hadn't lost her favorite pair in vain. She took a breath, vaulted up. It was touch-and-go at first, but she was tiny enough to finally squiggle through.

38

From his position in the Land Rover across the street, Ray tensed as he watched the form creep out from behind the shrubs surrounding the safe house. He hooked up his wireless mike and switched it on, was going to blare an alert into it when the guy ran in and out of the light from a streetlamp, and he saw it wasn't a guy.

He smiled grimly. When you're right, you're right. No way should he have trusted those bozos to keep tabs on Gillian.

He watched her hop on one foot as she struggled to zip up first one boot, then the other. Jesus, she didn't even have her shoes on. Where the hell was she going? She had no car, and unless those idiots had let her get hold of a phone, she had no way to call for transportation.

She crossed the street, scurrying down toward the subdivision exit. He let her get far enough ahead so she wouldn't spot him, then took off after her, cruising without his headlights. From two blocks away he saw her edge toward the subdivision entrance, which was brightly lit, and try to flag down a passing car.

Was she out of her mind?

Stupid question. Of course she was. But luckily that

was not true of the drivers in the meager traffic stream. After twenty minutes, not one had stopped.

When the only car for the last five minutes also zoomed by, her shoulders slumped, and he thought she'd given up. But she raised her head, straightened her back, and he lost her as she set off on foot toward Nashville. Quickly, he put his car in gear and eased down the street, out of the subdivision, and onto the highway. Was she going to walk back to town?

He followed at a sedate distance, pulling off the road when he had to in order to let her get far enough ahead. He was tempted to stop and pick her up, but hell, a long walk in those heels? Served her right. And as long as he kept her in sight she'd be safe.

Her little Boston Marathon ended at the first gas station she came to. He pulled past, watched her go inside. The store's interior lights blazed in the night, and through the plate-glass window he saw her speak to the clerk, who nodded to a phone on the counter. She picked up the handset, punched in a number, spoke briefly, and hung up.

Well, no one said she wasn't smart. Why walk the miles when she could ride? He turned the car off to wait for the cab to show up. Once it did he was prepared to follow her to Des Moines if that was where she was headed.

But almost immediately, she left the gas station and started walking.

Back the way she came.

What the—

Quickly, he started the car, followed.

It took her fifteen minutes longer to make the trip back, and she was limping as she turned into River Bend Estates. He parked a block away and watched as she sneaked into the house the same way she'd sneaked out.

That made no sense. No sense at all. Which made him very, very nervous.

It had taken her nearly half an hour to trudge back to the house. Ten minutes after she'd disappeared through the window, cars started arriving. Men with pads, cameras, and microphones tumbled out. Then the TV vans showed up. Reporters and photographers came together in an ominous crowd at the edge of the safe house. Finally someone—he thought he recognized Benton James, the reporter for the *Tennessean* who'd been at the museum—walked up to the front door and knocked.

Ray stared in disbelief.

The phone call. She hadn't called a cab. She hadn't called Maddie or her grandparents. She'd called a goddamn press conference.

When the knock sounded, Gillian marched purposefully into the living room. "I'll get that."

Landowe and the other guy had already drawn their weapons. They leaped to block her way.

"Take her to the back of the house," Landowe said to a beefy guy with a Kojak head.

"Who's he?" Gillian asked Landowe. "And where's Ray?"

"Move! Now!"

Kojak grabbed her arm and began to haul her away.

The knock came again. "Miss Gray! Miss Gray, are you in there?"

She jerked away from her captor. Turned to Landowe. "Open the door," she said.

"Are you kidding? We don't know who's out there."

"Last time I looked, killers don't knock first."

Landowe exchanged a look with the bald guy.

"Open the goddamn door, or I'll do it myself."

Kojak shrugged, pulled her away from the door's sight lines, and stepped in front of her. Landowe crossed to the door, stood with his back to one side, reached for the knob, and yanked it open.

A strobe flashed. Dozens of voices went off with it. Landowe slammed the door shut again.

"The press," Kojak said.

"How the hell did the press find her?"

Gillian stepped out from behind the shaved head. "I told them." And before they could say anything else, she ran to reopen the door.

Closing it behind her, she stood on the stoop in the glow of hot camera lights, raised her hands for quiet. "Gentlemen, I'll take your questions, but you have to let me hear them."

The cacophony subsided to a low din, everyone shouting at once. She pointed to someone in the middle of the pack.

"You're participating in an art auction at a charity ball for a local hospital. Given the controversy over your work, will you withdraw?"

"No." She pointed to a woman in front.

"Which Dead Shot are you donating?"

"None." She grinned. "Wouldn't want to scare anyone. It's a floral landscape. A favorite of my grandmother."

She began to worry. If the rest of the questions were as innocuous as this, she'd never make the morning news.

A man in front looked familiar. She called on him. "Benton James," he said, "The *Tennessean.* What do you think about the third murder?"

"Excuse me?"

"The third murder. How do you feel about it?"

"The third—" She looked out at the crowd, dread shuddering through her. "I think you made a mistake. There hasn't been—"

"No mistake," he insisted, and glanced down at a small notebook. "Linda Hayes."

The words "third" and "murder" were rippling through the assembly, slowly wiping out the noise.

"Got the photo an hour ago," the little newspaperman announced with a smug smile. "*Kiddie Pool,*" he added, referring to one of her photographs.

The silence exploded into thunder.

"Do you hold yourself responsible?"

"What do you want to say to the victims' families?"

"What do you say to Matthew Dobie?"

"Are you going to stop now?"

The crowd was pushing forward, nearly overwhelming her with the surge and the noise. She was being suffocated, overrun. The picture of the hanging child burst in her head, and she wanted to scream, to run, but she couldn't move. Couldn't think. Couldn't breathe.

"That's enough. Step back. Step back!" Ray pushed through the swarm, took her elbow. "Press conference is over," he said, and pushed her toward the door.

"Miss Gray! Miss Gray!"

"What are you going to do now?"

He got the door open, would have shoved her inside despite the clamor. But she wasn't going to let that slimeball son of a bitch win.

She pivoted, wrenched away from Ray's protective shelter, and turned to the horde. As if on cue, they hushed, salivating like vicious Dobermans waiting to attack. She didn't care. She stared them down, looked for the TV cameras, let the strobes explode in her face.

"You tell that bastard where I am," she said, the words slow and deliberate. "You print it in big fat letters. Show it bold on everyone's TV screen. I want him to know *exactly* where I am. You tell him I'm waiting for him." A tear slid down her cheek. "Do you hear me? Tell him I'm waiting." Ray wrapped an arm around her waist. "I'm waiting for him!" And dragged her through the door. "I'm waiting!"

"What are you going to do?"

"You gonna kill him?"

"Are you going to kill him, Miss Gray?"

Ray kicked the door shut.

"Let me go. Let me go!" She twisted, but Ray held her fast.

"I'm not letting you go, short stack." His strong arms wrapped around her. "So stop struggling." He held her head to his chest, and the flat plane absorbed her moans. "Stop," he said low and quiet. "Just... stop."

And as if he knew, as if he'd crawled inside her pathetic brain and tormented heart, and knew what she needed, he held her close. She collapsed against him and sobbed. He shushed and soothed and rocked her while the hard tears fell. And true to his word, he held on.

39

The phone woke her at eight the next morning. She was on the bed, fully clothed. A fully clothed Ray was spooned around her. For half a second she was disoriented; then the phone rang again, and the events of the night before rolled over like a heavy stone. Ray stirred, groaned, instinctively pulled her closer, his strong arms around her like a shield, hard and unyielding. A third ring. Ray reached over to the nightstand, where his cell phone—which she'd have given her eyeteeth for last night—sat.

"Pearce," he said. His shirttails hung loose over his khakis, both wrinkled and abused from holding her all night long.

She closed her eyes. Sat up. Braced her arms against the side of the bed, legs dangling. God, she had to stop this. Stop leaning on him. He'd only get the wrong idea.

"Yes, sir," he said into the phone. "She's here."

A tap on her shoulder and the phone was silently passed to her.

"Gillian?" It was her grandfather. "Are you somewhere where you can talk?"

She looked around the room, saw Ray watching her in

that concerned way, then slide his gaze away as though he knew he shouldn't. He disappeared into the bathroom, and a few moments later she heard the toilet flush and the water go on.

"What's wrong?" she said into the phone.

Her grandfather paused. "How do you know something is wrong?"

"No one calls at eight in the morning unless something is wrong."

Another hesitation. Gillian thinned her lips, waiting. Had there been a fourth murder? God, no, please. Her whole body went rigid with denial and expectation.

"I got a call from Tom Petrie an hour ago."

She stopped breathing. "The mayor called? Well, aren't we all lah-di-dah and refined."

Chip was better at ignoring her sarcasm than Genevra would have been. "I'm the head of the Board of Trustees at the museum," he explained levelly.

"The museum?" She let out a tense breath.

"He's asked me to put a motion before the board."

She tensed again. Asked cautiously, "What kind of motion?"

"He wants to close the show, Gillian."

She sucked in a breath, stared into the distance. Of course he does.

"I've called an emergency meeting in an hour," Chip continued. "I just . . . I wanted to let you know."

"Are you going to support the motion?"

The third silence of the morning. Finally, "Yes. I don't believe we have another choice. Not after last night."

Her heart cracked. Three dead. Her fault.

"I'm sorry, Gillian. We have to think of the larger picture here."

"Thanks for the heads-up," she said.

"Gillian—"

But she didn't wait to hear whatever else he wanted to say. She snapped the phone closed, ending the call.

When she looked up, Ray was in the doorway watching her again. "Problem?"

Somewhere in the back of her head, she remembered him carrying her to the bedroom last night. Her weakness shamed her, her need for him shamed her.

She schooled her face into neutrality, her voice into unconcern. "No problem." She got up and pushed past him into the bathroom. Her face was a mess. Last night's tears had run her mascara, and her eyes were black-rimmed, her cheeks sooty. She turned on the faucet, leaned heavily against the vanity while she waited for the water to heat up. "The mayor just wants the museum to close the show."

He turned toward her, brows furrowed. "Can they do that?"

She soaked a washcloth, ran it over her face. "If the trustees agree, they can. Sure." She punched off the water, dried her face.

"But that's like saying Matthew Dobie is right. Like saying the killings are your fault."

Off to the side, she saw a disposable razor. For longer than she should have, she stared at the edge with its small, sharp blades. Her fingers grasped the vanity in a taut, white-knuckled grip. She wanted to bleed. Needed to.

But another hand closed around the razor, lifted it up and away. She met Ray's gaze in the mirror.

"It's not your fault," he said to her image. "Not. Your. Fault."

"Tell that to Margaret Pullman," her mouth said back to him. "Or Dawn Farrell. Or Linda Hayes." She hung her head, away from the sight of herself. "Oh, wait, you can't. They're dead."

"You're not responsible for what that maniac does. Not now. Not then."

Her head snapped up. "What's that supposed to mean?"

"You know damn well what it means. You were seven. You couldn't have protected her even if you'd tried."

"Now that's the pot calling the kettle black."

He frowned. "What?"

"You can't be on guard every second. People do what they have to. They always find a way."

His eyes narrowed dangerously. "Like this?" He held up the razor. "You're telling me no matter what I do you're going to cut into yourself?"

"No, Ray. I don't do that anymore. I don't have to. If I want to hurt myself, I take a picture. I take a goddamn picture."

She rushed out of the bathroom before the tears could explode. Made it as far as the chair she'd used the night before to escape. Then her knees wobbled, and she sank into it, clinging to the sides because she was trembling.

Why was it always someone else who died?

She closed her eyes, despising the tremors coursing through her shoulders.

"Is there going to be an announcement?" The gentleness was back in Ray's voice. The quiet strength that always seemed to steady her.

"At the museum's board meeting this morning."

"We can go. Talk them out of it."

She opened her eyes, stared dully at the room. Vaguely,

she wondered if Ray, in all his planning and plotting, had brought her a change of clothes.

"This is going to be devastating for the museum," she said at last.

"Bad for them? What about you?"

"I don't depend on the kindness of strangers. They do."

"What does that mean?"

"They're a new museum, Ray, with no permanent collection. They use traveling shows. Censorship is a big crime in the art world, and closing a show is bound to be seen that way. This one in particular was put together by the Brooklyn Museum of Art, one of the most prestigious in the country. It will be hard to get anyone to work with them after this."

"Fuck 'em," Ray said. "They're fucking you."

She cut a glance his way. His callousness surprised her. But when she saw his big, solid frame filling the bathroom doorway, she understood that his heartlessness wasn't the inbred kind. His anger was for her.

She turned away. Why couldn't he be less beautiful? Less available? Less there for her?

She jerked to her feet, suddenly sick of the grief and the guilt. "You're right." She flung open the closet to see if she'd be wearing the clothes she'd slept in to the board meeting. "They are."

If anyone was going to be cold-hearted on her behalf, it wasn't going to be Ray Pearce.

Chip put down the phone after talking to Gillian and looked out into space, not seeing the room. His chest was heavy.

Grimly, he thought about another call he should make. That one, too, felt like a stone dragging him down. But it was a familiar weight.

He felt in his pocket for the number, ran the scrap of paper between his fingers. This time, he wasn't sure what the right thing was. But he suspected it wouldn't be the easy thing. Not for Gillian. And certainly not for Genevra.

Still unsure, he rose and went to find his wife.

Though she wasn't attending the board meeting, she was nearly dressed. Impeccably, as always.

"You shouldn't have gotten up," he murmured.

"I thought we could have breakfast together." But he knew she didn't care about coffee and toast, which was all she ate anyway. A bare piece of bread, not even buttered. She wanted to bolster him, make sure he kept his resolve.

He remembered her when she had a few pounds on her bones. She was born to be soft and curved, a lovely, feminine, pampered creature. But she'd been fired in tragedy, tempered by grief, and now she was a polished bar of iron, gleaming but hard.

"You're staring at me, Charles."

"Am I?" He ought to look away, but he didn't. Couldn't. He felt that paper again, hidden deep in his pocket.

And without him saying a word, she knew. The eyes that should have been soft were suddenly stark. "No," she said. "Absolutely no."

He drew her to the bed, sat down with her on the edge. Wrapped an arm around her. "We have to tell."

"I won't hear of it."

"It could be him."

"It isn't."

"Three murders, Gennie. Three women dead."

"He's weak and foul, but he'd never—"

"We don't know that. Not for sure."

She went rigid under his arm. Stiff and unyielding. "I will never forgive you, Charles. Never."

And he believed her.

40

The emergency meeting of the Gray Visual Arts Center's Board of Trustees began at 9:00 AM sharp, a full hour earlier than the usual time. Chip Gray took a deep breath, absorbed the heightened energy of the room. At most meetings, the long conference table was barely half-full, other obligations often keeping members from attending. But today all seats were occupied. Even with extra folding chairs, people were standing.

In addition to the board members, the museum staff was well represented. Will Davenport, the director, stood next to the head curator, Stephanie Bower. Naturally sandy-haired, she'd appeared this morning as a brunette. When Will had commented on the change of hair color, she'd shrugged.

"Better safe than sorry," she'd said.

Chip looked around. Noted the other women. Not a blonde among them anymore. The realization sent a ripple of dread through him. Dread magnified by the packed room, which had a stuffed, weighty feel he didn't care for. Bad enough to have to do this at all, let alone in front of a crowd.

But he hadn't made millions without knowing how

to deliver bad news. He pounded his gavel for attention. "Thank you all for coming."

The group he addressed was diverse, comprising those, like himself, who had the income to make things happen, and those, like the teachers and community activists, who had the passion to carry plans out. His circle attended the Swan Ball, the others attended the Swine Ball. But they all had the museum and Nashville arts education in common. "I received a call from Mayor Petrie. In light of the"—he hesitated, not wanting to use the word "murders,"—"tragedies that have befallen our city and their connection to our current exhibit, he's asked us to close the show and remove the Gillian Gray photographs from view."

The room exploded into noise, and, once again, Chip had to resort to his gavel. "Gentlemen! Ladies! Please!"

"We're a privately funded organization," someone shouted. "City government has no authority here."

"This is a request only," Chip replied, also shouting and pounding his gavel. Finally, the noise subsided. "Look, as trustees," he continued, "we can deny or comply with the mayor's request. All he asks is that we take community safety into account and give the request a serious hearing."

A teacher at the Art House spoke. "Will closing this show affect the police investigation or stop whoever is doing this?" No one answered, and she continued. "In fact, doesn't this madman want power and publicity, and by closing the show we're giving him both?"

Nods and murmurs went around the room again.

"There is precedent," Will Davenport said. "Other Museums have canceled shows."

"First of all," Stephanie Bower said, "Other museums are in cities in a deeper arts tradition than Nashville. If we do this, we'll never see another show from BMA."

"A split with the Brooklyn Museum of Art is the least of our worries," said one of the older trustees, a banker.

Stephanie turned to him. "Not in the long run. Remember who we are." She looked around the room, caught people's eyes. "Since our own collection is still small and not enough to maintain us, we're forced to rely on other museums. And how do they look at us?"

"Rednecks," someone called out.

"Philistines," shouted someone else.

"Dukes of Hazzard," said a third.

Bower nodded. "Once we do this, every museum will think twice before agreeing to work with us."

Silence greeted this prediction. It had taken many long years to get the museum built, and suddenly it seemed as if all the hard work would be for nothing.

"But this is entirely different," Chip said with an air of mild astonishment. "Lives are at stake."

"Community pressure is community pressure," said a sculptor. "If we set this precedent, who knows what will be up for grabs next."

"We are a museum," Stephanie argued, "a place to experience art. If some crazy man twists that experience, we cannot be held accountable. Catching that person is the responsibility of the police, not the Gray Visual Arts Center."

Scattered applause broke out, along with grumblings and an angry buzz. People were glaring at each other across the table and across the room. Chip hammered the gavel again, opened his mouth to call for a motion to end discussion. A bustle at the door stopped him.

Without warning, Gillian stepped into the room.

The bickering ended as if it had been choked off. Everyone stared at the newcomer, who was shadowed by

Ray Pearce at her back. Between dinner and the meeting, he'd found some respectable clothes and now wore a dark suit and tie.

"May I speak?" Gillian asked, cool and polite, as if Chip didn't know what she was up to.

He tried to keep his face expressionless. He'd felt it his duty to tell her about the meeting. After all, she was his granddaughter. But he'd hoped she'd have the good sense to stay away. He should have known better. Gillian liked nothing more than a public scene.

"I don't think this is the time—"

"She has a right to speak," the sculptor said, and the banker glared at him.

Mumbling around the room ensued, some supporting Gillian's right to address the meeting, others shaking their heads.

Chip's jaw tightened. The unity of the board, of the museum itself, was shaky enough. They were already fighting among themselves. The last thing he needed was for Gillian to make some kind of a Custer's Last Stand, defending her position to keep the show open. But though he sorely would have liked to, he couldn't deny her the floor. Not in front of the other trustees.

"Of course," Chip said, but with a reluctance he couldn't hide.

Gillian took a breath, stared everyone, including her grandfather, down. The girl had guts, he'd give her that. Not to mention her grandmother's steely eyes.

"Before you decide anything," she said, "I'd like you to know that I'm withdrawing my work from the exhibit."

A collective gasp, and the room burst into sound, everyone talking at once. For his part, Chip was so astounded, he didn't know what to say.

Gillian held up her hands. "I've already spoken with—" She had to shout over the racket, and finally Chip pounded his gavel again.

"Gentlemen! Ladies!"

"I've already spoken with BMA," she repeated when quiet had prevailed, "and explained the situation. They've agreed to allow the photographs to be crated and stored, either here or in Chicago, where the exhibit is scheduled next. And I've agreed to cover any extra costs."

Once again, whispers and mumblings began, but this time in approval and relief. Gillian looked around the room, ending on her grandfather's face. Her eyes softened, and all at once she reminded him of his beautiful Holland, his lost child. Tears suddenly stung his eyelids, and he had to look away. Clear his throat.

Did Gillian see his difficulty? He couldn't be sure, but she gave him time to recover by turning back to the meeting and speaking. "And, since I'm sure some of you are involved with the hospital fund-raiser, I think you should know that I've withdrawn from the art auction as well. And, I will, of course, stay home Saturday night." She smiled tightly. "That's all I wanted to say." She made a curt little bow and disappeared through the doorway.

Gillian closed the door behind her and paused in the hallway, leaning against the wall, her eyes closed. She was shaking and needed a minute to recuperate.

A touch on her shoulder, and she opened her eyes. Ray stood in front of her. He caressed her cheek, raised her chin to stare up at him.

"Sure you want to do this?"

She wanted to sink into his hand, revel in the comfort

he seemed so willing to give. But she turned her head to loosen his hold. "Don't."

For a moment he stood there like a fool, his hand in the air. But he was tired of stepping in and being pushed aside. She started to move away, but he wrenched her back. Pushed her against the wall and caged her there, a hand on either side of her. "Why not? Because you're so tough?"

"Because it wouldn't mean anything to some guys, and you're not one of them."

He could smell the soap on her, the sweat and sex washed away as thoroughly as yesterday's tears. A little laser of regret slashed through him, but he shrugged it off, more angry than nostalgic. "Are you saying I can't love 'em and leave 'em?"

"I'm saying you're the love-'em type, Ray. And I'm the type that leaves."

He stared at her. At her hard chin and doomed eyes. He was sick of falling for someone who needed him but didn't want him. Someone he could never make happy. And like a film rewinding at top speed, he backed off. Way off.

He held up both hands, and she pushed away from the wall. "Anyway," she said, moving down the hallway, "it takes the pressure off the museum. It's the right thing to do."

He watched her straight back and determined stride. "You always take the hard road, don't you?"

She turned, continued backward down the hall, shooting him a small, rueful smile. "I try, Ray. I try."

41

Jimmy Burke stared at the murder board in the squad room. The place smelled of long-dead biscuits, gravy, and fried okra. Some kind of breakfast for someone who was no longer there. Or maybe it was dinner. With the overtime and the overlap, schedules were out the window. But though the department had laid on the manpower, so far the extra poundage hadn't stopped the flow of victims or uncovered a connection between them.

For the moment, he was alone. He stared at the crime-scene photographs taped to the whiteboard, at the marks and slashes delineating questions, theories, statistics. He'd been staring at the damn thing for the last half hour, and the victims still had nothing in common.

The first was divorced, the second single, the last married, though her husband had been away at the time of the murder. Ages ranged from sixteen to fifty. Attacks happened at work, home, and on the street. A map showed locations getting closer to downtown, but in vastly different areas of the city, so whether or not the killer was closing in on a specific target, like the museum, was anyone's guess. None of the victims knew Gillian Gray, and they had nothing in common except their blond hair.

Now women were wearing scarves, wigs, and staying indoors when they could, but predicting the next strike was near on impossible.

Since the first victim, they'd been tracking the dozens of messages off deadshot.com. And there were still only three that could be connected to the murders. Each one closely followed a killing and was sent from the victim's own machine, either computer or cell phone. Off to one side, someone had tacked up the three Web site messages, each enlarged and on a separate sheet of paper.

I MAKE IT REAL.

MAKE IT REAL WITH ME.

CHEATERS NEVER PROSPER. THEY DIE.

Who was sending them? At the moment, the assistant seemed to be in the clear, though a phone call to her Manhattan apartment and Gray's Brooklyn studio had gone unanswered. Kenny Post was still MIA, which put him top of the list. But there was also the unsub from the 1986 murder of Holland Gray.

Jimmy had pulled the old files and gone over them. He'd talked to the cold-case guys, and also Harley Samuels. He'd passed the files on to some of the other guys. No new leads emerged. Just the vague uneasiness that whoever had done the mother was now after the daughter.

Why the long lead time? The favorite theory was that the unsub had been in jail and was newly released. So far, though, they hadn't found anyone whose dates matched.

The news had reported Gillian Gray's makeshift press conference three nights ago. Jimmy wondered how the hell Ray could have let her get away with that, but then Jimmy knew how Ray was with his women. Pliable. In any case, the damage was done and Gray's location made public. Saying they couldn't provide protection without client cooperation, Carleco Security had dropped the case.

He'd expected Gray to pick up and leave. But she hadn't.

He wondered what ole Ray was up to. Though they'd have to hold Jimmy's dick over a flame to get him to admit it, he wouldn't have minded a little of Ray's smarts right about now.

Because Jimmy kept circling back to the same thing. If the victims were substitute Gillian Grays, and the creep was after the real thing, why not give it to him?

Gillian frowned at the blowup of the photograph she'd taken at the lake behind Harley's cabin. She was in the basement of her grandparents' house, where she'd set up a small studio years ago. Remnants of her early work still hung from beams and posts. Stuff she'd done when she was seventeen. Huge black-and-white pictures of her palm, the life line scratched and hand tinted red. Close-ups of the scars on her arms. All experiments with film and color, light and shadow.

It had been ages since she'd been down here, but now she was back, reunited with her Nikon and her portable digital scanner. The camera hung from a hook on one of the posts in case she got a fast urge to shoot something. The scanner sat on a board between a stack of cinder blocks. She perched on a stool in front of a huge drawing board, and the lake stared back at her.

She wondered what Harley would say if she asked him for permission to do a piece back there. Her shoots were massive events—more like movie shoots—with large, intricate sets and dozens of crew members, including grips, best boys, lighting technicians, set builders, set dressers, carpenters, propmasters, wardrobe, and all their various assistants. The eight-by-ten color negatives she shot ended up as giant digital chromogenic prints, often more than seven feet wide.

She smiled, imagining that Harley would not care to put up with the disturbance to his routine.

Not that she'd get that far. At least not if she couldn't figure out what was wrong with the lake shoot. She set the photograph aside and pulled out a tracing of the blowup. She used this to play with composition, move components around, add set pieces or take them away. Heavy black lines on the white paper indicated trees, shoreline, and dock in simplified shapes. What looked like a crime-scene outline of a body stood in for victim, whom she'd placed diagonally on the shore, ankles still in the water. Gillian wanted her on her back, grit and pebbles on the dead girl's face, eyes open to the silent, uncaring sky. But something felt out of sync. Maybe if she twisted the body more?

She sketched in a new position. Stood back and gave it a critical look. That unsatisfied feeling still nagged at her.

Picking up the pencil again, she began reshading the contours of the corpse and the shore. Her hand moved in desultory fashion, and as if it had a mind of its own, a crude figure appeared beneath her pencil.

She stared at it. Peoplewise, she'd never had more than herself in a photograph.

She filled in the figure. A man. It was a man. Her heart began to pound.

Frantic, she scrambled for the three-by-fives she'd printed off the digital camera. Found what she was looking for, blew it up until the figure was big enough to excise. She grabbed the X-Acto, and with a few deft strokes, slashed it out.

Her cautious, trembling fingers placed the figure on the sketch. Standing on the shore over the dead body. Watching. Always watching.

Ray.

She wanted Ray in that photograph.

The shock of recognition hit her like a tidal wave, and she jerked to her feet, an instinctive reaction of denial. She yanked his picture away. Stared at the tracing paper sketch. Slowly, put him back in.

She hadn't seen him for two days. Not since the board meeting. Carleco had washed its hands of her, and so, it seemed, had Ray.

Well, she could hardly blame him. She practically threw him out the door.

She moved the picture of him slightly, testing the effect. It was the photo she'd taken of him that first day on the grounds. He was wearing his dark, G-man suit. He looked sober and a little annoyed but trying not to show it. She smiled. So very Ray.

An unwanted stab of regret went through her.

Thank God, her cell phone rang. Glad of the interruption, she grabbed it.

"Miss Gray? Detective Burke. Got a minute? I have a proposition I think will strike your fancy."

She couldn't imagine the hulking Detective Burke could have anything of interest to tell her, but listening to him was better than moping about someone else.

It didn't take Burke long. A few seconds, and she understood what he wanted from her. She clutched the phone, unable to stop the thrill that shivered through her.

"I'll do it," she said, cutting him off in midsentence. "I'll do it."

42

Ray poured himself a cup of coffee from the pot he'd just made in the kitchen. Taking it with him, he wandered into what was supposed to be a dining area, but which only consisted of a small table and a couple of chairs. In lieu of pulling one out, he arced a leg over the back and plopped down, a familiar shortcut. The paper sat on top of the table, still stuffed like a sausage in its blue plastic casing. He stared at it a minute, knowing it could make up the meat of his morning, on this the fifth day of his self-styled vacation.

Neither Landowe nor Coleman had ratted him out to Carlson, and since the company had already walked away from the Grays after the press conference fiasco, Carlson didn't protest too loudly when Ray asked for time off. He hadn't said so, but he thought he'd take the time to assess his possessions, figure out how long it would take him to pack everything up, and create a game plan for getting the hell out of Nashville.

Except it was days later, and all he'd done was take a single desultory walk around the house. Or cruise by the Gray mansion and check that the squad car he'd pushed Jimmy on when Carlson dropped the case was still keeping vigil. He felt like Hamlet trapped in the middle of to be or not to be. Shit or get off the pot, Ray, he told himself. Make like the wind and blow.

The clichés rolled on and on, and still he did nothing. Just picked up the paper, pulled it free of its housing, and began to read.

The stories above the fold were split between the progress of the police investigation into what reporters were calling the Dead Shot murders (none), and a proposed budget increase for the city's schools (plenty). But a sidebar below the fold caught his attention: GRAY TO ATTEND CHARITY ART AUCTION.

He read the piece with growing amazement and concern. Gillian had withdrawn from the hospital fund-raiser. Now, in the middle of a killing spree, she had changed her mind?

What the hell was she thinking?

He dropped the paper, shot up, grabbed his phone from the kitchen counter, where he'd left it on his way to coffee, and punched in Gillian's number. Just as quickly, he snapped the phone closed.

No. Not his problem anymore.

He shoved the phone in his pocket.

Returning to the table and the paper, he opened the sports page. The lead story was about a shake-up in Predator management and what that might mean to the hockey team. He tried to focus on the first paragraph, but the words swam in front of him.

Staring off into space, he pictured Gillian entering the hotel. Would her grandparents be with her? Or would she be unescorted and unguarded?

Damn, damn, damn.

He yanked out the phone and entered another number.

Before the receptionist could finish saying, "Can I help you?" he asked to speak to Carlson.

"You handling the security for the charity art auction tomorrow night?" He spoke before Carlson could finish identifying himself.

"Ray?"

"Yeah, it's me."

"I thought you were taking some time off."

"That's right."

"So event security shouldn't be on your mind."

"Are you handling it?"

"No. Why? What's going on?"

"Who is?"

"No one, far as I can tell. Whatever the hotel provides."

"You're kidding."

"No, Ray, I'm not. What's this all about?"

"You're going to let her walk in there unprotected?"

"Who are we talking about here?"

"Gillian Gray."

A pause. "My understanding was Miss Gray wouldn't be attending the auction."

"She is now. Front page *Tennessean* below the fold." Carlson always kept a copy of the paper in his office. Ray waited for him to scan the article.

"Uh-huh," Carlson said. "So?"

"So what are you going to do about it?"

"Nothing." Carlson sounded completely unconcerned. "You and I both know the woman won't protect herself or let us protect her properly. She's a walking time bomb. I don't want Carleco Security anywhere near her when she explodes. Besides, if I remember right, you said she was a pain in the ass, and you were glad to get rid of her."

Had he said that? He thought back.

"Right," Ray said. "Thanks." He ended the call. He *was* glad to be rid of her.

He reread the article. It not only mentioned the hotel in which the event was being held, but it also mentioned the specific ballroom. It was like giving the killer an address.

This time, he forced himself to stay on the line until Gillian answered.

"What the hell is wrong with you?"

"Well, Ray Pearce, nice talking to you, too."

"Did you see that article in the paper?"

"The one the police planted?"

"What?"

"The police. They worked with the paper to get it in."

"The police put you up to this?"

"Well, they didn't exactly bring me along kicking and screaming."

"That article is like putting a big fat target on your back."

"That's the idea, Ray. And a brilliant one, too, even if it was your pal Burke's."

"Jesus H. Christ."

"Now, Ray, don't be like—"

But Ray had already hung up and called Burke. "What the hell do you think you're doing?"

"I'm having me a cup of coffee, Ray. What's it to you?"

"You're going to get her killed."

"Get who—ohhh, you saw the piece in the paper."

"You're damn right I did."

"Slow down there, baby boy. She'll be wearing a wire. You know the drill. She'll be fine."

"Fine? She's going in alone. That's the way it's done."

"But we've got her back."

"My ass. You locate Kenny Post yet?"

"No, but—"

"You find a connection to her mother's murderer?"

"We're looking, but—"

"Truth is, you got nothing, Burke. Bupkis. Zilch. Which means the killer could be anyone. Anyone. By the time you get there, he could have her inside a plastic bag and suffocated, and you know it. And by tomorrow, Benton James will get another picture in his e-mail."

In another room, over a different cup of coffee, Maddie Crane also saw the article about the gala art auction. Shock mingled with concentration as she read it. Time, place. It was all there, practically a written invitation.

From the bathroom, Maddie heard the shower turn on. She gazed hard at the closed door, thinking about who was behind it. What would happen if anyone found out.

So like Gillian to splash her whereabouts all over the front page. Had she done it on purpose, or had some overzealous reporter done it for her? Every news station in the country had run tape on the midnight press conference, so Maddie had seen it. Probably on purpose.

Pushing her cup away, Maddie sat back. Needed to think. But the sound of the rushing water intruded. She remembered what she'd done the night before, and with whom. A flush of heat shimmered through her.

She focused on the paper, which sat like a roadside bomb waiting to be detonated. Gillian had provided the perfect opportunity. What was Maddie going to do about it?

* * *

Matthew Dobie tapped the morning newspaper thoughtfully, then allowed himself to be distracted by the muscular blond packing literature into a box for shipping.

The young man, sensing his idol's sudden attention, straightened. Squirmed charmingly with embarrassment. "Everything all right, sir?"

Dobie didn't like to admit he played favorites, but there was something about this one. Maybe it was the way his arms rippled as he arched over the cardboard. Or the strength and purpose of his jawline as he concentrated. Or that cleft in his chin. Whatever it was, Dobie couldn't help but appreciate it and had rewarded the boy with extra tasks. Tasks that would keep him close. Like packing up their mobile headquarters.

"Of course," Dobie said with a dismissive wave. "Continue."

"Yes, sir."

The young man bent back over the packing materials, and Dobie tore his gaze away. Now that Gillian Gray had withdrawn her photographs from the Gray Center, he'd almost won, and though he'd claimed victory loudly and clearly on as many networks as possible, there were still a few things left to do. It might be a cold day in hell before any reputable museum agreed to exhibit a Gillian Gray photograph, but he hadn't prevented her from creating them. And the article proved he hadn't stopped her from exhibiting either.

Once again, his eyes strayed to the young man's wide shoulders, and Dobie gave in to the urge to touch. He rose, came around the desk, and put his palm on the hard muscle.

"What's your name, son?"

The blond giant turned, stood at attention. "David, sir." He flushed, and Dobie repressed a smile.

"Take a break, David. Sit down." He pulled a chair to the desk for him, then went back to his own. "Have you seen this?" He showed David the article. Watched as his powerful neck turned a mottled red.

"I can't believe this." He looked up, indignation and outrage plain on his handsome face. "We should do something."

Dobie was enjoying the play of emotions in the younger man's eyes, so he encouraged it. "Do you think so?"

"Yes, sir. Absolutely."

This time, Dobie let the smile come, a slow, wide, satisfied smile. He reached out and lightly touched David's strong, powerful fingers. "You know," he said, "I was thinking the same thing."

43

That night, Gillian arrived at the downtown hotel to the sound of shouting. Hotel lights brightened the dark, but the black air split into a deafening clamor as protesters caught sight of her. Enclosed behind police sawhorses, they lined the walk up to the entrance. Their rabid faces and hate-filled eyes glared at her. Mouths twisted in loathing.

"Murderer!"

"God hates you!"

Her heart thudded in time to the chanted beat.

"De-cen-cy! De-cen-cy!"

The steady drumming was like an army of foot soldiers on the march.

Someone lurched over the barricade to wave a threatening fist at her. A uniformed officer rushed to beat him back. Another grabbed her arm and hurried her to the entrance.

"Why didn't you come the back way?" he shouted over the thunder.

Because she never took the back way. But it was too dark and too noisy to explain. She thanked him and slipped inside. Paused to steady the racket inside her chest.

People stared—bellmen, hotel guests—but she squared her shoulders and went to find the ballroom.

Her grandparents were huddled together just outside the door waiting for her. Like most of the women of her generation, Genevra wore a sequined jacket and long dress, while Chip wore his tuxedo. Gillian had on lavender again. A distressed velvet gown with a low neck that scooped her shoulders, skimmed her waist, and covered her arms.

"You look like something from the rag pile," Genevra said.

"Yes, but the color matches my eyes," Gillian replied.

She hadn't told either of them about the side trip she took to police headquarters or the arrangement she and Burke had worked out. First of all, they'd only try and talk her out of it, and second, she didn't want them breathing down her neck. But both of them had been baffled by her change of heart.

"I still don't think this is a good idea," Chip said.

"It's a terrible idea," Genevra replied, straightening her back and raising her chin. "Why else would Gillian want to do it?"

"You're not also going to change your mind about the museum?" Chip asked.

"No, that's a done deal," Gillian assured him, and in an effort to assure herself, she smoothed down her dress. Beneath it, she felt the vague outline of the transmitter taped to her skin.

Genevra inhaled. "Well, if we're going in, we'd better go." Like she was a member of the Light Brigade preparing to charge the enemy.

The ballroom was awash in Nashville glitterati. As Gillian and her grandparents wended their way across, business cronies of her grandfather high-fived him from across the room with highballs in their hands. A few of her grandmother's sequined compadres stopped to compliment her on the bash. A band played "All or Nothing at All," and Gillian looked around at the fat-cat crowd. Hard to believe a killer might be walking among them. The most threatening activity in this group was overeating.

But Gillian could still feel the deadly pulse of the crowd outside. Would Ruth be there again, disguised as a housemaid? Would Matthew Dobie send someone else? Would whoever it was do more than pull a prank with fake blood? Her gaze moved constantly, seeking out other possibilities. The waitstaff. Kitchen staff. Hotel staff. Must be a dozen ways to sneak in. She closed her eyes, heard the swish of a snare drum, and it seemed to match the rustle of her heart. She breathed, shook off the nerves, screwed down her resolve. Matthew Dobie or the mob, the mob or the monster, whatever was out there, she was ready.

And so was Nashville PD. They were in the room, though she didn't exactly know where. But Burke had promised, and she'd taken him at his word.

Not that rescue was high on her list. She knew what she was in for. Had known since she was seven. It was just a matter of getting the stars to align themselves. She hadn't thought to check the sky on her way in. City lights tended to obscure the planets, but, who knew, maybe tonight she'd get lucky.

She shivered with anticipation just as the band finished their song with a flourish, and the three of them reached their table. Since Genevra had chaired the event, and Chip was a major donor, it was centrally placed.

Or had the police arranged that?

A woman with pale green feathers circling her neck

tapped the mike. "Our totals are starting to move, so make sure you don't miss out. In the last ten minutes, the *Red Grooms* piece has had two new bids. It's all going for a great cause—"

"My living room," someone said from the floor, and everyone laughed.

"Not if I beat you to it," the MC said. More laughter.

The sound felt alien, threatening, its complacency disastrous. Around her, smiling faces stretched into distortion, like in a fun-house mirror. Stupid people. Didn't they know that tragedy was laughing, too? But not with them.

The band began again, another Lawrence Welk tune.

"I'm taking a walk around," Gillian told her grandparents, the announcement also for her invisible watchers.

"Really, Gillian, dear, it would be so much better if you stayed here."

"You mean hide my notorious face?"

"What your grandmother means is—"

"I know what she means," Gillian said softly, and with uncharacteristic warmth, squeezed Genevra's shoulder. "I'll be fine. No scenes. No public displays. I promise."

"Genevra, honey, don't you look a picture." A pudgy woman in a spangly top descended on the table, and before anyone could protest further, Gillian slipped away.

No way could she just sit there. Besides, people were watching out for her. It was creepy not knowing who or where they were. She never thought she'd want the Carleco guys back, but at least they were the devil she knew.

She crossed to the rim of the ballroom. The paintings and sculptures were displayed at the edges, giving the room's dark middle a furtive glow. She'd heard the committee had drafted someone from the Gray Center to help. This kind of thing was often put together in slapdash fashion that didn't show the art off at its best. But someone had done a decent job here.

Her own photograph was adequately lit and spaced between other pieces. She stared at it. It was a private piece, one she'd done years ago, that Genevra had always liked. It showed a corner of the estate in fading summer twilight. Grass and trees in fairy light. It had no point of view, except glossiness, was pure pabulum as far as Gillian was concerned, an interesting exercise at best. But it was always the one Genevra brought up to rebuke her with.

"Why can't you do more pictures like that?" she'd ask.

When Genevra had twisted her arm about donating something to the auction, Gillian had dug it out from the back of a storage cabinet in her studio.

The chair of the art committee had been relieved when Gillian had pulled the picture and unenthusiastic about accepting it back. In the end, Genevra's standing or Chip's dollars must have won out because she reluctantly agreed to include it without the police getting involved.

Gillian checked the bid books. Each piece had one associated with it. At the top was the starting bid. Below, dollar amounts rose in predetermined increments, with room for bidders to sign their names, thereby "outbidding" the name prior to theirs.

The piece next to hers started at five thousand dollars and rose by five hundred. Bids on her photograph began at fifteen thousand and rose in increases of five thousand. Nothing like infamy to hike up the price of gas. Four names were listed. No accounting for taste. But it was a nice chunk of change for the hospital.

Someone bumped into her, and she started, her heart racing. But it was only a woman looking at the photo. Geez, she had to stop jumping like that.

"Sorry," the other woman said. And in the next moment, she colored. "Oh—you're Gillian Gray."

Though she shouldn't be, Gillian was always a little surprised when people recognized her.

The woman was a few years older, her expensively highlighted hair smoothed beneath a black velvet and diamond band. She wore a cocktail dress, a strand of seed pearls, a thin gold watch. Private school sorority sister.

Gillian shot her a tight smile. "That's right."

"And this is your—"

"Right again."

The woman looked from her to the picture and back again. She clearly didn't know what to say.

Gillian helped her out. "Not what you expected?"

"It's very, uh..."

"Boring?"

The woman gave an embarrassed laugh. "Pretty," she supplied, then excused herself.

Gillian let out a breath. She would have settled for boring. At least it was honest.

Her eyes swept the room. Everyone seemed equally nonthreatening. Then why the film of sweat coating the back of her neck? Why so jittery?

"Gillian."

Another jolt of her heart, which she rapidly quelled.

She turned to find her grandmother approaching. "I saw you talking with Bailey Fawcett. You didn't say anything—"

"Dirty?"

"Provocative." Genevra frowned. "She's on the board of the Junior League. When I was sick last year, she brought over a casserole."

"Cook it herself?"

"Really, Gillian, I have no idea."

Gillian sighed. She hadn't known her grandmother had been sick. She didn't know Genevra could get sick. She wasn't human that way. The thought of it, of Genevra in bed, weak enough to need someone else's poppy seed chicken, shook Gillian's world a little. "I didn't know you were sick," she said, her voice smaller than she would have liked.

Genevra waved her concern away. "It was nothing. A little . . . a cold."

Gillian looked at her suspiciously. "A cold doesn't merit a casserole," she said. "Even if you do buy it. Or have the cook prepare it."

"Have it your way." Her lips compressed into a thin line. "You always do." Genevra left, and Gillian watched her retreat. Spine straight, shoulders back. For the first time in—well, for the first time ever—she imagined a universe without her. And it was like a wall had suddenly collapsed. Something solid and hard that had kept the world at bay, all at once, was gone.

She hurried after her. "Grandmother. Grandmother!"

"What is it?" The sharp question was a hissed reprimand, her gaze making sure no one else had seen her granddaughter break decorum in such unladylike fashion.

But now that she had her, Gillian didn't know why she'd stopped her. "You're all right now?" she asked. Lamely.

Genevra's gaze narrowed. Briefly, her eyes softened, then iced over again. "It was pneumonia," she said crisply, "and I'm perfectly well."

Gillian swallowed. "I'm . . . I'm glad."

"Thank you." She nodded regally. Their eyes held for a moment longer; then she was gone.

How strange to find out she cared for her grandmother on the same night she might never see her again.

Through the wide picture windows across the street, he watched the ballroom shine. Up where he was, the night air was dark and cool, but behind the hotel windows the light gleamed warm and golden.

He knew she was there. Everyone knew. Like them, he'd seen the newspapers, the news clips. He thought her brave to show her face at all, let alone at such a fancy party. He pictured her there, small and chastened. Withered in humiliation. He'd heard her enemies declare victory. They all hated her. All but him.

How could he hate her? He wanted to be her. Wave to the cameras. Nod to reporters. See his face on *Entertainment Tonight.*

It would happen. He'd already got the whole city talking about him. Got them to take down her pictures. That was strength. That was power.

Soon, he'd free her from her disgrace. Immortalize her, like he had the others.

He smiled at what he was going to do for her, his eyes stinging from staring so hard. But it was like TV, watching the party through the window. Real and not real. If only he could reach out and feel her skin beneath his fingers. So pale. So soft. The thought of touching her sent a hot shiver through him.

Soon, he would have her.

Soon, he would know what she felt like.

Mouth dry with anticipation, he felt an urge he couldn't resist. Through his pants, he began to stroke himself. And watch the people in their pricey clothes yammer and fawn.

He was always watching. It was what he did. What he liked doing.

Thinking about them. All those useless pretty people who thought they ran things.

But he ran things. He made it happen. Life. Death. It was in his hands.

Excitement hardened him, and he reached inside, licked his palm, made himself wet, then wetter, and stroked harder.

He would wait until she stopped kicking. Stopped struggling. They all struggled at first. Until they saw what a release it was to stop. That it was so much easier when they stopped.

She would stop, and he would place her. Frame her.

He stroked faster, panting at the images in his head.

He would frame her in his own design.

He would stand over her and shoot her. Over and over again.

And then, when he couldn't help himself, when it felt too good to help himself, then he'd come. All over her. All over that pale, soft skin. He gritted his teeth. Fuck, he said in his head. F-f-fuck her.

And with a grunt, he climaxed in his hand.

44

In the shadows of the ballroom, Ray tensed as Gillian circulated around the room.

Out of professional courtesy, or maybe for old times' sake, he told Burke he'd be there. And when his ex-partner made the standard protests—you don't work here anymore, you're a civilian, you'll get in the way—Ray called in his marker.

"I never asked a thing from either you or Nancy when it came to taking care of your father. He shows up in the middle of the night, I drop what I'm doing and handle it. So I figure you owe me, Jimmy, and now you can pay up. If there's trouble, I'll be there. If there isn't, I'll still be there. You know damn well I won't get in the way. And one more pair of eyes can't hurt."

So he put on his spare monkey suit and drove to the hotel, parking three blocks away in a tight squeeze between a lemon-yellow Beetle and a van from a window-washing company.

He arrived an hour before the gala's scheduled start time and half an hour before Burke's team showed. It would have been nice if this bash was at the same hotel he'd stayed in with Gillian. But it wasn't. So he'd memorized the new hotel's floor plan from blueprints Carleco had on file and used the extra time to scout the layout in person. He plotted escape routes from four different angles, then found a corner that gave him access to most of the room but would keep him hidden. And he spotted Burke's people—two men and a woman. The guys in rented tuxes, the woman in a long blue thing with puffy sleeves. All three looked like rejects from last year's prom.

At some point they caught each other's eyes, the only sign of acknowledgment or accommodation they made to each other. Truth was, they came at this from opposite sides of the same coin. They were there to catch the bad guy, and if Gillian got hurt in the process, they were still a step ahead. He was there to keep her safe, and if the bad guy got caught, that was gravy.

When Gillian finally entered the room, she looked her own offbeat, sexy self, and despite his promise to keep the emotions at bay, he felt winded when he caught his first glimpse of her in a week.

She looked healthy enough. Fuck it, she looked beautiful. The back of her hair was pinned up, as it had been that first time at the museum—blowsy and tangled, like she'd just got up from a wild round of sex. Like she'd looked after the wild round of sex with him. Eyes glittery, cheeks flushed.

Not like she was pining away for him. No way, no how.

He cursed under his breath and wanted to look away, but he couldn't. Not if he was going to ensure she survived the night. It sucked having to stare at her, sucked and took his breath away, but there it was.

He maintained his post for the entire opening meet and greet, while the men drank their scotch and the women their white wine. He saw Gillian move to the room's perimeter to check the art display and scuttled along the wall to keep her in sight. Saw the blonde bump into her, saw the interchange with Genevra. Moved back when the band stopped and people sat down for dinner. Kept a suspicious eye on the servers coming and going from her table. Salad. Entrée. Dessert. Someone he'd never heard of, but who was announced as a CMA newcomer of the year nominee, performed a half-hour set, reminding the room in between songs to bid, bid, bid.

By the end of the evening, sweat was dripping down the back of his neck, but no one had approached Gillian or her table. He was beginning to think the night would be a bust when the MC for the evening returned to the stage to give the auction totals. She wore some kind of sparkled top with feathers at the neck, and he wondered about the rich and how they managed to walk out of the house like that. But the MC made a special point of introducing Gillian, who rose, a spotlight catching her.

Ray groaned silently at the way the light pinpointed her. Anyone in doubt as to where she was would have no trouble finding her now.

As if the universe read his thoughts, at that exact moment he spotted a blur of vertical movement among the seated crowd. He refocused his sight line and blinked for half a second, his mind telling him what he saw was impossible, but his eyes making it true.

Maddie. Maddie Crane. Witch's hair flying as she ran. Calling out.

"Kenny! Wait! Kenny!"

Heads turned, people muttered. The feather lady's patter faltered, and Ray got a clear look at who she was pursuing.

Kenny Post, dark hair long and straggly, eyes gleaming wildly.

Gillian backed away. Kenny raised an arm, reaching out. Was that a weapon in his hand?

45

Ray bolted, legs hurtling faster than speed. He yanked Gillian backward, pushed her violently out of the way. Hustled her back, back, back. Out of the corner of his eye, he saw Burke's team converge on the table. The woman in blue tackled Post, and he went down.

"We got him! We got him!"

More cries and gasps from the crowd. Someone screamed. Someone—Maddie?—shouted, "Don't hurt him!" But it was all in the distance now. He'd dragged Gillian out a side door, down a short hallway, and into the steaming busy kitchen. Pans clanged, water swooshed. A chef in a high white hat scolded them for being there. Then they were out the back of the kitchen and into the night.

"Wait! Wait a minute!" Gillian jerked away.

He pushed her up against the building's outer wall, shielded her with his body, and scanned the alley. Empty. Quiet. Safe.

He released her. His hands were shaking, and he calmed himself by breathing. And by drinking her in. She was alive. Safe.

"What are you doing?" she asked, anger and astonishment in her voice.

"Getting you the hell out of there. Are you all right?"

"No, I mean—what was that? Inside?" She shook her head, looked him up and down. "Why—what are you doing here? And Kenny. That was Kenny. And did I see Maddie?"

"Are you all right?"

She took in a breath. Nodded. He let a breath out, relieved.

Before he could answer her questions, his phone rang. Burke, wanting to know where they were and if Gillian was all right.

"In an alley on the northwest back of the building. And she's fine." In the background a woman's voice. "Let me talk to her. Let me talk to her!"

Maddie. Her voice abruptly cut off.

"What's going on?" Gillian asked, but he ignored her.

Jimmy said, "They're taking Post and the Crane woman away as we speak. Bring Gray in, and we'll retrieve the wire, get a statement."

But Gillian had already reached inside her dress and was yanking off the device. The tape didn't release easily, and she cursed while she freed herself.

"Gotta go," Ray said quickly, and disconnected. "Hold on," he said to her. "Hold on!"

"I want this thing off me!"

"All right. Jesus." He spun her around, unzipped her dress, then peeled the tape off. His hands still shook a little, and as he turned her to the front, they brushed against her breasts. He looked up. Their eyes met.

She licked her lips, and heat blasted him. Before he knew what was happening, their bodies leaned forward and their mouths met. The kiss was explosive and shivery. It seemed to rock the night. It sure rocked him.

But when it softened, sweetened, and finally ended,

Gillian looked down. She was breathless, shoulders heaving, but refused to look at him.

He stared out into the night.

Right.

He stepped behind her, and, with a quick jerk, zipped her up.

She lurched away. "My grandparents must be going nuts. And I want to see Maddie."

He pulled her back. "What are you talking about? You can't go in there. Burke's already informed your grandparents that you're okay. And Maddie won't be there."

"What? Where is she?"

"She's been taken into custody. Along with Post."

She squeezed her head as if that would make sense of the night. "Oh, my God. This is crazy. She can't—"

"She did, Gillian. A whole ballroom full of people saw her."

She yanked her arm away. "Saw her do what? All I saw her do was chase after that slimeball, Kenny Post. Not a crime as far as I know."

"What was she doing there? If she's so innocent, why wasn't she in New York like she was supposed to be?"

"I don't know," she said grudgingly.

"And if she's such a great friend, why didn't she tell you she was here?"

"I don't know! But I sure as hell want to hear the answer from her."

"She'll only lie to you."

"She doesn't lie! There's an explanation. I know there is."

"Jesus, and whatever she tells you, that's it? You just say, fine? Okay? Or is it going to be like Ruth at the museum—confrontation for its own sake."

"It's not them."

"What?"

"It's not them. The maniac doing this killing. It's not Kenny. And it's certainly not Maddie."

He stared at her, understanding dawning, if slowly. "Why? Because you don't want it to be them? Because then you'd have to give up on your life's crusade?"

She glared at him for half a second, then wheeled around and stalked off.

He caught her in two quick strides. Wrenched her back until they were practically nose to nose. "That's it, isn't it? No matter who gets caught doing what, you won't believe it unless it's your—what did Maddie call him? Oh, yeah, your bogeyman."

"I don't know what you're talking about."

"I think you do."

"Let me go."

"You know exactly what I'm talking about."

"Let me go!"

He released her, and the shift made her stumble back a step. She straightened, glared at him with deadly intent. "I still want to talk to her."

"Fine," he said sharply. "Burke wants you down at the station anyway."

"But first—my grandparents."

This recklessness was exactly why Carlson had declared hands off. And exactly why Ray had come back.

So, against his better judgment, despite the first rule of protective service, which was to get the protectee the hell out of there, he escorted her back to the ballroom.

When they got there, they found Genevra sitting in a lone chair at the back of the room. Chip and another tuxedo-clad man, who turned out to be a doctor attending the gala, were hovering over her. As Ray and Gillian walked up, the two men were trying to coax Genevra into taking a mild sedative.

"It will just relax you." Chip held out a glass of water.

Genevra slapped his hand away. "I'm as relaxed as I care to be." Then she saw Gillian.

In all the time Ray had known the older woman, he hadn't seen many of the softer emotions cross her face. But at her first glimpse of Gillian, she cried out, rose on wobbly legs, and threw her arms around her granddaughter.

The surprise was that Gillian clung to her in return.

"I'm all right," she said, stroking Genevra's back. "I'm fine."

He found himself sharing a mildly astonished look with Chip. Not that the softness lasted long. Not with the two of them.

"Well, of course you are." Genevra released Gillian and stepped back. She brushed a stray piece of lint from Gillian's dress. "Even if you do look like a ragamuffin," she said stiffly.

Gillian smiled. "One woman's ragamuffin, one man's sexy muffin." She leered at him, ice in her eyes.

He recalled the kiss in the alley, and his face heated. Genevra stilled, as if seeing him for the first time. She shot her husband an accusing look, then turned it on him. "What are you doing here? I understood your company had dropped out."

"He can't leave me alone," Gillian said. "It's the dress."

Genevra turned to Chip. "Was this your idea?"

Ray didn't understand the antagonism behind the question but interposed quickly anyway. "No," he said. "It was mine. I thought you might need a little extra protection tonight."

"He was right," Chip murmured to his wife.

Genevra paid no attention to him. "Well"—she made the word sound like a dismissal—"I think we can take over from here." She put an arm through Gillian's.

"I have to go down to the police station," Gillian said.

"That can wait until tomorrow."

"I want to see Maddie," she said quietly.

Genevra paused, frowned. Finally, she said, "We can take you, then."

Gillian gave her a gentle, knowing look. "I'm not going to let you do that. Much as he annoys me"—she elbowed Ray in the ribs—"Ray has a car and is familiar with the routine. I'll be fine."

Genevra glowered at him, and he wondered what the hell he'd done to piss her off so much. Could she tell just by looking that he had a major jones for her crazy granddaughter?

"I'll bring her back to you safely," he found himself saying.

"Yes," Genevra said tartly. "So you've said." She sighed. Turned to her husband. "I'm tired. Take me home."

46

Gillian sat on the edge of the chair in front of Detective Burke's desk. She was breathing fast and trying not to. She'd turned over the contraption they'd taped to her. She'd made a written statement and signed it. But so far, she hadn't been able to see Maddie.

Ray had promised to talk to Burke about that, but he'd also made no guarantees. And he'd already been gone twenty minutes. Was it good news or bad that it was taking so long?

Truth was, he'd been right in the alley. She didn't want it to be Kenny. Or Maddie. It had to be the monster. She tightened her fingers around the edge of her seat. Had to.

When Ray returned, his eyes were grim, his mouth taut—signs that Burke hadn't gone down easy.

"Okay," he said, "you're set."

She blinked. From the look on his face, she'd been bracing for the opposite. "Really?" A relieved smile broke out. "Great." She jumped up and pecked him on the cheek. "Thanks." Immediately, she felt a flush creep up her neck. Geez, what was wrong with her? Why couldn't she keep her hands off him? She got very busy gathering her things. Purse, coat. Mind. Clutching her gear to her like armor, she said in as dignified a tone as possible, "Where is she?"

"There's a little catch."

She eyed him warily. "How little?"

"You have to agree to let the meeting be monitored."

"Monitored? Why?"

"In case she says anything to you she hasn't said to them. Anything contradictory to her statement. Or incriminating."

Incriminating. The word made the night even more somber than it already was.

"They didn't put her in jail, did they?"

"Not yet."

"And Kenny?"

"He's in a holding cell."

There was something in Ray's eyes, something he wasn't saying.

"You know what she said, don't you? That's what took you so damn long."

"They let me listen in on the interview," he admitted.

She searched his face for clues. "And?"

He shook his head. "One thing I've learned about you—you do better when you make up your own mind."

She hesitated.

"Take it or leave it," Ray said.

What choice did she have? She had to hear Maddie's story from her own lips. Gillian would never believe it otherwise. "Okay, I'll take it." Like he didn't know she would. "But I see her alone. If Burke wants to eavesdrop, tell him to put on a headset."

Ray took her to an interview room. Burke and two other men she assumed were detectives were milling around outside. A one-way window allowed her to see Maddie, who was slumped over a table, back bowed, black hair almost blocking her face. Almost. Enough was visible that Gillian could see how drawn Maddie looked. Worn down. Tired.

Despite everything, Gillian sent up a silent prayer. Please don't let it be Maddie. Please.

"Sure you want to do this?" Burke asked gruffly.

"Yes."

He shrugged and opened the door.

She stood in the open entrance with the cops behind her. It took Maddie a few seconds to turn her head and see Gillian. When she did, she hurtled to her feet.

"Oh, my God," she cried, and stumbled to the doorway, where for the second time that night Gillian had someone unexpected fling arms around her. "Thank you," Maddie sobbed. "Thank you for coming."

Behind her, the cops tensed. "Sit down, Miss Crane," Burke said. Thc other two began to pull her off.

"It's all right," Gillian said.

"I'm sorry," Maddie cried as burly arms pried her away. "I'm sorry!"

"It's all right! Leave her alone!"

"Wait," Maddie cried. "I'm just—"

"Sit down, Miss Crane," Burke said, then more forcefully when he'd separated them, "Sit down!"

Maddie looked from them to Gillian and back at them. She crept away. Timidly retook her seat. She was beaten. Cowed. Gillian never thought anyone could do that to Maddie. Not anyone.

"That's enough," Gillian told Burke and his crew. Maddie was weeping quietly in the background. "You said I could see her alone."

Burke didn't seem eager to go. Gillian sent a silent message over his shoulder to Ray.

Ray ground his jaw. He didn't like doing it, but he put a hand on Burke's shoulder. "Jimmy. We made a deal."

"Should have my head examined," Burke muttered. But he left.

When the door closed, Gillian took the chair opposite Maddie. She reached across the table and enclosed Maddie's hands in her own.

Maddie looked up.

"What happened?" Gillian asked. "When did you come back? What's Kenny doing here?"

"Oh, God," Maddie said in a shaky voice, and hiccupped. "I have so screwed up."

"Tell me, Maddie. You can tell me anything."

"You're going to be so mad at me."

"Better me than them." She nodded toward the door.

Maddie sniffed. "You remember when you kicked Kenny out?"

He'd had a little temper tantrum in her studio and wrecked a bunch of very expensive lights. "Oh, yeah, I remember."

"Well, he started sending you stuff."

"Stuff? What kind of stuff?"

"Messages."

"Like the one we saw?"

She nodded. "I suspected they were from him, so I went to see him."

"By yourself? Are you crazy?"

She gave a watery laugh. "I guess. But the thing is, I felt sorry for him. He seemed so lost. So I went back a second time. Just to make sure he was okay. And then a third." Her voice got small and wobbly. "And then..." She sobbed. "I . . . we . . . I love him, Gillian." She broke down altogether.

Gillian sat there stunned. Maddie and Kenny? Were the planets out of alignment? Did hell just freeze over?

"Okay, okay." She stroked Maddie's arm. "But why didn't you tell me?"

"I thought you'd hate me. I hated me. It felt"—she gulped down a huge lungful of air—"it felt like a huge betrayal. Like I was taking his side." She shook her head wildly. "But I wasn't. I swear. I wasn't." She looked away, ashamed. "I didn't mean for anything to happen between us. I just wanted him to stop bothering you. But he made me laugh, and he cooked me dinner."

"Kenny cooked you dinner? Geez, I couldn't get him to boil water." She looked at poor, broken Maddie. Thought about Ray. Was this what love did?

She shuddered, refocused. "So you fell for his bad-boy charm. So what? So did I."

Maddie shook her head. "Underneath, he's really an okay guy. And talented. Really, really talented."

"Yeah, but it's the same old, same old, Maddie. Too many drugs. Too much alcohol. Guys like that—they're trouble."

She sniffed. "I know. And that's why I told him—" She swallowed a sob. "That's why I told him I couldn't be with him unless he got help."

"Oh, Maddie. When are you going to stop thinking about everyone else and start thinking about yourself?"

"I am, Gillian. I swear. And Kenny is, too."

"Kenny Post never had a thought in his head that wasn't about Kenny Post."

"No, you don't get it." Maddie was wide-eyed and persuasive, a true believer. "He did it. He went into rehab."

Gillian wasn't sure she'd heard right.

"That's where he's been," Maddie said.

"Rehab?" It was hard to keep the astonishment out of her voice.

"He made me promise to keep it secret. He didn't want anyone to know. He was so ashamed. But Gillian, that's why he couldn't have done any of this. He was at the Canyon Rock Center outside LA until last night."

"So why haven't the police let him go?"

"I don't know," she wailed. "They don't believe him." She grabbed on to Gillian desperately. "It's all been this awful, horrible mistake. Please, you've got to help him. You've got to tell them to listen."

Afraid the police would burst in if Maddie kept hanging on to her, Gillian disengaged herself. "But what about you? You were supposed to be in New York. When did you come back? And why?"

"I never left." She began to cry again. "When the killings started, and Ray accused me and everything, I got so confused. I thought, maybe Kenny was behind them. See, I didn't trust him. I thought—I thought maybe he had done it. I called to make sure he hadn't left the center, but I wanted to make sure, so I stayed to keep an eye out. But I was wrong about him. I was so wrong."

"Then what is he doing here?"

"He had a weekend pass. A reward for all the hard work he's been doing. He surprised me. But I swear, it had nothing to do with you."

"Then what was that at the hotel?"

"Him being an idiot. You know how he is."

"Don't remind me."

"He's supposed to apologize for all the bad stuff he's done. And he saw the article and realized you would be here. He just wanted to"—she started sobbing again—"to talk to you. Say how sorry he was for being such an asshole."

Gillian sighed. "All right. Calm down. We'll figure something out."

She looked up with hope in her eyes. "You believe me?"

"Of course I believe you, stupid. The story's too after-school special and cheesy not to be true."

Maddie smiled through her tears. "I'll make it up to you, Gillian. I swear. I'll beat Kenny upside the head. Anything you want."

But Maddie had given Gillian back her monster. And that was gift enough.

47

Two days later, Gillian woke early, borrowed one of her grandparents' cars, and drove to the museum.

Since her photographs were only part of the exhibit and had been struck into isolation, she wanted to make sure they were packed and crated correctly. Though she was paying for it, and it was her idea, she didn't have to be there. Her grandparents had urged her to stay home—loudly and at length the night before. But supervising the task gave Gillian one more feeling of control. It would be the last official thing she did at the museum. The last tie, the last logistical reason to stay.

Maddie and Kenny had already left. The police had held on to them until yesterday, but their story panned out in every particular, so they were cleared and released. Not that Gillian had had any doubts. Whoever the black evil stalking her was, it wasn't Kenny Post or Maddie Crane.

Before they left, they stopped to say good-bye. Maddie was going back with Kenny for a few days to see him resettled in rehab; then she was going on to New York to check in with Gillian's studio and catch up on whatever she'd dropped to come to Nashville.

Gillian had been in the basement studio at her grandparents', working on the lake picture when the two of them clomped down the steps.

Kenny looked wan and shaky, but he was forthright in apologizing to her.

"Babe, I'm sorry. Truly. I was a jerk and, well, shit, you know." His long legs in their jackboots and tattered jeans shifted. "I'm going to pay for those lights, and you know, make up for everything."

She shook his hand, felt the hardened calluses at his fingertips from the guitar strings. "Just don't break Maddie's heart, you hear me?"

He grinned, his teeth white against beard stubble. "Loud and clear."

"Because you hurt her, I'll rip your tongue out."

"Whoa." He laughed uneasily. "No problem."

"And cut off your balls."

"I'd like him to keep those," Maddie said.

"Me, too." He squeezed her against him.

"Yeah, well, only if you behave."

He nodded and held up two fingers. "Scout's honor."

She and Maddie looked at each other and laughed.

He looked insulted. "Hey, man, I was a Boy Scout."

"I thought telling the truth was part of recovery," Gillian said.

"Okay, well . . . Cub Scout. Never made it to the big boys."

Maddie put an arm around his waist. "You will, baby. I promise. You will."

They looked at each other with enough heat to launch a hot-air balloon. Jealousy licked at Gillian, but she fought it. She and Ray had parted the night of the gala, and she hadn't seen him since.

"All right, you two. You're giving me a major sugar high. Scram!"

Maddie gave her a hug. “I’m just going to stay a few days to see Kenny settled. I should be back in New York by the end of the week.” She jabbed a finger at Gillian. “I expect the same from you.”

“Yes, Ma.”

“And stay out of trouble,” she said with a sternness that was only half-faked.

They both knew that wasn’t likely. But Gillian hugged her anyway. “Call me when you get to the studio.”

Maddie nodded, and they were gone.

Now, Gillian pulled into the parking lot behind the museum and wondered what she would do. How long she would stay. Used to be she couldn’t wait to get back to New York. But now… She knew the monster was out there, lurking close. Waiting. Just waiting. Leaving felt like giving up. Like letting him win. Again.

But what if she stayed, and the killer was never caught? That grim possibility had been played out her whole life. Would staying be a futile sacrifice? What if she went back to New York, and he went with her? What if he didn’t?

The museum hadn’t opened yet, and the lot was mostly empty. In the early morning stillness, the wide expanse of blacktop was unnatural. Impressions of former occupants flickered in her mind like the shimmer of heat waves. Museum goers now afraid to go out. Protesters who hadn’t arrived. Or maybe they were gone for good, now that she’d caved. She saw a couple of cars, and, near the service entrance, a van with its rear doors open, a yellow pail on the ground at its foot. Evidently the shipping company hadn’t arrived because she didn’t see the Artco truck.

Shipping artwork was highly specialized, and museums hired professional companies like Artco to handle it. Photographs were less complicated than paintings or sculpture, but her pieces were huge, so they needed custom wood frames built with hinged covers that were screwed on, not nailed. Two of the custom crates her work had been shipped in to Nashville had warped and needed to be rebuilt. They'd just completed them yesterday.

Before being crated, the photographs also had to be enclosed properly. Some foam wraps gave off damaging gases. Others trapped moisture and created mold. Water and snow damage, breakage, abrasion. Shipping was a big risk, so required as much art as science. Which was partly why she wanted to be there.

She parked and headed toward the service entrance, which was the only door open at seven in the morning.

She could see the lettering on the van now. HARPETH WINDOW CLEANING SERVICE, painted in green on the side. A skinny man, maybe a few years older than she, stood at the open doors, swiping the blade of a squeegee. His standard industrial green uniform—matching pants and shirt with some kind of embroidered name over the pocket—hung off his skeletal frame. He grinned as she approached, his face a death's-head. She saw his teeth were small and grayed at the bottom, like a row of sharp, dead trees.

A shiver ran down her back, and she passed him, heading around the van to the door. He spoke.

"Miss Gillian?"

She started, his voice was so close. His breath in her ear.

"Ye—?"

A cloth clamped over her mouth. She tried to scream, inhaled something awful, noxious. She gagged.

At the very last second, when she knew she was going under, she had one final thought.

At last.

48

Ray pulled up to the curb and stared at the familiar little house. He'd been there a thousand times, Christmas, Thanksgiving, Stanley Cup. All the major holidays.

But not lately. Not in a long time.

He grabbed the bag with the lemon icebox pie and got out. Trudged up the walk, went around the side to the kitchen entrance. Knocked.

Used to be he would have just let himself in. Now, he waited for the sarge to shuffle to the door and open it. Except it wasn't Mackenzie Burke who let him in. It was an overgrown farm boy, thick and wide, with a round, childish face and an open, gap-toothed smile.

"Can I help you?"

Ray stood there a minute, taken aback. "Uh, I'm looking for Sarge," he said, trying to peer over the giant's shoulder.

"Oh, you mean Mr. Mac?" The boy—no, man—grinned, opened the door wider. "He's here. Mr. Mac!" he called, stepping aside to let Ray into the kitchen. "Mr. Mac, you got company!"

"And you are?" Ray said.

"Oh, sorry." He closed the door carefully. "I'm Joseph. Mr. Mac's daughter, Miss Nancy?" He made the name a question, but after years of living here Ray knew the other man wasn't asking anything. "She hired me to stay with her father. Make sure he don't wander off no more."

Ray nodded, glad Nancy and Jimmy had finally found a solution to the problem. He could have wished one of them would have taken their father in, but doing something was better than doing nothing.

"Let me see what he's up to," Joseph said.

Ray handed over the bag with the pie. "That's okay, I know my way. I'll find him. Maybe you can slice up the pie? Make us some coffee?"

The prospect of pie lit Joseph's face. "Be happy to."

Ray walked through the living room, saw all of Gloria's knickknacks where'd they'd always been. Nancy must have hired someone to clean, or maybe Joseph kept the place spotless. Either way, no dust gathered on the little eggcups Gloria had collected, or the spoons from Washington, DC, and the Grand Canyon.

Family photos gleamed at him. Little snapshots of life come and gone—Nancy and Jimmy as kids, as teenagers, at high school graduation.

He spotted something on a set of shelves behind the sofa. Stopped, and parted the figurines in front. Hidden in the corner, but there, if anyone cared to look, was a wedding picture. His wedding picture.

He smiled fondly. Gloria always did have a soft spot for him. She'd been furious with Nancy at first, sympathetic to him. But, of course, Nancy was her daughter, and eventually they reconciled. But he noted she hadn't kept a photo from the second wedding.

The last time he'd been here had been the funeral. The house had looked different—strange—with people crowding the small rooms, holding paper plates and plastic cups of sweet tea. Perfume had hovered in the air like church music. And the smell, that lived-in smell of onions and laundry and old carpet had been overpowered by it.

But now the familiar smell was there again, sending the memories reeling. Sunday dinners, football games. Ghosts of Jimmy and Pam, his ex-wife, and their baby, Scott, crawling in front of the TV. Of Nancy sitting under his arm watching him open birthday presents.

Why had he come? What did he think he'd find in the dregs of what used to be his life? Carlson had called last night. For the past two days the news had been full of the gala and what had—or hadn't—happened there.

"You want to work so badly, I've got something for you," he'd said. "General counsel at Tenneco." He named one of the huge manufacturing plants in the wilds of Lewisburg outside of Nashville. "They're having labor trouble, and he's received some death threats."

Job was supposed to start tomorrow. If he was here tomorrow. Then again, he hadn't gotten far in packing. The boxes still sat in a flat pile in a corner by the armchair.

He found the sarge in the den, staring at the morning TV news with the sound off. He wore pants and a sleeveless undershirt. Slippers. But he looked clean. Shaved.

"Hey, Sarge, it's Ray."

The old man looked up, blankly, and Ray held his breath. Then recognition crossed his face.

"Well, I'll be." A smile broke out, and he thumped the couch beside him. "Ray Pearce, you are a sight for sore eyes. Sit yourself down, boy."

"Brought you some lemon icebox. Joseph's cutting it up."

His ex-father-in-law made a face. "Joseph," he scoffed. "Jailer more like it. Keeps me locked up here, don't let me go nowhere. No way to treat a man."

"Mr. Mac, now, don't you be getting grumpy," Joseph said as he bustled in, a shirt in hand. "If we knew we was getting company," he said to Ray, "we would have dressed more." He helped his charge with the shirt but refused to button it. "Go on, now, you do it yourself. Therapist said you should try. Getting all lazy with me doing everything for you."

Ray watched the sarge's thick, arthritic fingers struggle with the buttons and finally conquer them.

"See?" Joseph said with pride.

The sarge glowered at him, but the younger man didn't seem to mind. "Coffee be ready in a minute," he said, and left.

"So"—Ray turned to the older man—"how are you? You're looking pretty good for an old man."

The sarge gazed at him with big, hopeful eyes. "Do you know my boy, Jimmy?"

Ray laughed. "Sure I do. It's Ray, Sarge, Ray. Remember?"

The older man looked confused suddenly. "Ray," he repeated. But the understanding was gone from his face. Once again, Ray was a stranger, the past not even a memory.

Joseph came in with a tray. Slices of pie on plates, mugs of coffee. They ate together in the den, but recognition didn't return, and twenty minutes later Ray left.

"You take care of him," he said to Joseph, who waved the concern away.

"Oh, don't you worry about Mr. Mac. He's going to be fine. Just fine."

Ray nodded, hoping it was true. But whether it was or not, the sarge was no longer his problem.

The door closed behind him. Ray heard the latch click in place, like the last word in the final chapter of a long book.

Ray loped down to his truck, got in, and keyed the ignition. But he didn't go anywhere. He sat and listened to the engine whir. It was like the distant buzz of the past, a constant background noise he could never shake loose.

He should take the job Carlson offered. Go to the office, catch up on the threat assessment. Figure out where in the hell and beyond of Lewisburg the plant was. Drive out there, scout around.

But he didn't want to go to Lewisburg. He knew no one and nothing there.

So where did that leave him? Shuck the job? Go home? Start packing? And go . . . where?

He thought about the sarge and his broken memory. What would it be like to be free of your own history? Of those sticky ties that hemmed you in?

Why was it so hard to cut through them? He was a stranger to his father-in-law. Just as he was a stranger to Nancy and Jimmy. His reasons for staying were long gone. All he was missing was a reason to go.

He looked out at the street, at the small, neat houses. Not, he thought, like the lives inside. Lives that might have been small but were rarely neat. His own no exception.

But if he needed a reason, he had one, didn't he?

Maybe. Could be. Possible.

He smiled to himself. Nothing like a little certainty to get a man in gear.

He jerked the wheel, backed up with a screech, and turned the car around.

Fuck Lewisburg.

He headed west. Toward Belle Meade.

49

Gillian woke with the sting of pain. A man was bending over her. He was slicing a line into her arm.

"What the—"

She grabbed for him but came up short because her feet and hands were bound. Taped down with silver electrical tape. The attempt jerked her body, though, and surprised him. He lost his grip. The blade, a thin X-Acto knife, slipped, creating a jagged cut in her arm.

She hissed, and the man looked up. Smiled. She saw those gray, dead teeth again.

"Miss Gillian," he said. "So glad you're awake."

She eyed him warily. The face of the beast was like nothing she'd expected. Not huge and dark and animal-like, but thin, guileless. Empty.

And young. Too young to have been the cause of her mother's death.

He giggled. "You don't remember me," he said.

Her mouth was dry. Funny how that worked. All her life, she lived only for this moment, and when it came, it was like nothing she imagined. Not the monster she'd envisioned. Not the strong going down with the enemy. But weak and bound and with fear enough to suck her dry.

She licked her lips. "Have we met?"

Instead of answering, he pointed to the scars on her arms with the bloody blade. "How'd you get those?"

Second realization. He'd removed her sweater. She was lying in her bra on a dingy pallet blanket. Her jeans were still in place, thank God, but she was in some kind of large, deserted space. From her limited line of sight, she could make out oil or grease stains on the cold, concrete floor. Empty, rotted shelving in a couple of places. An old mechanic's shop? Factory? She listened for sounds that might help place her location. Traffic noises, air horns, train wheels. Heard nothing but the labored breathing of her captor. And her own heart, huge in her ears.

"Who did those to you?" he asked again, caressing the bumps on her arms with the knife.

She tried not to flinch. "I did."

He laughed, happy, delighted. "All by yourself?" He chuckled again. "That's something, that is."

She wiggled, trying to get comfortable. But she was lashed tight against something, her hands behind her. The tape cut into her shoulders and belly. "Can you"—she grunted—"can you put my hands in front?"

He looked her over, thought about it. "Soon," he said.

The word promised much more than a change of position. It promised everything to come. Everything anticipated. Everything feared.

A wave of dizziness rolled over her. Leftover, maybe, from whatever he'd forced her to inhale. Or from dread.

He rose and wiped the knife on his pants. Stashed it in the tool belt around his waist. A squeegee and a brush both had special pockets. A handle to screw into them. A cloth. A gun.

Goose bumps rippled across her. "I'm cold."

He touched her protruding nipple. “I see.”

He watched for her reaction, and she bit down on panic. “Who are you?”

He touched her other nipple. “Aubrey.”

In their bindings, she clenched her hands, digging her nails into her palm to keep herself perfectly still. “Aubrey, can I please have my sweater back?”

“You have pretty little titties, Miss Gillian.” He stared at them.

She swallowed.

“But, okay,” he said abruptly, and disappeared from her sight lines.

She had wild hopes of him unbinding her. He’d have to undo the tape to get her sweater over her head. It would be a chance to do something. Attack. Fight back. She braced herself for it, stoking her energy, drinking in air.

But when he returned seconds later, it wasn’t with her sweater. He held a heavy but worn cardigan, which he draped over her like a blanket.

He said, “I would have picked blue, you know.”

“B-blue?” She found her teeth chattering with failure and disappointment. She started to shake.

“For the picture. You chose brown, but my opinion? Blue would’ve popped more.”

She forced herself to concentrate, to make sense of what he was telling her. Brown cardigan. Brown cardigan.

A cry seized up inside her.

She’d draped a brown cardigan around a chair in *Kitchen in Suburbia.* Her mother used to keep one. Old and heavy with a zipper and a hood. Brown. She still remembered the smell of it. Pancakes on Sunday morning. Butter and maple syrup.

Her eyes widened. Aubrey was watching her, waiting for some pronouncement on his commentary.

"I couldn't find one in blue," she said at last, but she had trouble pushing out the words.

"If you could, you would have, though. Right?"

She nodded. Anything to keep him from touching her again. "Sure."

He frowned. "No, you wouldn't. Don't lie to me, Miss Gillian."

She shrugged, tired of the game. "It's art, Aubrey, and I'm the artist. I get to pick the colors."

"Not today, you're not."

"I'm not what?" Suddenly the fear and frustration overwhelmed, and she cried out. "Who are you? Where have we met? What do you want with—" Suddenly, crazily, the room began to spin. Was she dizzy? Drugged? No, she was turning. Moving.

Third realization. She was on some kind of pallet. And Aubrey was turning her around.

"I'm the artist today," he said.

50

The Gray mansion looked sedate and quiet in the morning light. The protesters were gone, and also the reporters. Ray cruised up to the gate, glad to see the squad car still there. The cop inside changed with the day and the shift; this time it was Carter something. Or something Carter. A twenty-year man, happy to slide by.

He saw Ray, rolled down the window, and called over to him. “You’re not careful, Ray, you’re gonna make a rut in the road,” he said.

A rut in his life more like it.

“Thanks for the advice,” Ray said.

“No problem.” Carter gave him a mock salute.

Ray pulled through the gate and parked in the driveway.

A maid escorted him to the living room. The silk drapes still hung over the window that looked out on the terrace, bathing the room in a warm, golden glow that contradicted the icy glare in Genevra Gray’s eyes.

“Mr. Pearce.” She frowned. “I thought we were finished with the incident at the auction.”

“We are,” he said. “I’m here to see Gillian.”

She stiffened her back, an animal about to strike. “I don’t see what you could possibly have to say to her.”

"No, ma'am." He weighed the hostility in her face. "I don't suppose you do."

He met her eyes, not challenging, but making it clear he wasn't going away until he got what he came for.

When he entered, she'd been sitting at a small writing desk in the corner, leafing through a leather-bound appointment book. She returned to it, dismissing him. "She isn't here."

Uninvited, he stepped farther into the room. "Where is she?"

Genevra looked up as though surprised to still find him there. "I don't know."

He came closer. Wondered what he'd done to draw her claws. Step over an invisible line and eat at her table? Fall for her rich granddaughter? Ask too many questions? Which sin was the greatest?

"I think you do." He smiled gently. "I don't think you'd let her out of your sight without knowing. Ma'am." He sat, a further goad to her hospitality. "I'm free for the rest of the day." He put his feet up on a coffee table, leaned back, crossed his hands behind his head.

"That's an eighteenth-century French antique you're crawling all over."

"I'm sure it is." He settled in for however long it took.

An irritated sigh. "She didn't bother to inform me," Genevra said tartly, "but I suspect she's at the museum. Seeing to the packing of her photographs."

"Thank you." He swung his legs down, stood, and was almost out the door when she stopped him.

"Mr. Pearce. Ray."

He turned. She was still sitting at the desk. Still looking at her book.

"You hurt my child, you'll answer to me."

"Me hurt her?" Ruefully, he shook his head. "You know her better than that. More like the other way around."

The dizzying trip on the pallet ended, leaving Gillian facing the wall that had been behind her. She went cold at the sight of the set in front of her. Not because it was a perfect reproduction of the kitchen in her photograph, but because it wasn't.

The kitchen in her photograph had a black-and-white tile floor. She'd chosen it to better outline the body. But the kitchen here had a strip of linoleum in front of the counter. Linoleum like in the house. Her mother's house. In her photograph, she'd used pink-and-green curtains to update and exaggerate the banality of the space. But here, they were thick, old-fashioned Venetian blinds. With a familiar red-and-white-checked valance across the top. A green wine bottle sat on a windowsill, with three yellow daisies in it.

In the center of the room, between her and the set, stood a camera on a tripod. Bile rose up her throat.

"Like it?" Aubrey asked softly.

Her lungs clogged. Her brain screamed. How did he know? How did he know?

"Who—who are you?" she choked out.

"I'm Aubrey, Miss Gillian." He stroked her hair the way you would a child. Or a pet. "You remember Aubrey, don't you? I used to come to your house with my daddy when he mowed the lawn. Or fixed the fence. That fence was always getting broke, d'you remember? I'd sit out in the truck because he told me to, and ain't no one didn't listen to my daddy and live. I'd sit out there when it was so cold I could see my breath or so hot I couldn't breathe at all. And I'd watch you through the window. You'd be out there playing. All twirling and laughing. Prettiest thing I ever saw in my entire life, you and your momma. I loved watching you."

The handyman? Aubrey belonged to the handyman? Nausea swirled in the pit of her stomach. She thought back, desperate for a single memory of the child he'd been, and came up blank.

"I'd sit out there and watch through the truck window and a feeling would wind up inside me. Like a snake. Like a rattlesnake, all snarly and mean. I didn't have no pretty momma, no house with green grass. I had nothing but my daddy. Oh, and his momma. Can't forget Grandma. Who prayed and prayed and never did nothing to stop him. And that didn't seem fair, Miss Gillian. Do you think it's fair?"

"I don't know."

"Yes, you do." He gripped her hair, pulled back on it. "I told you not to lie to me."

"If you"—she gritted her teeth at the pain—"if you stayed in the truck, how did you ever see inside the house?"

"Oh, that was your momma's doing." As if the mention of her mother was a call to gentler things, he released her. "Once, when my daddy was fixing the fence out back, she saw me in the truck. Felt sorry for me, I guess, because it was close to suffocating in there. She opened the door and took my hand and took me inside. I just about didn't believe my own eyes. Pictures and rugs. Everything neat and colorful. Like a fairyland. Like my own private Disney World." He paused, gazing out at the kitchen. "She gave me a can of Coke," he said dreamily, and smiled at the memory. "Best can of Coke I ever had." He sighed. "Sure was sorry about what happened to her."

He said the last in a funny, intimate kind of way. Gillian went rigid. Had he watched? Had he seen? He couldn't have been but ten or eleven. But his father...

"Was it..." She swallowed. Fear and anticipation mingled. Hope for an answer to the biggest question of her life. "Did your father—"

"Do her? Hell no. He was sleeping off a two-day drunk that morning."

Disappointment crashed into her. "Then what do you know about it?"

"Well, now, I know some." He knelt again, stroked the back of a finger down her cheek. "I know what it's like to steal someone's breath. To have them struggle beneath my hands. Their body go limp. The light in their eyes go out. I know more than you, Miss Gillian."

"Things I wouldn't want to know."

"That why you did all those pictures? Because you didn't want to know?" His finger traced her mouth, her neck, and she stiffened against his touch. "You're lying again. Don't think I can't see it. You're desperate to know." He ran his tongue up the side of her face to her ear. "What's it like to draw that last pinch of air? What's it like to know you'll never laugh again, never twirl again. Never see another second of misery, and wanting to more than anything." He tilted her head, his mouth an inch from her jugular. He held her there, like a vampire staring at the vein. "You think that little window in the camera keeps you safe? Underneath the phony rags and the New York galleries and the papers writing your name, you're just aching to know, Miss Gillian." His hand wrapped around her throat. He leaned in close and tight, whispered in her ear. "And I'm going to show you."

She struggled to keep from pulling away, to keep the terror at bay, to keep him from seeing how close he'd come.

"That's *my* work," he said, and flourished a hand toward the set. "My art."

She looked toward the faithful reproduction in front of her. She would die there. On the floor, like her doomed mother. Gillian had always known it. She would die at the hands of the monster. Call it fate. Destiny. Luck of the draw.

She flicked a glance at Aubrey's wet eyes and smiling mouth. The pride and glee she saw chilled and horrified. Was this what her mother had seen? Was this the last sight her eyes beheld?

No, not ten-year-old Aubrey. He was her monster, not her mother's. And if that was different, everything else could be, too.

Or maybe they were all the same. Every monster the same monster. Evil returning in a thousand disguises, but at heart all one.

She thought about Ray. About his pain and sympathy when he'd seen the scars on her arms. If he were here, he wouldn't hesitate to shield her. Protect her. Save her. If he were here, would she give him the next thousand years of her life? Would she promise her love, her hope if he saved her?

Wasn't anyone looking out for you? Ray had asked.

Only herself.

"Are you ready, Miss Gillian? Are you ready to find what you so desperately seek?"

Panic spiked, sharp as a spear. Not yet. Too soon. She

needed another hour. A day, a week. A year. Please. Just a little more time.

Did everyone haggle like this? Was every death scene set in a market stall? So, she thought, not so easy to die after all.

She struggled against the tape. It held her tight, helpless. She had no options. He'd given her none. And no time.

Ahead of her, he was waiting, eagerness in his face.

But there was always a choice. Always. It may be a tiny crack in the void, but slim was better than none.

So, she stopped struggling and turned from him. Deliberate, indifferent. Scornful.

"What are you going to do, Aubrey"—she mocked his name—"put a plastic bag over my head like all the others? Strangle me, suffocate me? Put me on the floor of my own kitchen?" She snorted. "Make another copy of a Gillian Gray photograph?"

His eyes narrowed, and the bottom fell out of her stomach, but she plowed on. "You're not an artist, Aubrey, you're a copier. A little Xerox machine."

He slapped her. Her head snapped back, her eyes watered.

"I do what you don't have the guts to do," he said.

"You want to talk about guts? Guts is facing the abyss and shaping it instead of falling in. Guts is a point of view. A single, original idea. And that's something you've never had."

He raised his hand again.

"But I can help you," she said quickly. "I can show you how to do what's never been done."

He eyed her suspiciously. "And why would you do that, Miss Gillian?"

"Because I never do the same thing twice. No true artist does. Because if you're going to kill me, and I know you are, I want a hand in it." She flexed her tired wrists, ignored the ache, and dug her nails into her palms. "Because you're right, Aubrey." She laughed hysterically and giddily, the tears so close she could taste them. "You are so right." She met his lethal, empty eyes. "I do want to know."

51

Ray pulled into the museum lot. The paper had announced the removal of the Gray photographs, and the long lines were gone.

He took the steps two at a time, eager to get inside, eager to get this over with. One last chance to talk Gillian into something he still hadn't talked himself into.

When he got inside, he found the exhibit blanketed with drapes and a sign that said "under construction." He tracked down a docent, explained why he'd come, and was directed to the design rooms, where the photographs were being crated.

He took the elevator up, hoping when the doors opened the madness that had rooted inside his brain would be over, and he could turn around, go back down, and never have to put his soul in the hands of Gillian Gray.

But the doors opened, and he stepped out of them, heading toward the firing squad or whatever else she had in mind. But Gillian wasn't there, and when he asked, no one had seen her yet. One of the staff members told him she'd be with the curator, so he took the elevator up two floors to Stephanie Bower's office.

Bower was polite and told him with a smile that Gillian was in the design room.

He blinked. "No, she isn't. I was just there."

Stephanie looked puzzled. "Well, she made arrangements to oversee the packing. I told her we'd begin this morning, and I was under the impression she wanted to be here."

"You haven't seen her?"

"Not yet. But we got an early start. The call was for seven. I'm sure she's just running late."

Ray left, stifling instinctive panic. According to Mrs. Gray, Gillian was supposed to be there. No, Mrs. Gray *thought* her granddaughter was there.

But Mrs. Gray was also unhappy about his interest in Gillian. And he was more than familiar with the games the Grays played.

He punched a number into his cell phone, waited with a mere scrap of calm for the call to be answered.

"This is Ray Pearce, Mrs. Gray. Where's Gillian?"

There was a moment's hesitation. Surprise or more games? "I told you—"

"No, Mrs. Gray, you didn't. And I don't appreciate being toyed with and lied to."

"Well, we are blunt this morning."

"I don't have time for polite. I'm going to find her. It's just a matter of how long it takes."

"As I believe I mentioned, she's at the museum."

"No, she isn't. Do you know where else she might be?"

"No, I don't." Worry crept into her voice. "Are you sure she isn't at the museum?"

An uneasy feeling crawled over him. "What time did she leave?"

"I . . . I don't know."

"Did someone drive her?"

"She borrowed a car. Drove herself. Why? Has something happened?" The swift fear in her voice said more about her truth telling than anything else. He took the stairs instead of waiting for the elevator, hammering down them.

He remembered the squad car. "Get one of the maids to run outside and ask Carter when she left. That's the cop watching the gates. And find out what kind of car she took."

"What kind of—? Why? What's wrong?"

He didn't want to jump to conclusions—Gillian could be anywhere—but he didn't want to be stupid either. "I don't know yet. Maybe nothing. But I won't know until you do what I ask."

"All . . . all right. Hold on." She returned a few agonizing minutes later, sounding breathless. Had she run outside herself? "She left around six-forty-five. The"—she took a moment to catch her breath—"the gray BMW. The sedan."

"License plate?"

"The license plate? I—"

"Mrs. Gray. I need the license plate on the car. Now."

She put him on hold again, and he reached the ground floor, ran down the slope of exterior steps, and sprinted across the drop-off drive to the parking lot. The museum had opened fifteen minutes ago, and the lot was half-full. He stopped short. There must be dozens of cars there. And Gillian's might not even be one.

But if she had been there by seven, hours before the museum opened, there would only have been a few cars parked at the time. She would probably have chosen a space close to the entrance. He dashed up the closest row, hoping he wouldn't find a gray BMW. "Come on, Genevra," he muttered into the phone.

He found three gray BMW sedans before Genevra came back and gave him the license number in a quavering voice.

"Thanks," Ray said, scanning cars.

"Wait! Mr. Pearce. Please. Do you mind if I stay on the line?"

And suddenly, he remembered that moment in the hotel ballroom, that brief, soft, loving moment between two flinty women, and he couldn't help feeling sorry for her. "Fine."

He raced down the aisle to the first of the sedans. Checked the plate against the number Genevra had given him. His heart sank. It was a match.

"I've got it. The car is here."

"Thank God. So she's all right?"

"I don't know. The car is here, but Gillian isn't. She never showed up inside."

Gillian knew instantly that he didn't have enough light, and it wasn't the right kind. There were a few small Fresnels on stands, but the set was wide. He needed more intensity and better distribution. The color was off. She would have used a minimum of three key lights, probably four, plus fills. And a special for the body. There'd be scores of practicals inside the set itself. Maybe some under-the-counter stuff, something reproducing a central ceiling light. And, of course, the window. She usually tented a powerful HMI to create the ominous glow that was her specialty. She'd experimented with all kinds of material and found an Indian muslin gauze that worked best.

But she didn't tell him that. Once the scene was set, it wouldn't matter how it was lit. Not to her. Instead, she concentrated on the composition.

"Forget the kitchen," she told him. "Put the table over by the window. Isolate that area and focus your light there." She grunted, craning her neck to see the right side of the set.

When he didn't respond, she thought she'd lost him. "Look, try it. You can always move everything back. You don't want this to be like all the rest. It should be special. Unique. Larry King isn't going to be interested otherwise."

He brightened at the mention of the interview host. That senseless smile lit his face so he looked like a kid anticipating a birthday. "Larry King? Whooee, Miss Gillian!" He rubbed his hands together and giggled. "You think so?"

"He wanted me. Why not you? Except he'd want something new. Fresh."

He thought about it. "I can always move it back," he said, as if it was his idea, and she hadn't just told him that.

She lay back while he lugged the table. The legs scraped against the floor, and she tried to breathe, but everything was jammed up inside. Then she remembered Ray's technique and began counting. Catching her breath was hard at first, but after two attempts, she could feel herself steady, her heart rate down enough to think.

Typical of Ray to give her that. Steadiness. Calm.

She would have liked to stay a while with Ray, siphon off his strength and compassion, but Aubrey was finished moving the chairs, and she had to find something else for him to do. "Only two." She shook her head. "This is someone who doesn't have friends for dinner."

He dragged the third and fourth chairs back across the room and out of the corner she was creating, giving her more time. More precious time to decide.

What would she do? Live or die?

"That good?" he asked, standing with his hands on his hips and looking it over critically.

"That's perfect," she said. If she'd been designing the photograph, there'd be a box of cereal on the table. Rice Krispies, maybe. And a quart of milk.

But she wasn't designing a photograph. She was designing a deathbed. Her deathbed.

"How we going to do it?" Aubrey asked.

She licked her lips. More than dry now. Cracked. "I told you. I explained it. Makes no sense any other way."

He put a hand on the gun in his tool belt. "I don't know..."

She shrugged, or at least she tried to within the confines of the tape. "Well, okay, then." She turned her head away, betting, hoping, laying it all down on the manipulation. "If you're not sure..."

"There's too much blood," he whined. "I don't like blood."

"Fine, then. Get out your plastic bag, rev up the computer, and wave bye-bye to Larry King."

"Okay, okay." He looked uncertain, but that was better than ten minutes earlier when he'd been adamantly against her idea. His pink tongue flicked out between those sharp little teeth and rested on the corner of his mouth while he thought about it. "But, I want to do it."

God, she felt sleepy. What a struggle to stay awake. To keep her brain working.

Patiently, she said, "Then it won't be me doing it, will it, Aubrey? Then you can't go on Larry King as the man who watched Gillian Gray die. You'd be the man who killed her. You do see the difference."

Quick as a whip he was at her throat. "Don't be nasty with me, Miss Gillian." His fingers pressed inward. Lights danced around the edge of her sight. "Ain't no cause to be nasty with me."

"Sorry," she managed to choke out. "I'm . . . sorry . . ." He shoved her away, and she coughed and wheezed.

"I'm having all kinds of second thoughts here," he said viciously.

"Check the shot," she croaked.

He stared at her malevolently.

"It's good," she told him. "Move the tripod and check it before you decide."

Grudgingly, he did it. Laughed when he looked through the lens. "My, my, my, it does look all bright and pretty." He hopped away, giggling with anticipation. "Okay, then." Turned to her. "You ready?" He pulled out the gun. "I'm ready." He drew in a sharp breath. "How you going to do it? Here?" He held the weapon to his temple. "Or here?" He held it underneath his chin. "Or . . ." He knelt and stroked her cheek with the muzzle. Forced her mouth open and slid it inside. "Here."

The taste was dirty and metallic. She nearly gagged with terror. But again, she reached for Ray's count. Breathe in. Two. Three. Four. Breathe out.

He chuckled. "Oh, I am so tempted, Miss Gillian." But he slid the gun out of her mouth, chucked her under the chin with it. "How's this? I'll put one bullet in the chamber, one tiny little bullet. So you won't see it coming. And then I shoot you with the camera as you shoot yourself."

She swallowed, stomach grinding. She'd not expected this. She'd expected one decision. One shot, over and done.

"I'll take all kinds of pictures," Aubrey crooned. "As you sweat. As you learn what you so dearly want to know. What it's like to stare Mr. Death in the face." He smiled, pleased with himself. "How many times you think you can pull that trigger?"

She gave him a clear, direct look, though she had to clench her bound hands and stiffen her spine to do so. "I guess . . . we'll find out."

52

The Grays arrived at the museum before the police did, frantic and demanding. They burst into Will Davenport's office, where Ray had already gathered the small crowd of people who'd arrived the first hour of the morning.

"What's happened?" Chip boomed.

Will raised his hands in a calming gesture. "We don't know yet."

Dissatisfied, Chip pivoted away from Will and set his sights on Ray, who was leaning on Will's desk.

"Where is my granddaughter?"

Coolly as he could, Ray said, "She made it to the parking lot. Something happened between arriving at the museum and getting inside."

"What?" Chip demanded.

"That's what we're trying to find out."

Suddenly, Genevra swayed and gripped the side of a chair to steady herself. "People don't vanish, Mr. Pearce." Her tone was icy as usual, but the quiver in her voice was unmistakable. "They just don't disappear."

"Chip," Will said in a soothing voice. "Why don't you and Genevra sit down."

"I don't want to sit down!" Genevra's voice wobbled on a shriek.

The outburst was greeted by an uncomfortable silence.

Finally, Ray said, "We were just going over some questions. Sit down and listen in. Maybe you'll remember something that could help."

Chip pulled out a chair for his wife, and, grudgingly, they both sat.

Ray turned to Will. "All right, you got here around—"

"Seven-fifteen."

"How many cars were in the lot?"

He thought back. "I think three. I recognized Stephanie's, and two others."

"Did you see a gray BMW?"

"I don't think so. I'm not positive, but I don't think so."

"Anything else?"

"A red car, I think. A minivan."

Steve, one of the design team members, held up his hand. "That would be mine. Gotta pick the kids up from school today, so I switched cars with my wife."

"Okay. We got Stephanie's Honda, your minivan, possibly Gillian's BMW."

"I was there by seven-fifteen," said Dan, the other design team member. "I've got an old green Volvo."

"So that gives us our four." Ray looked around the room. "Anyone see something else?"

The room went quiet. "I must have been the first in," said the minivan driver, "because I didn't see any of your cars."

Genevra burst out, "Something has happened to Gillian, and we're analyzing the parking lot!"

"Mrs. Gray—"

"No, I will not let this happen. Not again." Her voice caught, and Chip sent her a pleading look.

Ray saw some kind of signal pass between the two of them. Chip asking, her refusing.

"What?" Ray rose, his attention suddenly focused on them. "What's going on?" He waited, and the two older Grays seemed frozen. "If you know anything, anything about this—"

Chip's shoulders slumped. He turned to Will. "Excuse us? Please. I'd like to speak to Mr. Pearce in private."

"Don't," Genevra said to Chip. She rose stiffly to her feet. "Please. Don't do this." And now the plea was in her face.

"We no longer have that choice," Chip replied gently. He gestured for the others to leave. "Will?"

Davenport looked at him curiously, but only said, "Yes, of course. We'll wait in the curator's office." He ushered the three out and left Ray alone with the Grays.

53

Inside the now-cleared office, the air was charged. Ray looked between the two elder Grays. Chip had crossed to the window and was gazing out over the city. Genevra was clasping the back of her chair. Tense, white-knuckled.

Ray waited. It was like waiting for a land mine to explode. Your toes were on the trigger, and it was only a matter of time before you had to step off and detonate something. Your foot, your leg, your life. In this case . . . what?

"You had dinner with us," Chip said at last. "You remember that?"

"Yeah." Not likely to forget that evening.

"You asked about Gillian's father."

Inside, a little burst of surprise Ray was careful not to show. Whatever he expected, it wasn't genealogy. "The dead one."

"Yes, the dead one."

Genevra Gray was naturally pale, her complexion that of the fair Southern beauty who never meets the sun without a hat. But now, she looked beyond pale. She looked ghostly.

"He isn't dead," she whispered. More like a croak.

Ray's brows rose.

"He's here, in town," Genevra said. "And he wants money. A lot of money."

Chip turned from the window, his hands in his pockets. He shrugged, defeated, embarrassed. "We've been paying him for years, but now..." He exhaled a hard breath. "It seems he wants more. And I...I refused him." He hesitated, then drew himself up. "That's when the first murder happened."

A pulse in Ray's throat began hammering. "Who is he?"

"He's nothing. Nobody." Chip waved a hand as if waving the man's essence away. "A photographer. Runs a third-rate modeling agency, when he's in the mood."

Slowly, Ray said, "You're telling me you think Gillian's father, who, by the way, suddenly turns up alive, could be the killer? And you kept quiet about it?"

"We had good reason," Chip said.

"Three women are dead!"

"Don't take that tone," Genevra snapped. "This man is weak and vile, a walking disaster—"

"Disaster? He's a hell of a lot more than a disaster if he killed those women. If he's stalking Gillian. If he has her now."

Silence, rich with fear.

"At the least, you should have told her," Ray said. "Years ago." He thought of the decades of lying, the things Gillian had lost. Things whose value only she had the right to judge.

"Never," Genevra said.

"He's her damn father," Ray roared. "She has a right to—"

"No," Chip said adamantly. "She has no rights."

Ray wanted to punch him. “Are you kidding? Who the hell do you think you—”

“He raped her mother!” Genevra cried.

Ray stared at her. Inside the office, time seemed to thicken and congeal. “He . . . what?”

Genevra gasped and clamped a hand to her mouth. Tears welled in her eyes, and she looked away.

“He . . . he assaulted her,” Chip said quietly. “Gillian was the result.”

Ray stood speechless.

They were all trapped in silence. No one moved. No one spoke.

Finally, Ray recovered his voice. “Start . . . start from the beginning. What happened?”

Chip sighed. He looked as gray as his name. “We didn’t know at first. Holland refused to reveal the father’s identity.” He looked down at his hands. Age spots covered the tops. “I’m not sure she told anyone.”

“Except the rapist?” Yeah, that made sense.

“How he found out, I don’t know to this day,” Chip said. “Holland never told us.”

“And this was when?”

“Gillian was six.”

Six. A year before her mother’s death. “So somehow he finds out he has a kid,” Ray said, piecing it together, “and sees a way to make money off it.”

“He threatened to sue for custody unless Holland paid him off.”

“He didn’t stand a chance,” Ray objected. “No court in the world would have granted him custody.”

“The threat wasn’t about taking her child,” Genevra said with impatience. “It was about the publicity surrounding a court battle.”

The rape becoming public. The way her child had been conceived common knowledge. That hit hard. Even now, more than twenty years later.

"So she paid?"

Genevra had remained silent, only staring at nothing, the veins taut in her thin neck. Now she broke her silence with the single, curt word. "No," she said.

"She ended her career," Chip said. "She came home. If she was out of the public eye, she reasoned, he'd have less hold over her."

Ray looked away from the ravaged faces of Gillian's grandparents. What they were saying answered most of the questions he'd had about Holland's sudden disappearance from the celebrity world long after she'd had a child. He thought of the mythology Gillian had absorbed. Her beautiful mother giving up everything for her beloved daughter. Little did she know.

"Why didn't he make good on his threat? The tabloids would've paid a bundle."

"He didn't have to. He approached us," Chip said.

"And we paid," Genevra said bitterly. "Every month, like a mortgage on our granddaughter's happiness."

"She's had enough to deal with," Chip said defensively. "Finding out how she was conceived..." He gazed at Genevra, who shuddered.

"Unfortunately..." Her mouth turned up in a brittle smile. "Unfortunately, it cost us more than money."

Ray looked between the two of them. Saw acid knowledge in their faces.

"Holland was furious with us," Chip said. "She hated that man and the thought that he could benefit from what he'd done to her..."

"We did it to protect her," Genevra said, her eyes dark with hindsight. "And her child."

In sudden perception, Ray got it. "That's why she moved out." A chill went up his spine. It fit. It all fit.

"He's responsible," Genevra said with deep feeling. "He's responsible for what happened to her. He hurt her. He took her away from us." She began to weep. Chip laid a heavy hand on her shoulder.

"We were very generous," Chip said. "And he stayed away."

"Until now," Ray said.

"Until now," Chip repeated dully. "Honestly, I don't know if he's the one doing these awful killings. But he is a photographer. Or he was. I just... we have to be sure."

"What's his name? How are you supposed to contact him?"

"Sklar. Jerry Sklar. I have a phone number..."

"Sklar could have killed Holland. Why didn't you tell the police about him?"

"He has a rock-solid alibi," Genevra said.

Ray stared at her, but it was Chip who spoke.

"That morning..." He faltered. "I was paying him off." He shook his head. Tears swam in his eyes. "I was with him when Holland was... God help me, I was with him."

A swell of sorrow rolled over Ray. Pity for the things they'd endured, the decisions they'd been forced to make.

A knock on the door. Will cracked it open. "The police are here," he said.

"We'll be right out," Ray said.

Genevra clutched his arm. "You can't tell them."

Ray shook his head. "No choice. If this Jerry Sklar is a suspect, the police will have to investigate."

Her fingers dug deep in her arm. "If Gillian means anything to you, you will keep this to yourself."

"We have a sad history with the police," Chip said. He took out his wallet. "If there's any way we could persuade you to check this out quietly first. On your own. Make absolutely certain the authorities need to be told."

Ray clamped his jaw down. Chip Gray had waved his wallet around once before, using it to suck Ray in. And he'd let himself be persuaded. It pissed him off to know he'd do it again. And for the same reason.

"Put your damn money away," Ray barked.

He looked between the two of them. Old. Sapped. Enclosed in a shroud of the past. The same shroud Gillian tried to cut through with every dead shot she took. And it always seemed to pull her back. He wanted her free and clear.

And alive. Mostly, he wanted her alive.

54

Ray opened the door to Jimmy and another detective, Ned Mills, who was running the case. Steve and Dan had gone back to work, but the rest trooped back into Will's office. In the muddle, Ray stepped into the hallway, took out his cell phone, and punched in the number Chip had given him. It was long-distance, which, if Sklar was in town, probably meant a cell phone. No one picked up.

Odd for a blackmailer not to be at the contact number.

He called Carleco and asked them to trace the number and see what they could come up with on Sklar. Then he returned to the office.

"Mr. Davenport has filled us in," Mills was saying. He was an older man with gold-rimmed glasses, maybe ten years from retirement. Ray remembered him as steady and methodical. He was tempted to tell him about Sklar, then didn't. Until he got a lead on the phone number or the man himself, there was nothing the police could do that he couldn't.

Meanwhile, his ex-brother-in-law was eyeing him. "How'd you get involved?" he asked, only slightly belligerently.

Ray told him about his visit to the Grays earlier in the

day, how Mrs. Gray had sent him to the museum, how he'd found Gillian's car but not her.

Jimmy eyed him suspiciously. "Carleco is through with the Grays, and from what I saw at the station, Miss Gray is through with you. What was so important that you had to chase her all over town?"

Ray shifted. Truth was, he didn't quite know the answer to that himself. Whatever it was, whatever he thought he'd prove by clapping eyes on Gillian again, by seeing her smile or hearing some wisecrack come out of her beautiful mouth, he sure as hell wasn't going to confess it to Jimmy Burke or Ned Mills. "None of your business."

"Everything related to this case is our business," Jimmy said.

"Not my personal relationships."

"Personal?" Ned Mills said, homing in. "How personal?"

His face heated. He was acutely aware of Will Davenport and the Grays a few feet away. "Look, if you want my whereabouts this morning, I brought the sarge a lemon pie and stayed for coffee."

"You what?" Jimmy said, clearly taken aback.

"It's good you hired someone," Ray said to him. "He needs it."

The surprise on Jimmy's face relaxed into thoughtfulness.

Mills said, "That was real neighborly of you. I should stop by and see him myself."

"Don't expect too much," Ray said. "He recognized me at first, then lost track again."

Grudgingly, Jimmy said, "Thanks."

Ray waved off the gratitude. "No problem. And Joseph can corroborate the times. From there I went to the Grays, and you have the rest."

"I don't think you should be concentrating on Mr. Pearce," Genevra said cuttingly.

"It's okay," Ray said. "They have to cover all the bases."

"While they're covering their bases, or more likely a close anatomical object, my granddaughter is—"

Shouts from down the hall interrupted. Will stuck his head out the door. "In here."

The two men from the design team burst in, breathless from running down the hall.

"We just remembered something," the minivan driver said. "Well, Dan remembered it, and that clicked something with me and—"

"What?" Ray cut off the rambling. "What did you remember?"

"A van," Dan said. "Some kind of work van."

"It was parked near the service entrance," Steve said. "I think the back door was open."

"I didn't see a van when I came in," Will said.

They all took a moment to digest that, and Will introduced the detectives to the two men.

Jimmy turned to Will. "Were any workmen scheduled for this morning?"

Will shook his head. "Not that I know of." He made several phone calls to department heads, including maintenance. No one had outstanding work orders.

"Okay, let's figure out a time line." Ray pointed to Steve. "You were here first. What time?"

"Oh, maybe ten to seven."

"And the van was there?"

"Yes."

"And it was still there when you got in?" he said to Dan, who'd driven the Volvo.

"Yes."

"But by seven-fifteen, when you got here"—he turned to Will—"it was gone."

"I don't remember seeing it," said Will.

Ray, Ned, and Jimmy looked at one another.

"What kind of van?" Ned Mills asked.

"That's just it," Dan said miserably. "I don't remember."

Aubrey spun Gillian around to the right side of the set, where the table was located. The table that was to be her final destination.

"Having fun?" Smiling broadly, he bent down to her.

She looked at him coldly. "Not really."

"Now, now, don't be like that. Today's a happy day. All your dreams come true."

He whipped a long, lethal knife from the tool belt and made sure she got a good look at it. With a crafty smile, he lunged toward her, laughed when she flinched. "Oh, don't be afraid. I ain't gonna hurt you." Slowly, he cut the tape at her ankles, then straddled them, hot eyes observing her reaction. "I'm gonna let you do that yourself." She forced herself not to shrink away as he slid forward and slit the tape below her knees, then forward again to cut the tape at her hips. "You're so good at it."

Revulsion rose in the back of her throat, pungent and strong. It was all she could do not to vomit it up. But there was one binding left. It wound around her chest below her breasts, pinning her arms.

"You gonna run, Miss Gillian?" He transferred the knife to his left hand, took out the gun, and held it in his right. He sawed through the remaining tape, slowly, deliberately until she was free. "Now's your chance," he whispered.

He wasn't a big man, nothing like Ray, but it didn't take much to outweigh her. And he was pressing her down, knife at her ribs, gun at her throat. She could smell his breath, taste his excitement, feel his erection. The gamble she took seemed stupid now. Foolish. Lost.

Terrified, she denied it and stared him straight in the eyes. "You don't scare me, Aubrey." She put every ounce of strength she had into staying cool, bored, unimpressed. "I'm not afraid."

He yanked her to her feet, his pleasure dimmed. "Well, hell, Miss Gillian, pretend. I like it better when you are."

He pulled her off the pallet by one arm, uncaring when she fell to the floor and he nearly yanked it out of its socket. He just hauled her upright, pushed her over to the table. Held the gun to her neck and made her tape her legs to one of the chairs. Then he did the same with her torso, leaving one arm free. He found her sweater, yanked it on, so it covered the sight of the tape and stretched over the back of the chair. She was trussed, neat and complete.

He smiled. "How you doing?"

She didn't answer. What was the point?

He laughed and made a big show of emptying the bullets from the cylinder of the revolver. He shoved them in a pocket, except for one, which he kissed before loading back.

He spun the cylinder. "Let's see what kind of shot you take." He set the gun on the table and walked to the camera.

Gillian stared at the revolver. Six pulls, five empties. One lethal blast. Would she hear it before she felt it?

She would love to be calm. Love for her hand to be steady. She conjured up Ray, but the thought of all she might have had didn't stop the shakes. She wrapped her hand around the grip. Made contact with the hard metal. Heard the first snick of the camera.

She had one chance. Should she use it now? Or should she try to lower the odds?

Slowly, she pulled the revolver toward her. She saw a spiderweb in the corner. In the stream from the lights, fairy dust silvered the edges. It was all so sharp, so beautiful.

She looked over at Aubrey. Heard the camera click again.

She raised the gun to her head. And pulled the trigger.

55

"How about the color of the van?" Jimmy asked.

"Or words," Ray said. "Letters. Anything at all."

Dan and Steve exchanged a baffled glance. "White van, I think," said Steve.

"There was writing," Dan said. "Some kind of company name? Green pops into my head."

"Okay," Mills said. "That's good. Now, try to remember a word. Even a couple of letters."

Dan screwed his face up, thinking back. He shook his head. "Maybe... something with an 'H'? Harold or Harvey?"

That galvanized Ray. "Got a phone book?" he asked Will, and waited impatiently while the other man rummaged through two drawers before coming up with a Yellow Pages. Ray clamped his jaw to keep from screaming. "We need a White Pages," he said, and along with the rest, waited a two-minute eternity until Will was able to locate one in an office down the hall.

He scurried in and handed it to Ray, who dropped the heavy book on the desk and flipped through to the business section in the back half.

It took them half an hour and a painstaking, name-by-name search for Harold or Harvey to become Harpeth, and another fifteen minutes to separate the Harpeth Hills from the Harpeth Rivers and, finally, the Harpeth Valleys, which is where Ray stopped suddenly.

"What?" Jimmy said. "Go on, keep reading." Impatiently, he turned the book around, ran a finger down the page, and found Ray's place in the phone book. "Harpeth Window Cleaning Service," he read, then looked up at Dan.

"I don't know." Dan shrugged. "Could be. Sorry. I'm just not sure."

But Ray was picturing it. Night. Downtown. He was parking his truck.

"The night of the auction," he said slowly.

"Oh, yes, let's revisit that waste of effort," Genevra said.

"What about it?" Lee Mills asked.

"I parked my truck behind a van." He looked up. "A van from a window-washing company."

Suddenly every pair of eyes was on him. Shock ricocheted around the room.

Jimmy swore softly.

"Oh, my God," Genevra said on a sharp intake of breath.

"What?" Will said, looking from one to the other. "What are you talking about?"

"He was there," Ray said. "At the auction. He was there all along."

Jimmy exchanged a glance with his colleague. Both rose to leave, and Ray knew they'd go back to the station, check in with the lieutenant, hand out assignments, work the phones, and gather as much information as they could. They'd probably hit gold, but not for hours.

"Let me help. You could use it."

"Sorry, Ray," Mills said, not unkindly. "You don't work for us anymore. And we have to follow procedure." He left, but Jimmy hung back.

"Look, Ray." He pursed his lips, going through some inner struggle. Ray expected a barb, a further twisting of the knife, but when Jimmy finally spoke, he pitched his voice low, for Ray alone. "Someone has to check out the cleaning office."

Their eyes met.

"Someone who doesn't have to... follow procedure," Ray said.

Jimmy didn't respond. Just followed Mills out the door.

Ray headed straight to the little storefront office. It was located next to a liquor store in a decaying strip mall. The manager—one Floyd Burdette, if the name on the desk plaque was any indication—wore a stain on his tie and a comb-over.

Ray gave him a bogus business name and a phony offer of work. "Saw one of your trucks downtown Saturday night. Figured anyone working weekends must be worth checking out."

Burdette seemed pleased. He rocked back in his chair with an air of self-importance. "Saturday downtown? Sure, that was the Gray Building. Big job."

Excitement twisted inside Ray's chest. The Gray Building was across from the hotel where the gala was held.

Floyd was shaking his head, the enormity of the task sobering him. "Takes two to three days. Only send my best guys."

Ray restrained himself from leaping up and shaking the name out of the guy. "That's who I want, then."

Wide smile. "Well, let me check Aubrey's schedule for you."

Ray leaned forward. "Aubrey?"

"Aubrey Banks." Floyd consulted a computer screen. "Good worker. Polite. Quiet. Does an A-plus job."

"Yeah, it's always the quiet ones," Ray said dryly.

"Excuse me?"

He gave the man a tight smile, rose, and shook his hand. "Never mind," he said. "Thanks."

He hurried out, punching information into his cell phone as he raced to his truck. In less than a minute he had an address and was heading out the lot on a squeal of brakes.

He drove north, one hand on the wheel, the other speed-dialing Jimmy.

"I got a name," he told his ex-brother-in-law. "It's Banks. Aubrey Banks." He gave Jimmy the address. "I'll meet you there."

"The hell you will. You know damn well I'll need a warrant."

"Fine. Get your court order. I'll have been and gone."

"You stay the hell away from that house, Ray. Digging up information is one thing. You contaminate that evidence, we'll never convict."

"Maybe you can get him for murder, Jimmy. In the time it takes you to haul ass down there, he could kill her ten times over."

"Dammit, Ray, slow down. You don't even know he's our guy."

"That's what I'm trying to find out."

"Ray—"

But Ray had already disconnected.

He gunned the engine, heading around the capital and down Eighth. The Farmer's Market looked irritatingly inviting, yellow pansies and red tulips scattered like sunshine to draw you in. He resented the cheer but took it as a sign. He could just as easily despair as hope. Why not hope?

The address led to a cramped little house that looked like it had been there since Lee surrendered. Ray bounded out of the truck, hammered up the rotting porch steps. There was no "keep away" sign badly lettered on the door, but there didn't need to be. Whoever he was, Aubrey Banks didn't believe in curb appeal.

Ray knocked, waited, knocked again. "Mr. Banks!"

Just to make sure, he scouted around the decaying clapboard building. A chicken-wire fence enclosed the weedy rear, cutting it off from the back end of an overgrown rail yard. Neglected tracks slid by an ancient warehouse with several broken windows. Behind it, he could see the top of the U.S. Tobacco building. Had the warehouse once been used to house Skoal Fine Cut and Copenhagen Snuff? Not anymore by the looks of things.

He located a back door, which was covered in brown paper, felt around for the hole he assumed was behind it, and punched through. The opening wasn't big enough for him, not without a little help, but he was happy to provide it. Using his elbow, he cleared out the glass and climbed in.

The door led into the kitchen, tiny, damp-smelling. Empty.

"Gillian!"

Like he would be that lucky.

He waded to the front. The place was neater than

expected. Well, not neat exactly, with furniture in its appropriate place, but no hermit's pile of newspapers and dirty soup cans either. A worn rag rug covered the floor in the middle room, an armchair and a sagging couch staggered haphazardly on top. Plastic pails and cleaning fluid were scattered around. Squeegees, brushes, packages of wiping cloths.

Down a narrow hall, he found two other rooms, a bedroom with an open door and an unmade bed, and one with the door firmly locked.

His stomach did a little somersault.

"Gillian?" He rattled the knob, pounded on the door. "Gillian!"

He clamped his jaw down. If she was there, she might not be able to answer. Frantic, he used his shoulder to batter down the door. Didn't take much. The lock was old and gave easily.

But whatever he hoped to find—Gillian alive and tied up in a corner was first on his wish list—he was disappointed.

The room turned out to be another bedroom. Neat, pristine. Stale. Like a re-creation in a museum. A precisely made bed with a white chenille spread and a round pillow embroidered with curvy script: God Loves You. Next to the bed, a night table with lamp, a glass lamb nestling at its foot. A closet with wide grandma dresses and orthopedic shoes.

Ray swept the clothes back, felt around the back of the closet for unusual bumps, thumped the wall for a hollow space. "Gillian!"

Coming up with zip, he pounded the wall. He was close, so close. He wheeled around to face the room.

Who was Aubrey Banks? What would he want with Gillian? He could imagine no universe in which their two worlds collided. Was it random, then? Did he pick her out of a hat? Local celebrity? He could think of a dozen more famous.

Ray sank on the bed. There was something here. Something he missed.

Was this Banks's mother's room? The clothes seemed a generation older. Unless his mother had him old. That was possible. Or it could be his grandmother's. An aunt. Some female relation who raised him. There were no men's clothes, which could mean a spinster. Or a widow.

Why lock the door? That was obvious—to keep something hidden.

From who?

Outsiders.

But there wasn't anything here anyone couldn't see.

Who else do you hide things from?

He thought of his own mother, his own closet, the rooms inside his own head. There was plenty he liked hidden. Pain and failure and missed opportunities.

He panned around the room. So maybe Aubrey Banks kept the room locked not from other people, but from himself. So he wouldn't have to see it.

Why? What had happened here?

He rose on a hunch, braced himself, and jerked the spread down.

No bloodstain stared up at him.

Across from the bed, a dresser sat against the wall. A couple of photographs in wood frames stood on top. He picked one up. It showed a very young woman in a dark dress. Her hair waved in that deeply curled fashion of the forties. There was a shy look about her. Compliant. Submissive.

He picked up the second photo.

Blinked.

Looked away and looked back.

And that's where Jimmy and his cop shop found him. Holding a picture of Holland Gray's house.

56

The trigger clicked.

Gillian gasped, still alive.

In the distance, she heard Aubrey giggle his hyena laugh. Heard the faraway tick of the camera. His voice slowed as it reached her ears. "Go on. Do it again. Do. It. Again."

Sweat poured off her. The gun was slippery in her hand. She regripped it, staring out at the broken-down warehouse, its tired brick walls and boarded-up windows. Abandoned. Left behind to die alone.

Mommy!!! Mommy!!!

Her heart bucked as the screen door inside her head slammed shut behind her.

Mommy!

"What are you waiting for, Miss Gillian?"

She shifted her gaze to the man behind the camera. Four chances left. Four more times to decide who shall live and who shall die.

"Nothing," she murmured, the truest thing she'd ever said. Everything she'd ever waited for was here. Now.

She put the gun to her head. Wanted desperately to shut her eyes but refused to.

She inhaled one last time. Pulled the trigger.

"You're sure?" Jimmy asked.

"For God's sake, I was at the house a few days ago." And when Jimmy still looked doubtful. "Get the photos from the cold case file. It's Holland Gray's house." Ray put it down. "But there's something..."

"What?"

"Something different about it."

He took a step back, trying to get some perspective. Jimmy went to the bedroom door, stuck his head out. "Anyone find anything?"

"Roaches," one of the uniforms called back. "We got a little corral going in the kitchen."

Jimmy left to check out what they were doing, and the last words ricocheted around Ray's head. "That's it," he murmured. Picture in hand, he ran after Jimmy. "That's it!" He skidded to a stop in the kitchen, shoved the photo in the smaller man's hand. "Take a look at the fence."

Jimmy glanced at the picture, then up at Ray. "So?"

"It's a picket fence, right?"

"Uh-huh."

"Send someone out there. No picket fence now. It's split rail. And look." He pointed to the west side of the house. "No chimney. There's a big honking stone chimney there now."

The two men stared at each other. "You're saying this is the original house?" Jimmy tapped the photo. "What it looked like—"

"—When Holland Gray was murdered." Grimly, Ray nodded. "He knows her. He fucking knows her."

Click.

A small cry escaped Gillian. Her heart was pounding so hard she was sure the camera could capture the beat.

But once again, the pull of the trigger had left her alive. Still, God, still alive.

Why? The question hovered in the air, frantic for an answer.

She would never call herself lucky. Fated, doomed, whatever word you chose, she'd always been a pawn of the universe.

So why had the universe not lived up to its promise?

A frowning Aubrey stepped away from the camera. Even at a distance she could see the malevolence in his eyes. He started toward her, clearly unhappy with the way the hand was being dealt.

She licked her lips. Three more chances. Stay or hit?

Jimmy called Mills. "We found a connection," he said rapidly. "Get everything you can on an Aubrey Banks, dob 8-2-1969. LKA—" He relayed the current address.

"I'm going outside to look around," Ray said.

"Truitt." Jimmy nodded to one of the uniforms. "Go with him. See what you can find."

What they found was a root cellar in the southeast corner, butt up against the fence and practically buried in the weeds.

Truitt lifted the heavy cover and started down the steps

into the black hole. He was half-in and half-out when Ray heard a sound in the distance.

They both froze.

"You hear that?" Ray said.

"I heard something," Truitt said. "Firecracker maybe."

"Car backfire?"

"Possible." He nodded in the direction of the old warehouse. "Came from over there. And I don't see a car."

"I'm going to check it out."

Ray headed off, and Truitt spoke into his shoulder radio. "Detective, we might have something out here."

The chicken wire was only knee high off the ground, so Ray had no trouble hopping it. He listened hard for a repeat of the sound. Nothing but his footsteps crunching gravel.

Was it a gunshot?

Or his mind playing tricks?

Hunching low, he crossed the weed-strewn tracks, pulling his weapon. Backed against the warehouse's decaying brick wall. To his left, two wide steel doors, closed and rusting, a padlock wound around the handles. He sidled toward them.

Across the yard, Truitt was conferring with Jimmy. Truitt pointed, and the two of them looked his way.

Ray reached the doors as Jimmy started forward. The lock had been smashed, one door was cracked open.

Ray's heart started to thud.

He leaned closer to the opening. Listened. Only silence answered.

Jimmy reached the warehouse, inched over to him. "Anything?" he whispered.

Ray shook his head. "I'm going in."

Jimmy nodded. "Right behind you."

Ray twisted, darted inside, weapon aimed and steady. He went left, Jimmy, right.

Across the warehouse, a sight that stunned.

An ordinary kitchen, one corner brightly lit. A body slumped over a table. Another on the floor.

Ray stared, horror filling his throat.

He knew what it was. What it had to be.

Gillian Gray's last dead shot.

He stumbled forward on straw legs, but an arm blocked his progress.

"Don't," Jimmy said. "I'll go." Pity in his eyes. Not stopping him because of police procedure but out of kindness. To spare him.

But Ray didn't want to be spared. Carefully, he brushed the arm away, staggered another step.

Then the miracle happened.

Gillian moved.

Slowly, her head rose. He could see her face. Gray. Drawn. Tendrils of sweat-soaked hair framing it.

"Farm boy." Hoarse voice tinged in familiar sarcasm. "I knew you'd show up. Eventually."

57

Gillian watched Ray come. Watched him close the gap between them in three rapid strides. The shield of his body blocking her view of anything but him.

"Are you all right?" A pocketknife already in his hand, the binding around her chest, her arms, gone in a breath.

Shouts blurred, noise she heard, words she didn't. The edges of the world hazy except for the man kneeling in front of her. Cutting through the tape she'd wound around her ankles. Looking up at her with his strong, welcome face. The one that said he was here, and she could lean on him.

She reached down, traced the line of his mouth. Soft lips, hard chin. His brown eyes went all watery, and, she was ashamed to say, so did hers. Without knowing how, she was out of the chair and down on the floor. With a cry, she was in his arms. Safe. Alive.

And all she could think to do was ask for a favor.

It wasn't that she was morbid, though many were fond of saying so. There were just . . . certain things she couldn't turn away from. So before the entire police department descended on them, she made a simple request.

He tensed against her and she wondered how many

times over how many years she would ask him to do things he wouldn't want to do. And how many times he would do them.

He took her face in his big hands. She could feel the tremor in them. "Jimmy!" he called, his eyes locked on hers, still watching, always watching out for her.

"Cylinder's empty." Detective Burke walked over, holding the gun through the trigger guard with a pen. The chamber was open and he was looking through it. "What happened?"

Ray helped her to her feet, took Jimmy aside. Whatever excuse he made, he got his ex-partner out of the warehouse long enough for her to remove the camera's memory stick and the pictures on it.

Two days of wrangling followed. Explanations, statements, revelations. Aubrey Banks had washed windows at or near all the victims' workplaces or homes. Inside the root cellar the police found a collage of newspaper articles about Gillian, huge blowups of her photos, headlines from the murders, and a small elastic band from Dawn Farrell's hair.

They discovered a grave in the yard and identified the bodies as Aubrey's father and grandmother, both bludgeoned to death more than ten years ago.

And in a small box hidden in an alcove, a wedding ring and a necklace belonging to one Sarah Beth Henderson, along with a small newspaper clipping about the missing woman dating back five years.

And through it all, Gillian managed to keep the pictures to herself. Detective Burke suspected what she'd done, but the police didn't need them to prove their case, and she never admitted their existence.

Now, a week later, she was packed, ready to leave. Just waiting for Ray to show up and take her to the airport.

She pictured saying good-bye to him. Couldn't get the focus sharp enough.

She had one last thing to do. She slipped inside the bathroom and reached for the broken tile above the mirror. She'd had to remove the scissors to fit the small disc from Aubrey's camera behind it. When she took out the disc, the cubbyhole was empty.

She turned the digital card over in her hand. So small. Not much bigger than a stick of gum, if that. And yet big enough to hold everything she'd thought important.

With deliberate slowness, she tilted her hand. Watched the card slide forward and plop into the toilet.

The police still didn't know who killed her mother. Chances were, they'd never know.

But she'd faced the monster and come out alive. She didn't need pictures to prove it.

58

Ray stood in the shadow of the hospital doorway gazing at the man dying in the bed. It hadn't taken much to track down Jerry Sklar. He'd holed up at a flophouse across the river until he had collapsed and been hauled away to General Hospital, where all the uninsured went.

Ray could see why he needed the money, but it didn't look like he would have to worry about expenses much longer.

He stepped back, away from the room and its secret.

Half an hour later, the Grays' maid showed him into the sunroom, bright and cheerful, with its apricot walls and view of the terrace. A far cry from the oppressive air of the hospital room he'd just come from.

The Grays greeted him with caution but not the outright hostility of the past. Ray sensed the nervous tension between them and dispelled it as quickly as possible.

"I found him," he said.

Genevra clutched the back of the sofa, then sank to the seat.

"He's dying," Ray said. "Liver cancer."

It might have been cruel, but relief rushed across Genevra's face. She reached out to grasp her husband's hand, and they held on to each other like frightened children.

"Probably why he tried pumping you for more money. No insurance."

Neither of the Grays had invited him to sit. Chip himself still stood, large and imposing, standing over his wife's narrow form.

Ray handed Chip a slip of paper with the room number on it. "He's at General. You can see him if you want to. Or not. Up to you."

But the question that hung in the room was not about visiting the sick. Ray looked between the two older people. Gillian's people. Her connections, her family.

"She has a right to know," Ray said softly.

"She knows enough," Chip said.

Ray thought about how long and how hard Gillian's grandparents had fought to protect her. To stand between her and what could hurt her. Not so different from himself.

And yet, how much damage had they done at the same time? The scars on her arms marked the heavy toll of silence.

Which wounded more?

Before he could decide, Gillian waltzed into the room.

"Plotting attack?" she asked, and the air around its three occupants seemed to solidify. Genevra stiffened, Chip went rigid. Ray opened his mouth but nothing came out. They were all caught, specimens under glass. Gillian examined them. "Where's the cauldron?"

She smiled. Mischief and mayhem in a pair of lips. But there was courage, too. An open face, ready for anything. She might look like a fragile doll, but she always faced into the wind. And if it dared to knock her down, she got up again.

He turned to the elder Grays, his decision made. Genevra saw at once what he meant to do. Something in her face went dull with pain, but she fought it. It was their place to speak, and she knew it. She rose. Squared her shoulders, prepared herself for the coming ordeal.

"Gillian, we have something to tell you." She faltered. Looked at Chip.

"About your father," Chip said gravely.

"My father?" Gillian looked from her grandparents to Ray. There was something in the room. Something huge and burdensome pressing down on everyone. "You were talking about my father?"

Genevra took a quavery breath. "He's—"

"—Dead," Gillian said.

Chip stepped forward. "No, Gillian, he's—"

"A doornail."

"You should let them tell you what they have to say," Ray said.

"They don't have to," Gillian said.

"Yes, they do."

"No." She shook her head. Went to her grandmother's side and clasped the older woman's hands in hers. "They don't."

And there was this tiny moment between them. A moment of understanding and compassion. Did Gillian know the truth after all? Or didn't it matter?

"He's dead," she said quietly. "Let's keep him that way."

After that, there was nothing left to do but take Gillian's single bag out to the truck and say good-bye. Ray shook hands with Chip, nodded to Genevra, then stood back and let Gillian make her own farewells.

The drive to the airport took fifteen minutes, and they

didn't say much on the way. When they got there, he pulled up to the departure curb, got her bag from the truck bed, and put it on the curb. Absently, she toed it with her foot, then squinted up at him.

"Look, I could make a big speech. Say thank you and all that crap."

"You could."

"Here's the thing." She reached into her purse, pulled out a folded sheet of paper, and tapped it against one hand as if debating what to do with it. Abruptly, she shoved it at him. "I'd rather do it somewhere else."

He unfolded it. Saw the flight itinerary. Ray Pearce. Nashville to New York.

"If you're not busy," she said.

He looked at her. Heard everything neither of them was saying. "Guy's gotta work, short stack."

She nodded sagely. "Plenty of jobs elsewhere for an enterprising young man such as yourself. I believe there is a police department in New York."

He tried hard not to smile. Reached into his jacket and pulled out a similar sheet of paper. Gave it to her.

She looked at it, grinned smugly. Picked up her bag and walked toward the entrance. He called after her.

"So, who gets the refund?"

She held up a hand, waved his question away, and kept on walking.

He got back in the truck and drove away. He had a ton of packing to do. Calls to make. Another job to quit.

He was finally leaving town.

About the Author

A native New Yorker, **Annie Solomon** has been dreaming up stories since she was ten. After a twelve-year career in advertising, where she rose to Vice President and Head Writer at a midsize agency, she abandoned the air conditioners, heat pumps, and furnaces of her professional life for her first love—romance. *Dead Shot* is her sixth novel of romantic suspense. To learn more, visit her Web site at www.anniesolomon.com.